# missionary *No* MORE

AN EROTICANOIR.COM ANTHOLOGY
**PURPLE PANTIES II**

# missionary No MORE

AN EROTICANOIR.COM ANTHOLOGY
**PURPLE PANTIES II**

## EDITED BY ZANE

STREBOR BOOKS

NEW YORK LONDON TORONTO SYDNEY

Strebor Books
P.O. Box 6505
Largo, MD 20792
http://www.streborbooks.com

ISBN-13   978-1-59309-211-5
ISBN-10        1-59309-211-3
LCCN 2008937811

First Strebor Books trade paperback edition January 2009

Cover design: www.mariondesigns.com

10   9   8   7   6   5   4   3   2   1

Manufactured in the United States of America

For information regarding special discounts for bulk purchases, please contact Simon & Schuster Special Sales at 1-800-456-6798 or business@simonandschuster.com

# COPYRIGHT NOTICES

*This book is dedicated to the people in the world who have no problem admitting who they are, unlike those who play silly games with the hearts of others and put on way too many pretenses.*

# table of contents

# introduction

**M**issionary No More; I have been anxious to use this book title for quite some time. Glad I did it before someone else decided to bite my shit again; not that it worked the first time. I am so pleased to present this second volume of lesbian erotica. Once again, the stories are creative, the writers are vibrant, and it will leave readers hot, bothered, or at least wondering about the possibilities.

Purple Panties, the first volume, caused a ton of controversy. I was embarrassed that we live in a world where people continue to have so many sexual hang-ups instead of simply letting people be. Some bookstores said the book was "too racy." As compared to what? My book The Sisters of APF: The Indoctrination of Soror Ride Dick? Let's be serious. An online magazine claimed they would not feature any more erotica since some of their readers were offended by the book. To that I say, no wonder they only have a minimal amount of people on their email list in the first place.

Same gender loving relationships are not going to vanish. It is as simple as that. People will continue to live their way, and no one has the right to judge them; unless we are talking something so incomprehensible that it defies morality. How could love or passion ever do that?

Let me get down off the podium and return to celebrating the stories within this book. From "Ladies Night" where a young woman engages in a sexual adventure that will have people seeking out the secret parties to "The Namma's Nectar" where women decide to gain power by dining on one another, this book is off the chain.

It is time—it has long since been time—for women to embrace their sexuality and demand that their needs be met. The time of being missionaries for the pleasure of men is over. That is why the title fits this book so perfectly. This book is about female empowerment and not bowing down to what society—or men—deem acceptable.

I sincerely hope that you enjoy reading this book as much as I enjoyed editing it. This is my last anthology for many years to come. I have enjoyed the ride, but now I must get off and go back to my true love: novel writing. While I enjoy helping to bring the words of others to light—and will continue to do so through publishing—my greatest joy is being able to create characters and stories that express my views, my opinions, and my desires. Not to mention my sick-ass imagination. Thus, this is both a moment of greatness and a moment of sadness as I type this. But trust that we will all still be together for a very long time as I revive the characters that have meant so much to my many readers and give birth to new ones that I hope will continue to touch lives and, more importantly, spark thought and discussion.

Blessings,

Zane

# ladies night
## LOTUS FALCON

I look forward to Ladies Night every month. At one time I would shy away from the local club scene because it was hard to find a reputable venue that would be anything but a funky little bar filled with women covered with piercings, tattoos and clothes that looked like Saran Wrap. The clubs in San Francisco and New York were off the chain. The booty was abundant and everyone came to get their party on. I met some of the finest black women on this side of the hemisphere in some of those clubs, but upon returning to my hometown of Washington, D.C., or rather the Chocolate City, I felt a little disconnected to the party scene.

It wasn't until a friend of a friend turned me on to a group of women who were throwing private parties that I was able to feel connected to my party roots again. These sisters would rent a suite of rooms at numerous hotels downtown. We would register on the internet and pay a cover charge via PayPal. This particular party was being given at a Four Seasons Hotel. It was well-organized and the only way you could gain entrance was by referral. All the rules and guidelines were spelled out on their website and we even had to submit references and respond to an online questionnaire. This was one of the safest parties in town; one where a sister didn't always have to be watching her back.

The first time I went to Ladies Night, we were greeted by topless hostesses that were there to check us in. I don't know where they found those sisters, but they had the firmest, most succulent breasts I had ever seen, with nipples the size of cupcakes. I was hypnotized and immediately knew that I wanted to sample some of those breasts before the night was over.

Before even getting through the door of the hotel room, we had to go through all the preliminary check-in stuff, like showing a picture ID and displaying a confirmation or verification of payment. I even had to sign an agreement to verify that I understood the house rules and that I was participating on my own free will. These sisters ran this operation like a true business and had all the bases covered. There were also bracelets provided that gave us an opportunity to identify the level of participation we wanted to be involved in.

There were three colored bracelets that could be selected. The red bracelet was for voyeurs, women who wanted to watch and not participate. The yellow bracelet was for those who only wanted to participate partially, by either being a receiver or giver of pleasure. You had to be specific on which you preferred. The green bracelet meant you wanted to fully participate and that you were ready for whatever was going down for the evening.

Since this was my first night, I decided to get a red bracelet, at which time I could upgrade at any time during the evening. I heard that this party had the best pussy in town and I decided that I would take my time and cruise the joint before settling into any one spot. It had taken me months to get on "the waiting list" and I had masturbated for days in anticipation of this night. Now that I was in, I wasn't about to take anything for granted.

There was wall-to-wall pussy from Diesel Dykes to Femmes. Huddled in the corners, eyeballing everyone from the back of the room, were the Baby Dykes. It was easy to figure out that they had only recently come out of the closet, so to speak, by the way they were holding up the walls with their hands between their legs. Every now and then, I stumbled across a sister that had only had sex with one other woman in her life and, for some reason, was holding out for "Ms. Right." We called those sisters Lone Star Lesbians and would steer clear of them; we pretty much knew that they were just there to sightsee.

Then there's the Stone Butches that like to suck, lick, fuck and everything else, but don't want to be touched sexually. That's alright by me as long as I know what the deal is beforehand. I don't usually have to sweat them since they usually pair up with the Pillow Queens, who only like to receive sex. So the Stone Butches and Pillow Queens are enough for each other and make a hell of a sight to watch.

Then there are the women that are married to "beards," which is what we call those brothers married to sisters who are living the illusion that they are straight, just so that they can cover up the fact that they are lesbians. These are the true freaks-of-the-week. They usually come out to swallow up as much pussy as they can get, so that it will last them until they are able to get out again. They eat pussy all night long and I have even seen a couple of them tear up two and three at one time.

My favorite freaks of all are the Gold Star Lesbians that have never slept with a man in their whole life and have no intentions of ever sleeping with one. Unlike myself, I have dabbled with a few dicks in my day and don't have anything against them, except I just like pussy better. If I had to choose between a pussy and a dick, then undoubtedly I would have to go with the pussy. I love the way it looks. I love the way it feels. I love the way it smells. I love the way it tastes. I love the way it pops when air gets caught up in it. I love the way it fills up and bubbles over at the right time. I love the way the lips swell and protrude when they get hot. I love the way pussies come in so many different shapes and sizes. What can I say? I just love me some pussy!

The music was jumping and the sound of "Do Me Baby" by Prince was blasting out of the speakers. The smell of Nag Champa incense was going straight to my head and the diffused lighting made shadows dance in time to the music. I had the option of walking around fully clothed, partially clothed or butterball naked. There was a changing room that we were encouraged to use and there wasn't any pressure one way or the other about wearing or not wearing clothes. The temperature was a little on the cool side, but when I noticed all the erect nipples, I figured that was probably by design. Bowls of lube, mints and condoms were plentiful. The condoms made using the dildos and vibrators easier, because it made the clean up a lot less messy.

Sex toys were always an arm's length away and were inconspicuously available in bookcases throughout the suite. There were vibrators of every description from G-Spot Vibes to Vibrating Rings, from Jack Rabbits to strap-ons. Safe sex was of the utmost importance and proper hygiene was indeed a must. Washing up and cleaning "the coochie" throughout the night was highly recommended and there were baby wipes and towelettes available in every room. DVDs and homemade movies were playing all around the joint, so that we were surrounded by pussy in every direction. The party was off the chain and by the end of the night, I wanted to be up to my neck in pussy.

When I checked in, I thought I was at some organized conference or something. The "hostess" escorted me around, showing me the layout of the rooms, and alerted me to the different "playrooms" that I could choose from. There were four major rooms that consisted of a room for masturbation, a room for erotic massage, a hot tub room for water play and the master bedroom or the "Fucking Room." There was also a room off to the back that was designated for "Performance Porn," which I was told I would learn more about later in the evening.

Since I had to warm up to the whole public nudity thing, I decided to keep my bra and panties on and with my "red bracelet" in place, I was ready to get my "party on." There were wall-to-wall sisters by the time I had finished my little tour and even though the incense was thick in the air, I smelled pussy and it smelled sweet. I followed some big-breasted women to the masturbation room and it took a few minutes before my eyes could get adjusted to the darkness. There were so many sisters, there wasn't even enough space for me to hardly inch my way inside the room. The smell of pussy was potent and from moans and growls I heard coming out of the room, I decided that I would double back to this spot before I left for the evening.

The erotic massage room was slowly filling up by that time and one of the hostesses suggested that she was free to give me a massage before it got too crowded. Even though I showed her my bracelet, she said she was having a "newcomer's special" and it would help to loosen me up for the rest of the evening. I eagerly agreed and was led by the hand into a dimly lit room that had soft music playing, candles burning and pillows everywhere. I was helped onto a table and the next thing I knew my panties were coming off and my bra was being removed. Since I was still wearing my "red bracelet" I figured I would be watching an erotic massage rather than participating in one, but here I was lying on my back, with my pussy in the air.

The hostess was a fine, coffee-colored sister with the softest locks I had ever seen. Her nipples were the size of silver dollars and the hair on her pussy was shaved into a neat triangle; the way you see them in those porn videos. After looking at her little patch of hair, I wished that I had trimmed mine back a little closer, so a sister could at least see what she was working with. However, in most of my experiences, I had met a lot of sisters that liked hairy pussies and didn't find it a problem, but I still tripped over it when meeting someone for the first time.

The hostess warmed some oil between the palms of her hands and began running her hands all over my body, beginning from my head and working her way down to my toes. As she carefully rubbed the oil into my skin, she alternated with rubbing hard and with rubbing soft. Each time she rubbed me, she would get closer to my inner thighs and breasts, barely touching them. As she got closer and closer, I would anticipate each stroke of her hands. Even though I tried to play it cool, the desire was building between my legs and I wanted her to stop all that damn teasing and make a move.

As my hostess noticed how my body was starting to twitch, she started to kiss my neck and then planted light kisses down toward my stomach, then back up to my lips. Her lips were soft and as she kissed me behind my ears, she told me how much she liked the hair on my pussy and how hard my nipples were. On cue, my nipples doubled in size as she touched them and began stroking them from my left nipple to the right one.

She took her thumb and index finger and encircled my nipples with a soft, pulling motion and continued to rotate them counterclockwise until I found my hand between my legs. She wouldn't let me finger myself and when I protested, she handcuffed both of my wrists to each side of the table. I could feel the blood in my pussy kick in, causing it to tighten up as she began stroking my nipples with her index finger while she started rubbing on hers.

As she applied more oil to both of our nipples, she leaned over me and pulled her nipples across mine until they both were hard and swollen and standing at full attention. She squeezed her breasts together as she ran them across mine, making her nipples look like small torpedoes. It felt so good, the way her nipples rubbed up against mine, that I begged her to let me taste them, but she kept on rubbing mine and rubbing hers and then suddenly stopped when I was about to cum.

After my intensive "tittie massage" she turned her attention to my pussy which was hot, heavy and swollen and in need of some immediate attention. She opened my legs to expose my clit and told me how big it had gotten. She used her forefinger to work the head of my clit out of its tight hiding place and lifted my head onto a pillow, so I could watch her work my nubby clit into a convulsion. She licked her fingers several times as she tried to get my clit to swell beyond the size it had already gotten. Homegirl then oiled up a silver bullet and turned it up full speed and worked it on, in and across my clit and down my pussy until I was shaking like a junkie.

By that time, my inner pussy lips looked like the petals of a flower. They were plump and thick. The more she stroked them, the plumper they would get until they had changed to a deep shade of red and then to purple. She worked my outer lips as well and fondled and stroked them until they were completely hanging out of my pussy. She kept complimenting me on how pretty my pussy was and how wet I had gotten.

At that point she asked me what I wanted her to do next, as if I was ordering from a menu. Since I was given a choice, I told her that I wanted her to "fuck me." So, without further ado, she put on a strap-on dick and not one of those baby dicks either, but one of those long, wide, thick ones that can drill a hole straight through your pussy. She climbed on top of me and parted my knees. Before entering me, she opened me up with two lubricated fingers and parted the lips of my pussy so she could insert the strap-on in just the right angle. She entered me slowly and kept asking me, "Does this feel good?" and all I could do was grunt and moan, because sister-girl was working that strap-on like she was born to fuck.

The head of the strap-on was curved in such a way that it was able to go deep into my pussy, finding its way into every nook and cranny inside of me. She was fucking the shit out of me like she was looking for buried treasure. When she came to the edge of my pussy, she pulled toward me and pumped two more times deep inside me. That got me off to the point that my pussy was bubbling over, like a volcanic reaction. As I was trying to push the orgasm through my body, she took the silver bullet and lit me up again for a second orgasm.

My hostess didn't even give my pussy time to cool off before she asked me if I had ever experienced fisting. When I said that I had tried it a few times and didn't like it, she convinced me that it wouldn't hurt and would even walk me through it step by step. She took the handcuffs off of me and placed a pillow under the small of my back. She then put on a latex glove and soaked it with plenty of water-based lube.

I had never used lube and figured that's why it probably had hurt the way that it had before; not to mention the other sisters actually trying to jam their entire arm up in me, making the experience quite numbing. My hostess started with a couple of fingers at first, one at a time, and massaged my clit as she was doing it.

She kept asking me, "Does that feel good?" Checking in with me every now and then, I heard her but couldn't answer. It was feeling too good to talk, but she got the message just the same.

After working my pussy for awhile, she formed her fingers in the shape of a teardrop and slowly worked her hand into my slippery hole by slowly rotating her wrist in and out of my pussy. On contact, my pussy swallowed up her hand. She kept rotating her wrist until her whole hand was buried deep in my pussy. She then slowly moved her hand in and out and carefully twisted her wrist from left to right. I can't say that fisting was ever something that I usually volunteered to do, but this shit was feeling incredibly right tonight and it didn't even feel like the end of a baseball bat like usual. Her hand actually filled my pussy up with the exact amount of pressure that soon had me humping her fist on every down stroke.

Even though she slowly eased her fist out of me, it stung a little when she finally removed it. It wasn't a bad thing; it was just a throbbing feeling that made me want to rub my pussy to cool it off. Homegirl must have sensed that my pussy was on fire, because she started rubbing her thigh on my pussy in such a soft way that immediately cooled it down and then heated it back up. The more she rubbed her thigh across my pussy, the more I rubbed my pussy against her thigh. We went from thigh to pussy rubbing, to knee to pussy rubbing, to ass to pussy rubbing, and finally to pussy to pussy rubbing.

She positioned herself over me as if we were a pair of scissors. She pulled back slightly to show me how to pull my pussy lips back far enough, so the inside of our pussies were wet enough for us to feel the soft sticky flesh rubbing up against each other. The more we pushed into each other, the stickier we became until both of us busted the biggest nut that is humanly possible. I don't know who nutted the most, whether it was me or her, but after getting into a "69," we then started a race to see who could eat "the pussy" the fastest.

As I ate her pussy from the top, she tore mine up from the bottom. She smelled musty and tasted salty and I couldn't get enough of her sticky juices. The lips of her pussy were hanging out of her like "balls" and the more I sucked on them, the more she drove her pussy into my mouth. As she nibbled on my clit, she fingered me at the same time until both of us were twitching and moaning.

When she was finished with me, she turned me over and gave me a full body massage, fucked me one more time from the back with a glass dildo, and left me alone to recuperate until my jelly legs became firm. When she left the room, all I could do was get in a fetal position and suck my thumb like a baby. I could hardly move and my pussy was numb, but I was feeling better than I had felt in a long time. As the feeling began to come back in my pussy and in my legs, I slowly rubbed my nipples and clit, because I was experiencing those aftershocks that usually happen after good fucking.

I suddenly heard something that sounded very familiar and as I looked up on the big screen in front of me, there I was with homegirl with a mouth full of pussy. Beside me was a release form giving permission to feature my video during the "Performance Porn" portion of the evening. I immediately signed it, because I didn't want to deny anyone the opportunity to see two divas at work and I certainly didn't want any of that good pussy action to go to waste. Once I was able to regain total consciousness, steady my breathing and stand on my own, I was immediately going to turn in my "red bracelet" for an upgrade.

ဆၤၚ

*Lotus Falcon is a native of Washington, D.C. who holds a bachelor of science degree in education and a masters of public administration. She is an educator in a public school system who also leads women empowerment/sexuality workshops and sells adult toys and products in her spare time. She is currently working on several writing projects for children and adults and is married with seven children.*

# she loved a girl
## COLE SULLIVAN

Danielle "Danni" Goode was twelve years old the first time she experienced that tingle between her legs. At every opportunity, she had been sneaking and reading her mother's hot erotica novels. She always found them to be hot and steamy, but her heart would especially race each time she read the stories involving two women making love. Even at such an early age, Danni recognized right away that the thought of being with a girl made her vagina contract with excitement. It didn't take her long to realize that she was different from her female counterparts; the ones constantly giggling about the cutest boy band member of the week.

Growing up, Danni soon came to realize that her sexual preference was not a likely conclusion for a woman of her stature. Females who looked like Danni were typically assumed to be attracted to the red-blooded, chiseled male species, those who were hung like horses. She stood five feet nine, and her curves were often compared to a Coca-Cola bottle. With a short, sassy haircut, mocha-brown skin, thick full lips and a beautiful smile, she was on every man's agenda. Little did they realize that her agenda was nothing of the sort. Despite innocent flirting, Danni had never actually been with intimate with either sex. She had experienced plenty of orgasms; all by her own effort. Imagining what it would be like to touch and feel the soft skin of a woman always ended in late night one-on-one finger matches with her vagina. It wouldn't be until freshman year in college that Danni would share her first sexual experience; with a woman no doubt.

It was love at first sight when Carmen Evans walked into the initial session of her biology class. Danni's pussy thumped hard, a feeling she was all too familiar with. THUMP! THUMP!

"Down, girl," Danni whispered to her pussy. *Thank goodness I don't have a dick*, she thought. Otherwise she would've long been *exposed*. Carmen Evans was gorgeous. She had honey-colored skin, big gray eyes and light-brown, shoulder-length hair. The short denim miniskirt she sported modeled her long, beautiful legs. She was curvaceous and had a smile that could light up any room. Residing in the state where everything is bigger, Carmen's rack definitely helped to sanction that expression. Right then Danni knew that she would do whatever was necessary to make Carmen Evans a part of her first taste-testing.

Danni and Carmen became instant BFF's—best friends forever. Danni soon discovered that disguising her true feelings for Carmen would prove a tough challenge. She repeatedly watched Carmen go through a series of different men. After each one disappointed Carmen, Danni was there to offer a shoulder to lean on and an ear to listen. Each time, she hoped for an opportunity to give Carmen the orgasms the men had failed to deliver. She wanted so badly to be the one who pampered and stimulated Carmen's vagina until she shook from uncontrollable bliss. Fortunately, for Danni, she wouldn't have to wait much longer. The first time she and Carmen were together was a long time coming, but well worth the wait. It was a moment

Danni would never forget. The experience turned out to be everything she had hoped it would be, and much more.

Danni had invited Carmen to spend Thanksgiving break with her family. The night they arrived, they were both exhausted and decided to retire early to bed. Since the other guest bedrooms were occupied by visiting family members, she and Carmen shared her old bedroom. Danni showered first and hopped into her usual sleepwear; a tee and panties. When Carmen came to bed, Danni nearly climaxed at the sight of her beautiful image. She wore a tiny, light-pink tank top with adorable matching boy shorts. Her skin was still damp from the shower and her nipples were protruding through her shirt, once the cool air hit them. Danni drooled at the sight and fantasized about how badly she wanted to suck and caress her breasts. Carmen's pussy lips formed a well-defined camel's toe through her tight-fitting shorts. Danni couldn't help but steal a few glances at the vision of beauty.

A swift knock on the door quickly zapped Danni from her lustful gaze. Her parents were peeking in to say good night. Danni giggled to herself when she saw the embarrassment on her father's face, after he caught a glimpse of how good Carmen looked in her pajamas. It was obvious that even *he* couldn't deny that the girl was *fine*!

THUMP! THUMP! Damn! "She" was calling again! But there was no calming her down tonight. No way could Danni forfeit this opportunity. She had to take the chance to make love to Carmen.

Danni's heart was beating a trillion milliseconds per minute as she lay there, strategizing the best move to make toward fucking Carmen. As Danni watched Carmen sleep, she became moist when she noticed how the sateen sheets conformed to the shape of her body, exposing her curvaceous silhouette. Danni began to inch closer and closer to Carmen. At that moment she was unsure if Carmen was completely asleep or not, but she didn't care. Her urges had taken over. She slowly eased her arm around Carmen's waist and began caressing her silky, smooth thighs. Carmen did not protest.

Danni moved her hand a little higher and began to gently caress Carmen's juicy ass. Still, she gave no reaction. Feeling a bit more confident, Danni began to massage Carmen's breasts. Her nipples became hardened and erect, encouraging Danni to slip her hand underneath her top for complete access to Carmen's perky 36DDs.

By this time, Carmen could no longer pretend to ignore Danni's advances. Danni's touch was so soft and gentle; much more stimulating than from any man she'd ever experienced. She had always been curious about making love to a woman. She decided, right at that moment, that she would allow Danni to taste her.

Carmen turned on her back and spread her legs. Danni slowly glided her hand over Carmen's boy shorts, teasing the moist crevice Carmen made available. She eased off her shorts and guided her tongue down toward Carmen's navel, depositing wet kisses on her stomach and thighs along the way. Once she reached the dampened jewel, Danni didn't waste any time penetrating her tongue inside Carmen's warm pussy. Danni gently teased the opening of her wet lips and dipped her tongue as deep as she could. Hungrily, Danni spread her lover's vagina, searching for her feast. She began to gently suck her clit, applying a soft pressure that made Carmen squeal and moan with excitement. Elated that she was the guilty culprit responsible for serving up Carmen with this dish of pleasure, Danni relentlessly continued tongue-fucking Carmen's pussy. Now ready for a new position, she instructed Carmen to turn and lay on her stomach. Danni began kissing and licking the back of her neck, all the way down to her curvaceous buttocks. Eagerly, Danni started sucking Carmen's pussy slowly from the back access. With a long wet upward stroke, Danni guided her tongue and naughtily started to tease the crack of Carmen's ass. The intensity of Danni's skillful tongue proved to be too much for Carmen and, through muffled screams captured by the pillows, she released hard and long. Danni scurried her tongue down to her vagina, to ensure she captured every drop of Carmen's release. As soon as Carmen regained her composure, she turned over and gave Danni one of the softest, most intimate kisses that she had ever shared with anyone.

Eager to return the favor, Carmen climbed on top of Danni and began softly grinding her moist pussy lips into hers. She playfully ran her fingers through Danni's hair and teasingly sucked her bottom lip as she slipped her tongue in for another intimate kiss. Carmen's hands felt like silk gliding her fingertips up and down Danni's body, causing her to shiver in sheer pleasure. As she continued her finger play, she gradually slid two inside Danni's vagina. Lost inside her slip-n-slide, she offered finger number three and Danni lost control. Soon, Carmen exchanged her tongue for her fingers. Danni's body suddenly tensed with an unexpected displeasure. Much to Danni's surprise, Carmen was far from the natural she had assumed she would be. Danni was quickly reminded that this was Carmen's first taste test—as it was hers. It was clear that her lover would need some assistance to complete the mission.

To avoid the night ending in disappointment, Danni regained

some control and suggested the sixty-nine position. She decided she would initiate a little game of sexual Simon Says; this was her way of disguising the "Oral Sex 101" course that she would secretly begin instructing. It was now "game on" and Danni, of course, was Simon.

Assuming the position, Carmen straddled her pussy over Danni's face and Danni began to softly suck her pussy lips one at a time. "Simon says, one at a time, softly suck each of my pussy lips."

Danni, now Simon, instructed Carmen to repeat the same action she had just performed on her. Carmen followed "Simon's" directive and effortlessly delivered the same pleasure. Danni initiated the next command and demonstrated with long, intense strokes as she maneuvered her tongue in and out of Carmen's melting pot. Danni gripped Carmen's hips to allow her tongue a deeper dive into the split between her legs. Carmen started bucking and fucking Danni's mouth, from the pleasure she was delivering. She obediently followed "Simon's" demonstration and performed the act verbatim.

Danni completely immersed herself in the enjoyment of Carmen's amateur-turned-pro skills...and selfishly lost focus on maintaining her end of the sixty-nine deal. Danni had long retired Simon and it was now a one-woman show. Carmen had stolen back control and, with her newly learned talents, she handled Danni's clitoris like an expert as she softly sucked her to a hard orgasm; followed by a deep sleep.

Throughout college, and even after graduation, Carmen and Danni continued to enjoy each other sexually and romantically. They worked overtime to guard their sexual relationship and attraction for one another from their family and peers; Carmen more so than Danni.

ဢༀ

"Why, Carmen, why?!" Through clenched teeth, Danni demanded an immediate explanation. She grabbed Carmen and pulled her in so close that their breasts made contact.

Carmen pulled away and stood firm. "For the last time, Danni, I *am not* in love with you."

Danni shut her eyes and shook her head, attempting to erase Carmen's words. Unable to control the tears streaming down her cheeks, Danni was convinced that she had lost her lover forever.

ဢༀ

"Do you take this man to be your lawfully wedded husband?"

Carmen nervously looked out at the sea of her close friends and family, all anxiously awaiting her response. Her body tensed as she wavered at the pastor's question. She directed her attention toward Danni, who was also a part of the congregation; after she had refused Carmen's offer to be her maid of honor. She stared at Danni for what seemed like an eternity before finally whispering a faint, "I do."

Hearing this, Danni felt, at any moment, she would flee the church in disgust.

"What was that, dear? Will you repeat your response a little louder, please?"

The pastor asked Carmen to reiterate her answer three times before she finally stuttered, "I...I do...yes, I mean, I will, I do."

The pastor paused and raised a questioning eyebrow at Carmen before continuing. She nodded her approval to proceed and the pastor moved on with the ceremony.

Although Carmen secretly still loved Danni and had enjoyed making love to her more than anything over the years, she realized that she would never be at ease with exposing their relationship. She was heterosexual, and planned to stay that way—on the surface anyway.

So when Cort Jameson—the biology professor who had instructed the class where the two women had first encountered each other—asked her to marry him, she agreed without hesitation. One day, Carmen had stayed after class to discuss a failing exam grade. When they hit it off, she continued to secretly see Cort behind Danni's back.

"If there's anyone here who sees just cause why this man and woman should not be married, speak now or forever hold your peace."

Danni wished she had the nerve to stop the wedding. As she sat there watching Carmen commit to a lie, she couldn't help but remember what had taken place in Carmen's dressing room, less than an hour earlier. She toyed with the idea of letting the guests in on their little secret, of how she had finger-fucked Carmen while helping her get into her dress. Danni wanted to inform them all of how she had cupped her breasts and tongued her nipples before zipping her up. She wanted to tell them all how Carmen had allowed her to camp underneath her wedding dress and suck her delicious clit one last time. Instead, Danni's tears created a steady flow as the pastor finalized her worst nightmare.

"I now pronounce you man and wife."

80C3

It had been several months since the wedding and Danni hadn't heard a single word from Carmen. Sadly, she wondered if she would ever get to enjoy her lover again.

*"Don't 'cha wish your girlfriend was hot like me?"*

Danni jumped as her cell phone's ring tone blasted her current favorite song of the month. The caller ID read "private", so Danni allowed the Pussycat Dolls to sing until they were finally interrupted by her voicemail picking up the call. One short beep meant the caller had left a message. Danni dialed in to listen to the voicemail. Immediately, she recognized Carmen's soft sultry voice.

Danni listened and her heart sank. She replayed the message and slid her hand inside her velour sweats, teasing her moist slit. Carmen's voice always had that effect on her. Penetrating two fingers even deeper, she replayed her lover's message for a second time.

"Hello, Danni. It's Carmen...I miss you...and...and I'm *hungry*."

As Danni listened, she withdrew her fingers from her vagina. As she sucked remnants of the sweet chocolate flavor that remained on her fingers, she whispered aloud to herself, "So am I, Carmen. So am I."

## part 2: she loved a girl...and a boy

Danni knew she wanted nothing more than to make love once more to Carmen. Even though she yearned to taste her lover, she was still bitter by her abrupt marriage to Cort. She wondered if Carmen's call was a result of the happy couple's short-lived marriage. Had Carmen really meant it when the message she left implied that she wanted to taste her? Did she plan to cheat on Cort with her? So many unanswered questions. Danni's curiosity guided her fingers to begin dialing Carmen's cell phone number. She was curious to find out what her former lover had in store.

Carmen picked up on the third ring. "Hello?"

"Hi, Carmen. It's Danni."

&cap;&cap;

D anni was equally nervous and anxious as she waited for Carmen to answer the door. Carmen was even sexier than Danni remembered. The ex-lovers didn't waste any time acclimating themselves to each other again. Right away, they indulged in a long tongue lock and clothes immediately began falling off, as they made their way to the couch between kisses. Danni sat back and relaxed on the plush cushions, widening her legs to better enjoy Carmen's soft lips. As she moaned from Carmen's tongue rippling through her vagina like an ocean wave, she reminisced about how she and Carmen had played "Simon Says" during their first time together.

She licked her lips and moaned even louder as she thought of how well it had paid off. She pushed Carmen's face further between her legs, pleading for her to go deeper. As Danni almost reached the point of climaxing, the pair was abruptly interrupted by a male's voice.

"May I join in?"

Danni's eyes sprang open to see Cort standing over them, excitement bulging from his pants and dancing in his eyes. He had obviously been watching for some time and, immediately, Danni realized she had been set up for a surprise ménage a trois!

Once Danni got over the initial shock of the couple's complete manipulation, her body was still on fire; she wasn't yet ready to stop. Although Danni had never actually been with a man, she assumed those nights she had spent experimenting with her dildo were probably all the preparation she needed for the real thing. Besides, something told her a long, hard dick would be the perfect addition to the sexual adventure. And since she would do anything to be with her lover again, she decided to give the two of them an experience they would never forget.

Lustful eyes were on Danni as the two of them anxiously awaited her reply. She did not say a word. Instead, she grabbed Cort and passionately kissed him; a clear indication that she was ready. Danni immediately took the star role and instructed both of them to lie on the bed. She began to simultaneously orally stimulate the couple. Danni pulled away, careful so that neither of them would climax too soon. She walked over and stood, facing the wall. Then she posted her hands on the wall and spread her legs, as if she were being frisked by the cops.

She demanded Cort to fuck her from behind. Excited by her request, he slowly teased the opening of her wet vagina with his head before giving it all up to Danni. When he slipped his entire huge dick inside, Danni's knees almost buckled from the shock of the penetration. She bit down hard on her lip, to capture the pleasure screams dancing on the tip of her tongue. No dildo could have ever prepared her for the massive log Cort had deposited into her tight hole.

Carmen took her own position by sliding against the wall, facing Danni, and began stimulating her nipples and clitoris.

The pleasure was so overwhelming from the duo that Danni reached her climax in record time.

The threesome headed to the shower to cool off, quite the contradiction of what really followed. The steam from the water was the perfect aphrodisiac and the threesome took complete advantage of it. Carmen and Danni began to tag team Cort. Danni took backstage and swarmed his entire backside with wet, passionate kisses. Carmen positioned herself front and center, sucking his dick so good that, after only a short time, she had Cort pleading for her to relent. Ignoring his pleas, she continued engulfing his penis until he liberated the thick, warm ecstasy onto her tongue.

After they exited the shower, they dried one another off and collapsed back onto the bed. They finally gave in to their exhaustion and fell asleep. Danni was awakened a few hours later by Carmen's soft lips teasing her hardened nipples. She rolled over to extend an invitation for Cort to rejoin the activities; softly massaging his already erect penis. Bringing Cort to his climax, as well as her own from Carmen's gracious finger, she smirked as she thought to herself how, this time around, she would stop at nothing to get her lover back all to herself.

ഇ෮

*Cole Sullivan a.k.a. Bridget C. presently resides in Dallas, TX. The thirty-two-year-old single and sassy "authoress" is new to the writing scene and is currently working on many enticing short stories to share with the recently acquired fans of her work. She welcomes all comments and can be reached at mscain28@yahoo.com or www.myspace.com/bridgetmechelle*

# caged

YVETTE SIMMONS

## chapter 1

Whoever's out there reading this, you're probably a nosey-ass person with nothing else to do but peruse the story of a bitter, black woman. Five years ago my name was Adrianne Green. Now I'm a bunch of numbers, locked up from the outside world like the animal they make me out to be.

All the major issues inside made me fight anyone who challenged me. I fought hard, daily, to gain my respect until I became worn and broken. I've been stabbed, my hair was cut off, my eyes were blackened; many, many times. All broken up and abused, my heart and soul are damaged the most. After all my efforts to earn my respect, I've become someone's bitch inside this hellhole. If you knew me by face before I came here, you wouldn't recognize me now. I've been repeatedly disfigured.

Some feel you end up in here because of your upbringing. I'm beginning to think they're right in my case; this is the best place for me. Even though both parents were in the house growing up, I would've preferred my father alone. Nothing I did pleased my mother, causing me to rebel and take my frustrations out on others.

Bitch...bitch...bitch is the only way to describe my demeanor for so many years. Instead of crying, I sucked it up and dealt with my fate. When I finally let out all that I had kept inside, I knelt down beside the tiny unsanitary toilet that sat in a corner of my old cell and told a story of how sorry I was for being an awful person; complete with tears and loud sighs.

I hated to leave the cell where all my sorrows were released. My new cell was like breaking in a new pair of shoes that hurt the hell out of your feet but can't be returned because the bottoms are scuffed.

It took me a long time to realize that beauty is on the inside; I have none of that. My insides are as rotten as sour milk.

Thinking back, the first day of high school was when I realized that I desired a woman's touch. Relly was sweet, soft, quiet and sexy as hell. Her hair was nappy and short, but soft. The way she licked my wet self, outside for all to see on a picnic bench, was satisfying and uplifting.

The A-line dress I wore that day was long, down to my ankles that covered Relly's lap on up. Those who watched, I could tell wanted me to raise my dress, so they could see more, but only my intense expressions, soft sighs, and Relly's legs showed; the rest they had to imagine.

The top of my dress was low-cut; exposing my breasts without shame. My classmate, Kenya, watched by a tree as I rubbed my nipples and blew a kiss her way. Not enough time that day to get with her too, but I watched her masturbate, leaning against the same tree where we would cross paths the next time. The stress I endured from my mother, I felt settled inside my vagina. Relly's touch, with Kenya's help, soothed a distressed twat all through high school.

After graduation, I became an accounts supervisor at a hospital.

Needless to say, I became the bitch that I always was after my probation. Right after probation, Relly and I grew apart for no other reason than taking different paths in life. Her path relocated her out of state and I wasn't prepared to go.

My housewarming; only my father showed and we had the best time. After he left, the sadness set in. Refusing to cry, I occupied myself with stuff.

My selfish ambitions pushed aside my needy and neglected twat. One day I walked in the house, looked around, sat in front of the TV, and stared at the front door. I imagined a very attractive woman opening my front door, like she had both the permission and keys to enter.

Her profession, how she lived, and where she came from didn't matter. She stopped in front of me and undressed. Her breasts reminded me of beautiful porcelain pieces. Her curvaceous backside made me blush and the perfectly shaped triangle sitting pretty between her legs, covered with dark strands of hair, made me scoot to the edge of the couch; my back at attention and mouth open. I looked around the room and thanked God that no one else was watching me reach for something that wasn't there. When I think of sex, my body becomes warm and my gates open as cum flows through my dark passage. If sheets felt pain, they would hurt from my tight squeeze and teeth marks that I embrace them with.

Thanksgiving dinner every year was at my parents' house. Whoopee! Every year I came alone and was teased because of it. This particular year was no different, but I found peace and sexual healing with Kenya, who yearned to feel me instead of watching from afar as we did in high school.

She lay on the bed, facing me. Her face so close I could feel air when she breathed on my lips. Because she was there with my cousin Andre, and we were in my parents' house, in my old room, doing nasty things, made what we did endearing and daring.

The following Thanksgiving I found out Kenya and Andre were getting married. Kenya wasn't ready to expose her desires for a woman to the world, nor was she willing to let go of what we shared behind Andre's back.

My mother and Andre were close. I overheard my mother telling him that something wasn't right between Kenya and me, to keep his eyes and ears open. He told her thanks, but he knew Kenya very well. I chuckled a little and listened on. She also expressed the fact that she wished she had birthed a son instead of me. Andre was quiet, and catered to her bullshit. Her words hurt me at first, but I got over it, and treated her like I always have; like she wasn't my mother.

## chapter 2

The last Thanksgiving dinner I spent at my parents' house, I bought my new groove, Grace, with me to flaunt. Because my father loved me unconditionally he accepted my lifestyle. I didn't give a shit about how my mother felt about me being with a female, or anyone else for that matter.

I had no desire to be with Kenya any longer, but her desperation to feel what we used to do on a regular basis caused her to do the unthinkable.

She slammed the bathroom door behind us and proceeded to take off my clothes without my consent, and then bit my nipple as hard as she could. I hit the side of her head hard, with my fist. It dazed her momentarily, but she soon came at me again, trying to place her finger inside my vagina. I slammed her against the wall and ran out the bathroom, straightening my clothes.

The struggle seemed long, and unwanted scratches were visible on my face. Grace asked what happened. I told her a snagged fingernail accidentally scratched me twice. The look in Kenya's eyes told the story of being betrayed and thrown away. She licked her lips that I used to enjoy. I watched them chap as I licked Grace on the side of her face before we walked out the door.

Kenya began stalking me at work, but stopped after three months. Just as I began to live without being bothered, I could see her car when I reached the corner of the hospital. Before I knew it, she was in my office, closing the door behind her with a gun pointed in my face. I trembled as she spoke soft and caring words as she placed the gun to her side. I thought maybe she was going to leave. Instead, she gave me the gun and told me to shoot her with it. That, I could not do. She then walked up to me and held my hand and placed my finger on the trigger pointed at her chest. The gun went off, shooting her straight through the heart.

I was left, standing alone, as her dead body lay there lifeless and pitiful. She left my ass to be punished for something I didn't do. My body shook so hard that, if I were a tree, my once filled branches would now be bare.

Kenya wore gloves; my hands were bare. Too scared to move, I didn't think to wipe the gun off before authorities arrived. I've always been the one to talk shit about what I would do, if someone did this or that. Yes, I could have tried to escape with the gun. There were a lot of things I could've done, now that I think about the shit. What the fuck; I didn't. My ass was scared.

When the police did arrive, I was still in disbelief, the gun still in my hand. I lost my freedom—and all that mattered to me—that day.

The woman I loved, the twinkle in my father's eyes, my career; I lost it all. During sentencing, I looked behind me at my father, who stared at the ceiling and never looked my way. My mother never showed. Grace came the first day of my trial; after that, she never returned.

Twenty-five to life, they gave me in this bitch. The first day, I realized that I wasn't getting out; not even for good behavior. The second day, I beat the hell out of this bitch who challenged me in the shower with a bar of soap. Now I know what her intentions were but, back then, I was still green. A tongue, a dick, or fingers are the only things that will ever enter my holes; that's my theory on life. One chick figured pinching my nipple without asking was the thing to do. I knocked both of her front teeth out.

"Pretty Girl," they called me; all who wanted a piece of my pretty ass. My father taught me how to fight when I was a small child, and I did just that.

Most of the guards and inmates wanted to see me at my lowest. Those who liked my looks and wanted my sex desired to see my ass beat by others so I would seek out protection for a price. The price of safety was my sweet pretty self.

The guards are mean. I'm not the only one on the shit list of misfits, but I feel like it. I used to be the finest thing in here, even the guards are ugly. Women who used to have good looks were no more. Now, I've become one of those women.

The guards constantly shove me hard in the back when it's time to go eat. "Move it, pretty bitch," they used to say to me;

until I lost my pretty features. Now they just say, "Move, bitch."

My cellmate, with her scary ass, told others what day my father was coming to visit me. They made sure I greeted him with a bang. My father's visit was pushed back because I needed time to heal. When the time came for my father to come, I was still a broken woman with dark bruises, swollen body parts, and a limp from being hit in the leg one too many times by the guards for being disobedient, so they say. My father broke for the first time, as he watched me make my way to his arms. I never saw my father again after that day. A few months later, I read about his passing in the newspaper.

All the anger that had formed inside of me was forced to show its ugly face inside this place. Every time I hit someone, I fussed like a mother would when you did something bad and had to listen to the preaching as well as endure the butt whooping. My father was the only person who believed in me; I miss him.

It broke my heart; my father left me and I was deprived of knowing about his passing when he first departed this place. I'll probably never know how he died. I'll meet my mother in hell someday and, if I recognize her, I will lay my burnt ass on top of hers to burn her even more. It broke my heart to know that I was a disappointment to my father by being locked up behind bars; even though he knew it wasn't my fault. No damn body better not had fucked with me during my time of grieving, and no one knew how long it would last.

My father dying, the reason I'm in this hellhole in the first place, nightmares of guns going off, and the mess Kenya left on the floor as she lay there. Too many things were hitting me at once. Three months passed, and they felt that was long enough for me to grieve. They decided I should be buried along with my father, but I wasn't finished grieving yet. I whooped all three of their asses. Their ribs I broke, their faces I stomped, and their legs I tried my best to break. I lost my mind on those bitches. Not until then did my grieving subside a little. Yes, I was punished. I'm always the one punished. Good behavior. *What the hell is that?*

My eyes blackened for the hundredth and something time, I have permanent marks that make me look like a raccoon. Dislocated jaws constantly have left my face slightly crooked. The guards cut my hair off when they think it's getting too long.

Many times I've thought, *before I die in this hellhole, I'm going to pin one of these bitches up in a corner and make her wish that she was dead.* Because they're able to go home at the end of their shifts, cut my hair, and push inmates around and tell us what to do, they think their behavior is alright and justified.

My bottom grill is false now; the dentures are not cut right for my mouth and they give me an unattractive look. Ugly? Yes, I am. At least, I blend in now with the rest of the hard faces in here.

My body is covered with scratches, permanent bruises and reminders of war; it is no longer flawless. Although my shapely legs, full breasts, flat stomach, and round perfect ass are still present.

I'm tired of fighting, tired of watching my back and having no one on the outside for support. I'm alone, angry as hell and I long for the feel of a man again; sometimes. The love and comfort from a female that I once shared, she fucked with my morale by making sure my life is ruined. A man can and will cause the same pain, if not greater, which brings me back to a woman's touch and not a man's, although missed.

Tired of fighting, yes, but I had one more ass to beat. My cellmate who ratted about my father's visit. I beat the hell out of her one night when the spirit hit me. She explained to me that "snitching" had kept her alive; even though it was at my expense. I refused to apologize, but understood just the same.

Later that same night, my cellmate and I had a long conversation for the first time ever. Both braless, I couldn't help looking down at her cleavage; she watched mine as well. For a brief moment Kim and my eyes met. Which one was going to make the first move? She placed her finger between my breasts and ran it down to my navel as I took off my shirt. Both breasts were exposed and begging to be touched as she rubbed my nipples with tenderness. I appreciated her gentle touch with her hands but I desired more than just hands on me. I wanted the warmth of her mouth to embrace the soul embedded inside my nipples. For the first time, my nerves were rattled when sex was involved. Being watched by criminals, those who belonged behind prison walls unlike me, unnerved me somewhat. I managed to put all that aside, propped myself against the wall, and waited for her to crawl between my legs. I imagined her to be Grace. I licked my finger, then rubbed my nipples, hoping she could read my mind. The warm insides of her mouth placed my nipples in a comfort zone. She had read me like a good novel.

She placed her legs on the outside of mine, folded them back. Her behind rested upon my hands that were placed on my thighs, waiting for her to sit down with our twats mere inches away from touching. Her butt felt great in my hands as I squeezed her cheeks like Charmin. Raising up her lengthy breasts herself, so that they could reach my mouth, my hands still gripping her behind, I returned her gestures as she did mine to her nipples.

Each stroke with our tongues, licking and sucking, she began to hump. My hands squeezed her backside even more aggressively, matching her every grind.

Nothing in here is a secret. Ears are open, the guards on duty watch us, probably wanting to sample a taste themselves. Some pretend to be disgusted by what they see. One late night, I unbuttoned one guard's shirt, took off her bra, and caressed both nipples evenly before placing my tongue down her throat. Later, I licked her pussy better than any man ever could. She and I are cool now. Other guards, I still have to endure but in time, if given the chance to sex them, life inside will hopefully get better for me.

Back to Kim; she wanted to be licked between her slender thighs. A flower, sugar cane, snow cones, and biscuits with grape jelly and butter between describe what sat on my taste buds during and after I ate her open and wet vagina.

It then became my turn to be pleased but, before I released myself, I wanted to feel something other than her tongue, something stiff that would remind me of a dick; the kind that I had once felt. I asked her to love me with two fingers, which made me come shortly after. When finished, she lay beside me with one hand covering my breast, snoring like she had asthma. What we shared was good.

Ever since the first day I entered this place, there were those who wanted my sex. I wondered how long it would be before I was forced to do others, now that I'm tired and weary.

Kim, my cell-mate, was already the bitch of many others. It was only a matter of time for me. I had hoped when that time came, maybe I could at least enjoy it; if their stuff was clean and I didn't have to kiss those who had rotten teeth, or no teeth at all. If so, they would have to beat my ass, or reverse, before I gave in.

Like a picky person who has their limitations about who they lay down with, I wouldn't donate air to most of the women in here. An ugly woman stood in front of me in the shower one day. She was a hefty woman with large hands and I had never seen her before. *Oh shit!* I thought to myself, *here we go*. Another stranger—just as stout—approached me from behind. It was either fight or give in. The one in the front was a sight to look at, but gentle when sucking my nipples. The one in the back opened my legs wide, rubbed my tight ass, and then licked the outer lining of my back hole. As I held my head back, my arms extended out with my hands resting upon the shower wall, I accepted all that they gave. The one in the front left my nipples, then squatted down and licked my twat. Both my holes were sealed with two tongues that made sighs escape from me that no other had managed to do.

My grind was hard; the audience that watched made my love come down even more. I want to feel what they shared, daily. Yes, I became their bitch, or maybe we are all each other's bitches. It doesn't matter, the shit is good. This place is about survival. I've lost track of time. No need to know since I have years to go. Maybe I'll get an appeal. Will it free me? Who knows?

ഓരു

*Yvette Simmons is a single mother of one son, Markel. Born in Martinez, California, she resides in Richmond, California. A Richmond High graduate who works as a maintenance assistance associate at a college campus, she finds writing to be a favorite pastime and began writing books in February of 2006. She has since written three novels entitled* The Game is Ova', Don't Call Me No Damn More, *and* Janitors + Master Keys = Relationships and Sex. *All have since been self-published.*

# eve's secret
## PRE'CISE

Moving to a new city was a drag after my breakup with my girlfriend, Crystal. The new scenery—especially all the beautiful women surrounding me—was enough to scratch her completely out of my mind. I moved from Kansas City all the way to sunny California, where it never rains and the sexiest women walk the sandy beaches. It was time for me to move on. I was thirsty to find another woman to fill the void that Crystal had left behind in my life. So, I began to hit up the nightspots, hoping to intrigue a new lover. That's when my eyes first met Eve's.

She was a sight for my sore eyes, as I watched her body sway from side to side on the dance floor while the brothas drooled at her feet. Eve Williams was five-eight with long, luscious legs and thick, curvy thighs that screamed for me to travel toward her. Her skin was the color of brown sugar and her palm-sized tits were as perky as they wanted to be. Her face was the epitome of beauty and her smile melted my panties as I sat at the bar mesmerized by her body.

Her eyes caught mine as I sat sipping and watching. She flashed me a sexy smile as her body moved to the music. I wanted to walk up to her and touch her all over, but I couldn't do that in the club. So I sat back, fantasizing about all of the things I wanted to do to Miss Eve Williams. My mouth watered and my mind wondered how delicious she really tasted.

I slammed my empty glass on the bar and lifted my ass from the barstool as I walked toward the dance floor. With my eyes engaged on her, she studied me from head to toe. As I was veering closer to her presence, my journey was distracted by a Southern, chocolate cat trying to holler all in my face.

"Say, Miss Lady, I was watching you at the bar and I have to say that you are one sexy thing. Can I have this dance?" he asked.

I jerked my wrist from his grip. "No, I'm here with someone! Sorry!"

When I felt a soft touch reach for my hand, all of my attention was diverted back to her.

"Hey, I saw you staring at me from the bar. Do you like what you see?" she asked as her fingertips rolled up my arm, causing chills down my spine.

"Yes, I do. I think you're sexy as hell, but I didn't want to approach you like that. I didn't want to offend you because you may not be *that* way."

We walked arm-in-arm toward the private booths in the back of the club.

After we sat down, Eve became mesmerized by my looks just as a tall, chocolate, fine fellow came into view.

"Hey, baby. I'm sorry I'm late. I was trying to get here as fast as I could. Oh, who's your friend?" he asked, his arms wrapped around Eve's body by that point.

"This is…" she began as I yelled out my name.

"Dana! My name is Dana Hill!"

He reached for my hand. "Nice to meet you, Dana. I'm Chris Williams, Eve's husband."

I was shocked by his introduction. *Who would have thought*

*that the woman I craved was a married woman?* I could tell by the way she looked at me, and the way she touched me, that she wanted to get to know me better. I was both ready and willing to oblige. I craved to get to know her from the inside out.

"Would you ladies like some drinks?" Chris asked as I watched Eve stroke his chin with those same fingertips that had sent chills down my spine.

"Yes, baby," she replied. "Get me an Apple Martini and for Dana… What would you like?"

"I'll have the same."

He slid out of the booth, making his way toward the bar through the thick crowd.

"I didn't realize you were married. I was so busy looking at *other* things, I overlooked your ring. I don't mean to pry."

I attempted to slide out of the booth. Eve's hand wrapped around my arm, as she pulled me tighter and closer. "No, don't leave, Dana. We're still getting to know each other. You're not prying. I envision us becoming *real good friends.*"

After whispering those sweet nothings in my ear, she slipped her tongue seductively into my ear. I turned toward her and gazed into her sexy face as she guided my hand up her dress.

I slid my fingers between her satin panties as I caressed her clit gently, feeling her wetness while I slid my finger deeper into her hot body. Eve's legs opened wider as her hips grinded my hand. I watched her enjoy the pleasure that I was bringing her as she moaned in my ear.

"That shit feels so good!" she purred.

Eve was hot, wet, and most definitely ready for me to have a taste as I slid my fingers out of her sweet, sticky nectar. She tasted like sugar and I was on my way downtown when Chris' presence distracted the groove.

"Here you go, sweetie!" he shouted, passing her a drink.

"Thank you, honey," she replied, planting a kiss on his lips.

I instantly became jealous as I watched Chris' tongue tangle with hers. Time passed us by and the D.J. was yelling, "Last call!"

While we sat in the booth, drinking and enjoying the vibe of the conversation, she leaned into me and whispered in my ear, "Do you want to come back to our place?"

My smile was her answer as I excused myself from the table and headed toward the bathroom.

"I'll come with you, Dana. Hold up. I'll be back, baby," she expressed to Chris as she kissed him on his lips and slid out of the booth.

We walked to the bathroom and waited for the six bitches to come out. The handicap stall freed up. I slid into the stall and was working my zipper down with a quickness when I heard all of the gossip and echoes of the ladies disappear, the door slamming shut behind them.

"Is anybody in here?" I shouted out.

Her voice responded instantly. "I'm still here."

As I opened the stall door, my eyes locked onto her nude body, sitting on top of the sink with her legs gaping open and her back leaning up against the mirror. She was massaging her pussy and palming her left breast.

"Don't you want to taste me real quick?" she asked as I slid my body between her legs, letting my fingertips scroll up her silky thighs.

I confessed, "I've wanted to since I first laid eyes on you."

I fell down to my knees, pulling her pussy close, then falling in tongue first. I split her pussy open and let my tongue roll up and down her creamy center, tickling her swollen clit as she moaned and rocked her hips.

"Oh shit! That feels so good, Dana!" she gently voiced as she continued fucking my face.

I sucked her clit and swallowed her cream, leaving her trembling and panting for more.

"Come on, let's go. You're coming with me," she said as she quickly dressed and exited the bathroom.

By the time we had finished playing with each other, the club was practically empty and the lights were on. Eve and I walked toward our booth to retrieve our belongings. After that, Eve walked over to Chris and fell into his arms. He embraced her lovingly as he carried on a conversation with the club owner.

"What was taking ya'll so long in there?" he asked.

"Oh, we were fixing our hair and got caught up in our conversation. You know how ladies do, sweetheart."

I walked past them.

"Are you coming back home with us, Dana?" Chris asked, his eyes making a journey down my cleavage.

"Sure, that's if you want me to come...with you."

Chris licked his lips and kept his eyes engaged on my breasts. "Oh, you're more than welcome. Besides, my wife wants to play and...so do I."

His moist palms ran up and down my back as we headed out of the club together toward the parking lot.

"Follow us!" Eve shouted, hopping into their silver Lexus SUV. They pulled out of the parking spot and I stayed on their bumper all the way to the freeway. Fifteen minutes later, we entered the condominium parking garage and took up spaces side by side. After we got out, we headed toward the elevator. As the doors closed, Chris pressed me up against the wall with his body, and shoved his tongue down my throat.

He pulled up my dress, placing his fingers inside my panties as he massaged my clit. Eve stood next to us, getting turned on as she watched her husband molest his willing victim. Chris pulled down the straps on my dress, letting it fall past my tits as he palmed them.

He instructed Eve, "Suck on them, baby."

"My pleasure," she said, following his request by rolling her tongue across my hard nipples while Chris helped himself to my pussy.

Eve's tongue danced up my chest to my mouth as our tongues clung to each other. Her touch was electric and her tongue was relishing while Chris's tongue worked magic on my clit. The elevator buzzed and came to a stop as we all gained control and headed toward their apartment. Chris unlocked the door and as soon as we walked in, it was on.

Eve and I both slipped out of our dresses as Chris watched in amazement.

"Let's get in the Jacuzzi," he suggested.

Chris directed as we followed his lead toward the pool room. We slid inside the heated Jacuzzi as the buck wild orgy commenced to take place. I enjoyed the way Eve kissed me, and especially how she touched me. I was so into her, it was almost like Chris wasn't even in the room. While we played, Chris pulled out a camcorder and began capturing the girl-on-girl show as his wife sucked on my nipples and finger banged me until I climaxed.

"You two, come to Daddy," Chris ordered as we both hopped out of the Jacuzzi and over to the lounge chair where Chris was chilling naked down to his asshole. "Dana, come put it on my face and Eve, put Daddy's dick in your mouth," he commanded.

I straddled his face backward, letting his tongue pleasure my pussy while I watched Eve gorge on his thick, long meat. I watched her suck while I ran my fingers through her hair. When she came up for air, I pressed my lips against hers as we kissed and fondled each other. I cupped Eve's perfect breast in my hand as I licked her erect nipples softly.

My tongue rolled up and down her chest as I worked my way down to her pussy. She lifted her hips and I let my tongue taste her passion while I jacked Chris off.

"Turn around and slide that pussy down on this dick, baby. Let your friend lick you from behind," Chris directed as her body turned and her pussy slid down on his hard shaft.

His tongue kept rolling around my clit as I watched Eve's ass wiggle and bounce up and down on his dick. I licked her ass while Chris kept smacking mine until it was sore.

"Oh shit, I'm coming...put it in your mouth, baby!" Chris yelled.

Eve hopped up and assumed the position as he exploded in both of our mouths. We sucked and lapped up every drop from his dick as we caressed the head with our tongues.

"I want you to watch us now, baby. Do you want to see me lick her pussy?" Eve asked her husband sexily.

As he held the camera in place, Eve's tongue went to work.

*Now that's what I'm talking about; Eve and I making love without Chris. This is how it should be*, I thought to myself as she sucked on my pussy like a pro.

"I want you to come, Dana!" she moaned.

I gave her what she wanted. I came all down her throat; she remained in place, taking in every sip.

"Let me taste you," I said, pulling her body up toward my face.

She straddled me as she prepared herself for the ecstasy ride I was about to take her on.

I licked her exactly like I had at the club. She moaned and

grinded like she had when I tasted her the first time. Her body began to flow and I tasted her appreciation as I licked her inner thigh.

We lay on the lounge chair together in full embrace, tonguing each other down. I glanced over at Chris, who was sitting there stroking his dick in suspense as he watched his wife navigate my body. Simply having her body next to mine made me think about how Crystal and I used to make love. After we would finish making love, we would always lay together, holding each other just like Eve and me.

Even though Eve was married, I could tell that she wanted a woman more than she wanted a man. I could tell because it was in her touch, in her kiss, and in her smile. They all told the true story.

Morning came and Chris was off to work. I was awakened by Eve's touch as she played in my pussy and helped herself to my breasts. Eve couldn't get enough of me and she yearned to explore me every chance she got. Eve positioned herself between my legs, placing them on her shoulders as she inserted her strap-on dick inside my pussy. She worked it in slow and rolled her hips with ease as I held my legs in place.

She began to work me like a man as she stroked me, continuously making my body wet. We spent the whole morning fucking each other. It was now afternoon as I laid between her legs, devouring her sweet pussy until her clit was sore. Since Eve had plenty of toys to enjoy, I extracted the vibrator that had caused her to climax multiple times. She then turned the vibrator my way, making me squirm until I came. Before we knew it, hours had elapsed and we were still licking and experimenting with each other.

"My husband will be home in a minute. We've got to hurry, okay?" she said as she posted up in the doggy style position and I slid on the strap-on.

"Why do we have to hurry when he knows I'm here? He didn't seem to have a problem with it last night, so why rush?" I questioned as I stood behind her, ready to penetrate.

"He doesn't know that I'm a lesbian, Dana. I love women but he doesn't know that. The only reason we had a threesome last night was because I convinced him to try new things. I told him that I wanted us both to experiment with another woman. I had to pull teeth, just to get him to do that. He had fun, but he'll lose his mind if he found out that we were here doing this without him. It's okay if he's involved, but he doesn't want me to get with a woman like that," she expressed as I slid the dick in her slowly.

"So, you're saying that you're a lesbian, even though you're married and have sex with him?" I questioned in confusion.

"I'm bisexual, but I love women more than men. That's why we're doing this now, because I can't get enough of you. But we've got to keep this a secret from Chris, okay?" she asked as I held on tightly to her hips and plowed into her with force.

I fucked her like she wanted to be fucked. She enjoyed each stroke as she clung tightly onto the sheets, biting down on the blanket. I grabbed a handful of ass as she humped back while I knocked at her G-spot's door.

"I'm coming, baby! I'm fucking coming!" Eve mumbled in the pillow as I slid out, dropped to my knees, and took her clit between my teeth, sucking all of her sugar until there wasn't anymore. Her body shivered with passion.

After I had sucked her dry, I got dressed and was heading out the door. Before I left, I gave Eve my number and told her not to be a stranger. I tongued her down seductively and ran my fingers through her soggy pussy, with a quick rub of the clit.

"Every time you touch me, I melt, Dana."

As my fingers picked up speed, she moaned and let her body melt in my hand as her mouth dropped and her eyes rolled into the back of her head.

I didn't want to leave, so I stayed right there by the door, with Eve's pussy in my hands while I manipulated her body with my finger tease. Just as she was about to come for the umpteenth time, we heard Chris' keys jiggling at the doorknob. "Oh my God, he's home. You've got to go, Dana," she whispered as my hands remained lodged in her pussy.

"Not until you come for me."

I continued massaging her phat pussy. When Chris unlocked the third lock, Eve had caught her nut and straightened herself up as we sat, talking and laughing like girlfriends do, as he entered.

"Oh, hello, baby. Dana was just leaving. How was your day?" she asked, engulfing him into her arms.

"See you later, Chris." I stepped out of the door. "Eve, call me tomorrow. Maybe we can hook up for lunch and finish our talk."

She waved me off. "Okay, girl, I'll be calling you. You take care."

৪০৫৪

**M**onths went by and Eve and I had become the best of friends...more like friends with benefits. Chris remained in the dark about our true relationship and Eve's secret was safe with me. I got what I wanted and she got what she wanted; the best of both worlds. Every now and again, we would all three hook up and have our sessions but, most of the time, it was just Eve and me; doing what we do.

Months turned into a year and Eve and I were madly in love. It was time for the secret to come out of the closet. Eve was prepared to leave Chris for me; I was excited to have her all to myself. Eve didn't know how to tell him that it was over—at least, not in words—so she decided to let him find out with his own eyes as we fucked on the dining room table. What a visual way to break the news.

Chris was in shock when he caught his sweet little wife eating my pussy on the same table where they enjoyed their meals.

"Eve, what the fuck is going on?" he yelled.

She stood before him, wiping her mouth.

"What does it look like, Chris? Your wife is enjoying herself; that's what she's doing," I responded, scooping her body closer to mine.

"So, this is why you've been spending a lot of time with Dana? Because you're fucking her? Without me? What does this mean, Eve? Are you a lesbian?" he inquired in distress.

"This *means* that I want a divorce. I don't want to be with you anymore. I'm in love with Dana, Chris. I want to be with her." She slid the ring off of her finger, throwing it to Chris and pointing toward the direction of his packed luggage in the corner. "There are your bags, Chris. Leave and don't come back."

Eve turned to engage me with a French kiss. I adored her kiss as my hands fondled her tits. My body was on fire and I was ready to come. I couldn't have cared less that Chris was standing there watching, this time with a different expression on his face than normal. I saw pain and confusion in his eyes as he watched me suck on Eve's nipples, making her moan while she whispered dirty little things to me.

"I like it when you suck on them like that. That feels so good, baby."

I massaged her breasts with my hands while she massaged my clit. I opened my legs wide, allowing her to have her way with my pussy as I took her tongue into my mouth, tasting her sweet juices. I felt the cream come oozing out of my pussy while she continued masturbating my swollen clit until I begged her for some head.

"Get down there and finish your job!" I demanded, pulling her down to her knees as my back fell back onto the table.

Her tongue parted my lips as her tongue worked circles across my clit. Wrapped up in the moment, I massaged my breast and moaned sexily while Chris took his last and final look before gathering up his things and walking out the door. As the door slammed, Eve's head shook like a pit bull while she knocked my G-spot over and over again with her fingers.

My body exploded as I gripped onto the edge of the table, letting my ecstasy flow while she stared into my eyes with a smile. Eve Williams was now open and out of the closet, with no more secrets. We were together and in love; Eve's marriage was officially over.

Chris was finally kicked to the curb with a torn-up heart and a head full of confusion, as I'm sure he was sitting somewhere gazing at their wedding picture. His world went from fabulous to disastrous and with a constant thought in his mind. *My wife left me for a woman!* Tough shit, but that's how the cookie crumbles. One man's loss is another woman's gain.

ଽଠଔ

*Pre'Cise was editor and head writer of her high school newspaper with well-known, talked-about poetry and short stories that have won her many awards and recognition from others. Pre'Cise's bad decisions in life—including her initiations and leadership role in her former blood gang—never stopped her creativity and her ability to produce the satisfying work her fan base craved. Pre'Cise modeled from 2003-2005, but quickly gave up her title as a model to become a full-time mother of three and a focused writer. With her first book,* Pleasure and Pain, *finished and self-published through lulu.com, she launched her own fragrances for men and women inspired by her steamy tale. There is indeed a luminous future in store for the temptress of tales, so don't sleep on her. She'll be on the literature map very soon.* Pleasure and Pain *will keep you begging for more.*

# caramel latte

## N'TYSE

"Will you be having the usual?" the friendly waitress asked Dolce, whose face was buried into that day's Dallas morning newspaper. Dolce lowered the paper, folded it, then placed it back on the table the way she'd found it. "Yes, caramel latte, please."

"With whipped cream and a sprinkle of nutmeg?" The young waitress smiled, hoping that she had impressed Dolce with her good memory. Dolce returned a pleasant grin, then turned her attention back to the article she had been reading earlier.

The smell of French toast, fresh banana muffins, and coffee brewing filtered heavily throughout the diner. Waiters and waitresses hustled the floor to accommodate their morning regulars.

"Excuse me, but I believe I was sitting here," a voice said behind Dolce. She ignored the woman, not concerned if she was speaking to her at all. She was too interested in the Macy's thirty-percent-off sale that she'd come across. "Excuse me," the lady said again, this time walking in front of Dolce. "And is that my newspaper?"

She couldn't believe how bold people were nowadays. *I leave to go to the restroom and she flops down in my seat*, she thought.

"Here you go, guys. Two caramel lattes, both with whipped cream and a sprinkle of nutmeg. Enjoy!"

The waitress smiled; she had taken both of their orders separately. She guessed the two were meeting there on business, judging by the way they were similarly dressed. Dolce wore a stylish white and mauve pantsuit, with a pearl necklace and earrings to complement her attire. Her open-toe sandals showed off her fresh pedicure and a silver dangling toe ring.

"Thank you," they both replied in unison, eyeing each other in a peculiar way.

"I'm sorry. I didn't realize this table was taken," Dolce admitted, rising from her seat. "I'll move." She began gathering her belongings, along with the saucer her cup of breakfast sat on top of.

"No, I'm sorry. Don't leave," the woman suggested. "Please sit and enjoy your coffee with me."

Dolce eased her things back down and got comfortable in the chair. She stared at the beautiful woman across from her. Her slightly doubled chin; pierced, narrow, diamond-studded nose, and her slanted, warm brown eyes. Every feature this woman owned, Dolce admired. Her smooth, cocoa-brown complexion made Dolce wish she possessed the same. Instead of inheriting her parents' rich, milk-chocolate skin, she had skin the color of buttermilk.

While this beautiful woman's hair before her was long, black and straighter than a Pocahontas Barbie doll, Dolce's was short and sandy-red with waves deeper than the Pacific Ocean. Labeling herself as a vanilla Oreo, she was nonetheless a beautiful Albino.

"So, you come here often?" the woman asked Dolce, making the effort to spark a conversation after initially coming off so rough. She took a sip from her cup.

"Yeah, I guess you can say I'm a regular." Dolce brought her mug back up to her lips. The woman was dressed tastefully but could have used some pointers from Dolce. Dolce wanted so badly to tell her that the dress she had on was from several seasons ago, and that the scarf around her neck clashed with the rest of her outfit. But she figured she'd cut her some slack because her sexiness made up for it all.

"Well, I'm not from here but when I'm visiting Dallas, and I do come here, it's always so crowded," the woman commented, observing the patrons entering and leaving Sugar Mama's Café.

Dolce smiled and nodded in agreement. "Yeah, this is the norm for a Monday morning. It's best to get here *really* early if you want a seat at all," she hinted.

Dolce tried her best to turn her attention elsewhere and not hold a stare, but she couldn't help it. This woman's body language was talking to Dolce; forward and backward. She tried lowering her eyes as soon as she caught a glimpse of the woman's bare-breasted chest. She couldn't believe this woman wasn't wearing a bra. She felt the heat and, in her nature, she was scorching hot.

"I'm sorry. Is everything okay?" the woman asked Dolce, whose eyes seemed to be rolling around in her head.

"Yeah, um, woo…" She cleared her throat and swallowed that dirty thought. "I better get going. I'm heading to a meeting that I can't be late for," she remembered.

Dolce finished her beverage that now seemed as cold as ice compared to the heat she was fending off.

The woman stood up with her, making eye contact with Dolce as she licked the whipped cream from around her lips. "Please let me pay for your drink," she offered. "I feel horrible about earlier."

"No, it's okay. Don't worry about it. Really."

"I insist," the woman told Dolce. "And I'm not taking no for an answer." The woman placed a twenty on the table.

Dolce looked down at the money, then back to her Coffee-mate. "Alright, if you insist." She grabbed her purse and headed for the door.

ഇൗൽ

When Dolce arrived at the office, everyone else had already made their way into the conference room. She was the last one to enter, taking a seat between Yolanda and Vicki.

"Now, before we get started, I want to introduce you guys to the CEO of Speckwith Marketing. This marvelous woman has taken it upon herself to come down and personally assist us with our latest campaign. Please welcome Ms. Calice Matthews."

Everyone applauded; everyone but Dolce. She was too occupied with entertaining her naughty thoughts of the woman she had enjoyed coffee with earlier. Mr. Hamilton stepped away from the podium and in walked Calice; the woman Dolce had running through her mind. She couldn't believe it. Now she had every reason to give the meeting her full attention.

After everyone had asked and had their questions answered, Calice decided to make her rounds around the large room. She wanted to meet the entire staff that she would be spending the next few weeks with.

"So we meet again?" She gestured to Dolce.

Dolce was speechless, not to mention this woman was breath-taking.

"So we do," she was able to let out.

"I'm Calice." She grinned, extending her hand to Dolce. "I never had a chance to formally introduce myself."

Dolce wanted to do a whole lot more than simply shake her

hand but, given the circumstances, she settled for what she could get. "And I'm Dolce. Dolce Hills, as you may already know."

The ladies carried on a conversation about nothing more than what they were there for.

Calice and Hamilton decided they would partner the group up so that they could hear out everyone's ideas and marketing strategies to promote the new ladies lingerie apparel campaign. Mr. Hamilton agreed it was best that Dolce work with Calice, after Calice expressed to him the conversation the two had engaged in. She told Hamilton Dolce's ideas were very impressive and that she wanted to spend more time with her to lay out marketing strategies.

When Dolce found out she would be partnering with Calice, she wasn't surprised. After all, she knew what to say to lure Calice in. All she wanted was the extra time with her that becoming her partner would allow.

"So, where would you like to meet and discuss everything?" Dolce asked Calice, who was collecting the remaining handouts of her Powerpoint presentation to put back into her briefcase.

She stopped what she was doing to face Dolce.

"Ughh, let's say Sugar Mama's. Naw, that probably wouldn't work, huh?" she asked Dolce, already knowing the answer.

Dolce was lost in her eyes. "Probably not. It can get pretty loud in there," she told her.

"Well, if you're okay with coming to my hotel, we can do everything there. I mean, talk about the ideas for the campaign," she corrected. She gave Dolce a smile that she had not quite seen earlier.

"That sounds great to me," Dolce responded, trying her best not to sound too excited about Calice's invitation.

"Well, let's do nineish."

Although wondering why so late, "Nine it is," Dolce agreed.

Calice pulled out the hotel card where she was staying and jotted down her room number. "Come with your thinking cap already on. I wanna get creative," Calice remarked, walking off and looking back at Dolce.

"Oh, I will," Dolce mumbled. "I'd like to bring more than my creative cap."

☙❧

It was thirty minutes until and Dolce wanted to make sure she wouldn't be late. She arrived at the hotel, parked in the garage, and hung out in the bar until it was time. Five minutes before the hour, she took the elevator up to the twelfth floor. She walked down the hall; briefcase and laptop in hand. She knocked on the door for room 12-B. She really couldn't figure out why she was so nervous. She tried drying her sweaty palms on her skirt.

Calice opened the door dressed in a long, black, silk robe. Her long hair was pinned up with a Chinese stick.

"Come on in. I hope you don't mind the look but I wanted to jump into something comfortable."

Dolce wanted to get out of there and go hide under a rock. "No, it's fine… what you have on," she lied.

"Good, I didn't want to make you uncomfortable or anything."

"No, you're fine." *And I do mean fine*, Dolce repeated the thought.

"Great, well then, let's get started."

Dolce followed Calice around her presidential suite. "I ordered us up some wine," she paused, allowing the possibilities to float between them, "and I made sandwiches, and whipped up a fruit tray. I hope that'll work for you."

"That's more than enough. Thanks. You really didn't have to do that." Dolce looked the room over, wishing one day she would have the money to spend on something as nice. Her attention was immediately directed back to Calice. The room she could not care less about any longer.

The two engaged in small talk, far from the conversation they should have been having. After four glasses of Merlot, stimulating conversation, and jazz to soften up the mood, Dolce's eyes found their way to the clock above the bar area. It was late. Very late. Three o'clock in the morning.

"I have to go," Dolce said quickly. She sat up from the laid-back position she had been in on the sofa.

Calice clumsily brought herself to her feet. "Don't go, Dolce."

Her long silky hair, once pinned up in a neat bun, was now draped across her shoulders. She grabbed Dolce by the hand and pulled her toward her. Dolce, not knowing what to think, looked Calice dead in her eyes and wished the woman wasn't inebriated.

"Calice, you're drunk," Dolce told her sternly.

"No, I'm not. I've wanted you from the moment I saw you," Calice confessed.

Dolce widened her eyes.

"Kiss me, Dolce," she asked, almost begging.

Before Dolce knew it, her fingers were tangled in Calice's strawberry-smelling hair and her lips interlocking with hers, exchanging tiny pieces of strawberries, melon, and grapes. She kicked off her heels and the two fell to the floor.

"Fuck me, Dolce," Calice whined.

Dolce willingly unwrapped the robe Calice had covered herself in and, to her surprise, Calice was already butt naked.

"I told you that I wanted you, Dolce. Please, have me."

Those words were enough to drive Dolce insane. She kissed and sucked on her chin, her earlobes, and then worked her way down her neck. Calice wrapped her legs around Dolce, pulling her into her. Dolce made her way to her nipples. *Whoever her Creator was*, Dolce thought, *I could kiss Him right now.* She snaked around her breast, using her tongue as a compass. Calice's breasts reminded her of two Hershey's chocolate kisses in a 3-D image. They were perfectly designed and developed for sucking pleasure. She cuffed each breast in her hands. The way Calice's nipples swelled upon contact with her lips made her own juices pound at her door.

She watched Calice squirm underneath her and beg for more. Dolce did what she thought to do next, she slid her finger into Calice's mouth and watched her suck it seductively in a manner that turned her on even more. She kissed her way down Calice's tight stomach, tonguing her belly button along the journey, then headed south of where she had started.

"Umm, umm…" Calice moaned.

Dolce released the temptation that had been taunting her all that day. She seized the moment. She placed her hands under Calice's round, soft ass and devoured her early morning snack. Once she was completed there, she flipped her over and tasted her dripping maple syrup from behind, inserting her wet and readied finger into Calice's pussy in slow, deep thrusts. She stroked it and dipped it until Calice's body began to shake in an epileptic convulsion. Dolce thought she had caused her to have a seizure, until Calice begin crying out a beautiful song that would forever play in Dolce's head.

"I'm cumming. Ummm, I'm cumming."

Calice gave into her but wanted to showcase her skills as well. She ripped off Dolce's blouse, walking her fingers down the small of her back. Dolce was very attractive to her. She had never seen such beauty stand out before. She slowly licked the soft, tan freckles that were spread about Dolce's body, from her cheeks to her belly ring.

Dolce lay there and enjoyed the tenderness of each touch.

Calice continued. She wanted to please Dolce the way she had pleased her. She eased her hands into Dolce's heated middle, then began caressing her midsection with her fingers.

"Do you like that?" Calice asked her.

Dolce couldn't talk. All she could do was nod.

Calice slid down Dolce's skirt. She turned her body around and her face was now in between Dolce's thighs while the tip of Dolce's clit brushed against her lips. Calice wanted to mouth-fuck Dolce until the sun came up.

With a few drops of Merlot left in the bottle, Calice poured it over Dolce's hairless pussy, pacifying and drinking the cum out of her like it would be her last supper. She then commenced to working overtime on her.

Dolce climaxed over and over. When she thought they were done, Calice had other things in mind. She went to the fridge, pulling out a fresh banana.

Dolce, relaxed and feeling overworked, lay there on the floor on top of Calice's robe, with her legs spread eagle. She couldn't believe what had happened.

Calice came back over. The coldness of the banana made Dolce flinch when it touched her leg. When Dolce finally opened her eyes to see what Calice was doing at the other end, she knew she'd be calling in to work for sure. Calice peeled the fruit, broke it in half, then began stuffing it inside Dolce until it had vanished. Dolce tightened her ass cheeks.

"Relax, sweetie. Let me show you how I make love to a woman," Calice told her.

Dolce's head fell back and Calice's face fell in, disappearing between her legs. She ran her tongue in Dolce as deep as it would go and began sucking and eating the banana out of her until it was completely gone. A banana malt never tasted so good.

৩০৫

During the days that followed, Calice and Dolce entertained each other every morning, every afternoon, and every evening. When their project was completed, Calice flew back to her Chicago home and Dolce remained in Dallas. Until the two could meet again, Dolce nearly lived at the place they had first met: Sugar Mama's Café.

৩০৫

It had been over a year and Dolce still couldn't get Calice out of her mind. She hadn't heard anything from her since she had left Dallas.

Dolce brought the newspaper down from her face when she saw the waitress walking over in her direction.

"Here you go, Miss Roslan." The waitress stopped at the table right before hers. "A caramel latte with whipped cream and nutmeg sprinkled on the top."

Dolce got out of her seat and walked around to see who this woman was. It was not Calice; although she had hoped that it would be. Heading back to her seat, she heard another woman say, "Excuse me, I believe I was sitting here."

She turned around and the woman resembled *the* Calice Matthews from behind. Only her hair was shorter and she appeared a little thicker. Dolce was sure it was all in her mind.

That was, until she heard the lady say, "And is that my newspaper?"

Dolce walked back over to the table and tapped the lady—who sounded like her former lover—on the shoulder. "Calice?"

Calice's mouth spread and she hugged and kissed Dolce on the lips.

"I'm sorry, I'll move. I didn't realize this seat was taken," the woman apologized to Dolce and Calice, figuring the two were there before her and that maybe she had intruded. As she started to get up from her seat, Dolce pulled up a chair and sat next to her.

"You don't have to leave." Dolce smiled.

Calice motioned the waitress over to the table. "We'll have what the lady here is having," she told her.

"Okay, two caramel lattes, whipped cream on top, and a sprinkle of nutmeg, comin' right up."

&#8526;&#8419;

*N'Tyse is the author of the novels,* My Secrets Your Lies *and* Stud Princess, *along with several short stories and collaborations that are featured in some of the hottest and best selling anthologies to date. She currently resides in Dallas, Texas where she is hard at work on her next big project. Visit N'Tyse at www.myspace.com/ntyse to get updated on the latest.*

# the namma's nectar

## TIGRESS HEALY

Diva raised her face to the Sun God and wiped the salty liquid that ran like the Tigris down her golden bronze neck, between her divine bare breasts, before gathering in her navel on its journey southeast. She looked in the direction of the palace and let out an exasperated sigh. Threw her spading fork and watched the other women toil.

She surveyed the plot of land she had cleared and mourned the abuse of Mother Earth. Soon, the men would import gravel or sand, or worse, lay another smelly black pavement. Each year they required more parking for the festival.

"I hate this shit," she said, peering toward the palace. She sucked her teeth in disgust.

"Hate what?" Suma asked, as if she didn't already know. She looked up from the soil she tilled with her bare hands.

A jubilant woman, she wasn't working, she was playing in the dirt. Gold-toned and naked like Diva, her hair was braided in cornrows that went straight back, stopping two inches above her plump ass.

"I hate preparing for this festival. The rich just get richer!"

"Diva, you know how the Namma feels about—"

"Look, I don't give a *damn* about the Namma! I just—"

"Hush!" Suma scolded. Checking to ensure her co-worker

hadn't been overheard, she whispered, "You must never speak out against Her Royal Grace or abomination and bad luck will follow you."

"Follow me where?" Diva scoffed. She believed the stories even less than she believed in the finality of death. Clearly, they had been created to reduce the power and significance of commoners.

Sure, the Namma was a bad bitch but then so were the rest of them, only they hadn't been fortunate enough to marry a King. And even at that, the Namma's title "Goddess" had been reduced to "Queen"—somebody's wife. The consort of the explorer who discovered their island. The only thing that made her different was her supposed Sweet Nectar.

Suma dusted her hands. "I know you're not a believer but I am. We're doomed to be destitute unless we're fortunate and blessed enough to be able to—"

"I know, 'Drink the Sweet Nectar!' But have you ever wondered why that privilege is only available to men?"

"I have but I don't question it. It's bad for morale."

"Chuh!" Diva sucked her teeth and spat.

The next fifteen minutes, silence ensued. Diva pitched rocks toward the fortress while Suma smothered her body in volcanic soil to benefit from its nutrients.

The sun was going down, which meant it was time to head home and care for the ungrateful husbands that were assigned in exchange for the freedom of being naked all the time. For their protection, unmarried women had to wear clothes. As a rule, no woman was required to have children but if she did, she could breastfeed in public and bring her children to work. That alone made island life better than living on the mainland.

"I want to confide in you. Lay here," said Suma, patting the earth. Diva stretched on her back, breasts spilt like milk; mound shaved as bald as a man in the electric chair. Suma's pussy secreted at the sight.

"You know how the story says the Namma's Nectar gives you prosperity and everlasting life? Well, sometimes I want to see if it's true."

"But that would require you to—"

"I know, but honestly, I wouldn't mind. If there was really something in her pussy that will make me happy, independent, and rich, I would gladly drink it from the reservoirs of her ass!"

The women laughed heartily, despite disapproving stares from the elder women.

"You think it's worth a try?" Suma asked, playfully pressing her filthy breasts against Diva.

"Nope," her friend responded, brushing the dirt off.

"Why?"

"I don't *try* anything. Either I do it or I don't. And I need *nothing* from the Namma. I also possess the Sweet Nectar."

She stood, retrieved her tool, and was ready to go.

"The legend says there's no substance more powerful than hers."

"It's bullshit! A tale. A myth. A story told about one that represents us all. I know, for a fact, my nectar is strong."

"How?"

"Have you never tasted your own nectar?"

"No, but every man who has became successful. I thought it was coincidence. Aju became wealthy, Yoki has attained land, Wandoo got a herd of cattle, and Digo acquired his own island, or so he says."

"Right, so he says! Nonetheless, it sounds like your power has already been proven. You can tell the potency of the nectar by the success of the men."

"I am nothing like the Queen."

"That's because you're yourself!"

"Come on, Diva. You really don't think we should try?"

"Alright, you got me. I confess. Sometimes I want to participate, to quench my curiosity, if not my thirst, but *not* because the Namma has something I don't."

"Then I think we owe it to ourselves to—"

"Exactly! Find a way for women to experience the Namma's Nectar. But how the hell are we gonna do that?"

༄༅

"I don't understand why she would let herself be exploited," said Suma, swatting insects with one hand and carrying a small wooden container with the other.

"Who?" Diva asked, holding an identical box. Leaves rustled and twigs cracked as they made their way through the woods.

"I'm talking about the Namma."

"Exploited how?"

"By letting strange men from strange lands drink from her vagina for money and gifts, but with no lasting gratification."

"I beg to differ. Isn't all sexual gratification short-lived? Do you believe that the Namma, with her luscious breasts, chocolate chip nipples, and beach ball bouncy ass...thick legs and incredible intelligence, would allow herself to be exploited if there was nothing to gain? It must *feel* good, at the very least. After all, the juices don't work if she doesn't cum."

"I've never heard that stipulation. Where'd you get that?"

"Last year, while serving food, I overheard a client talking to his friend. Apparently, he didn't make her cum during his allotted time and was told her juices wouldn't work. And get this: he wanted a refund but the kingdom wouldn't give it. They kept all his money and charms!"

"That's big pimping, if I ever heard it. I guess I'm right to want to sell my shit! No refunds on my homemade Sweet Nectar Juice!"

"Or tea."

"Or wine."

"Mmm," escaped Diva's lips. Eyeing Suma seductively, she said, "I want to be your first client."

"I'm open for business. Use your mouth as a cup."

"Mmm," Diva moaned again. She hoisted Suma against a tree, letting her legs wrap around her waist. She greedily sucked her titties, pulling each nipple with her teeth.

"Bite my nipples, sweetie! I like it rough!"

"Shit!" Diva moaned, as she felt Suma's thumb on her clit and middle finger ease in her wet pussy.

Diva lifted Suma again and placed her on top of a shallow pile of leaves. Threw her legs open to feast.

"Eat me, baby," Suma cooed, spreading her pussy lips widely. Like a bully, Diva pushed and teased the bulging clit with her tongue until Suma cried.

She threw her legs over her shoulders, smacking her ass. "You like this, baby?"

"I love it!" Suma sobbed.

"Get on your hands and knees. Hurry up! We don't have all day!"

Suma scrambled to get in place while Diva gave that ass another smack. Watched it jiggle and flow in oceanic waves.

"Let me do you," Suma said sexily.

"Oh, you want to drink my nectar? Cool, but when I cum, I usually squirt."

Diva stood while Suma kneeled, burying her face in her pussy. "That's right, baby! Lap it like a kitten!"

Suma fondled her own clit while Diva gyrated, holding her head. "Lick me, Mommi. Mommi, make me cum!"

"Back on your knees," Diva ordered. She mounted Suma, doggie-style, pressing her clit against her ass. Pulling her hips back in rhythm, she said, "I've always wanted to hit this shit. Suck those fucking tits. Fuck this juicy pussy...ahh...oh, shit...fuck...shit...," she screamed as she came.

"Sit on my face. I'll make you cum."

Suma only lasted a few seconds before she exploded. The women kissed vigorously before rendering the session complete.

Satisfied, they arrived at the neighboring village forty minutes behind schedule, to collect deposits for the Annual Sweet Nectar Festival.

&)CR

"Maybe we should kill him."

"Don't talk like that! You want to get us killed?"

"Then let's make him sick. What about food poisoning?"

"What good would that do?"

"If he's sick, he won't be able to supervise the event, or tell the Namma what to do or what *not* to do. He can give orders, but he won't be there to see."

"What about his chiefs?"

"We can manipulate them. Tempt them with a little bit of ass."

"Just because they're men doesn't mean they'll risk their jobs. They're loyal to the king and they're accustomed to having pussy. What'll make ours so special?"

Diva thought for a moment. "You're right. We'll have to reason with the Namma. Have her make the King lie low during the festival."

"How do you suppose we'll do that?"

"Let her worry about that part."

"No, how do we get *her* to listen to *us*?"

"Appeal to her ego and greed. Feed her some mainland women's lib. Talk about exploitation. You know, 'pimps and hoes.' Tell her she doesn't need the King as a middle man to collect her money."

"Sounds like a death wish to me. What if she tells him what we've said? Do you know what'll happen if we're charged with treason?"

"We mustn't think the worst."

"Okay, but how are we going to get past the guards?"

"Sometimes it seems as though you know absolutely nothing at all. By posing as wealthy men, how else?"

&OR

"These are the best I could find," Suma said, dropping the hideous brown and gray suits on the bed. They each had a matching vest, hat, tie, and shoes.

Diva inspected the items and scowled. "They smell like mothballs!"

"Again, *best I could find* that would fit. I got them from a thrift shop on the continent. Now check this out," she said, digging into her pocket. "I got fake mustaches from the gag store."

The women giggled like children. Being sneaky was such fun.

Diva said, "The only thing left to do is exchange our currency. Get as many American dollars as we can."

ᏠᏣ

The plan went off without a hitch. At the gate, the disguised women flashed two weeks' pay to the guards—in all ones—handing them a note. It read:

*We're businessmen from The States and would like to participate in the Annual Sweet Nectar Festival but we must appraise the goods before we invest and notify our colleagues.*

The guards notified the King, who was too noble to meet them but sent the Namma into the courtyard with an armed escort.

"I am the Namma," the woman said, approaching them slowly and sensuously. Adorned only in a hand-beaded amber gemstone creation that draped her thick body, and clear stilettos with embedded Swarovski crystals, the Namma entranced the women, making their pussies cream.

Suma's jaw dropped, staring at those globular tits and sexy black areolas, succulent brown thighs, smooth legs, and phat ass.

"We need to talk in private," Diva said in a man's voice. The Namma snapped her fingers and her protection was gone.

"Nice Afro," Suma said in her regular voice.

"Shut up!" Diva hissed.

"Ladies, what can I do for you today?"

"Damn, you got us!" Suma exclaimed.

"Shut the hell up!" Diva chastised.

"You ladies certainly deserve to see me, if you've gotten this far."

"Thank you. Can we go somewhere inside?" Diva asked, squinting at the sun.

"Every majestic woman has a room of her own. Follow me but don't speak. Keep up your masculine facade."

The women passed several male servants, who graciously bowed to the Queen. Diva wondered why there was no female help.

They entered a cozy, dark office with couches and advanced technology. There were endless bookcases filled with texts about business, government, and matriarchy.

"I don't have much time, ladies," the Namma said, taking a seat on the edge of her desk. Her legs dangled, swinging gently like a pendulum. Hypnotized, Diva stared at her royal pussy, with its neatly trimmed pubes.

"I see why they pay all that money for your nectar," she began.

"Do you?" the Goddess asked. She was obviously thrilled with her own excellence.

"Yes, and I see you're an entrepreneur and leader. We're here to offer you free business advice."

"I'm all ears."

"Actually, you're all ass. Ain't nothing wrong with that! Not at all... Your Royal Grace."

"Please forgive her," Diva implored.

"No need. I'm interested in what she has to say."

"Suma?" Diva pressed.

"Well, as women, we'd like an opportunity to benefit from

the Sweet Nectar, too. Why should men be the only ones allowed? We feel they should be prohibited from participating in the festival to see how it feels. This sexist policy is keeping us oppressed."

The Namma was expressionless. Didn't speak for several minutes. Instead, she lay on her desk, kneading her nipples and sucking them. Grazed her fingers along the contours of her body. Whimpered as she finger-fucked herself while her visitors struggled to remain composed. She had fantasized about this for many years but never thought she'd have the support of the women. She relished the idea of endless lines of gold-toned females paying to serve her sexually.

Finally, she said, "So I should take pity on you two?"

Diva answered, "Not pity, Your Royal Grace. *Advantage* is more like it. We're willing to do anything you need." She paused for effect. "This is a great business opportunity, organizing an exclusive affair for women. You can charge them astronomical amounts and increase your profit by refusing to let *any* intermediary take a percentage of your pay. No collectors going into villages, no promoters, no bodyguards—do everything yourself. Benefit from direct sales to the untapped market... women."

"What if they can't pay?"

"Have the married ones get money from their husbands. Anyhow, women are always useful. Let the unfortunate pay a little, then work off their debt."

"And what do you ladies want from the deal?"

"The opportunity to drink from your vagina first."

"According to the legend, if I allow you and the other women to have me, you'll develop the same powers and would threaten my position. Certainly, that wouldn't be a good business move."

"Certainly, but with all due respect, we already have the same powers," said Diva. "It's just that most women exalt you so they don't know. As long as we don't say the power they'll derive from your nectar will be comparable to yours, most will never realize or try to compete. Sound like a plan?"

"I haven't decided yet."

"Please don't tell the King."

"Of course not."

"What about the money already collected from the men?" Suma asked.

"I can assure you it's not substantial. Most men like to pay the day of," the Namma informed.

"Your Royal Grace, can we satisfy you now by drinking from your magnificent cunt? It'll be a gesture of good faith from you to us," Suma posed.

"What kind of fool do you think I am? My escort will see you out now! I'll send for you when I've reached my imperial decision. In the meantime, do not return here again."

∞∞

Diva lit into Suma as soon as they were alone. "What the hell is wrong with you? This was supposed to be methodical and slow. What if she backs out on us now?"

"I doubt it," she said casually.

"Girl, you're starting to act like me!"

"Probably because I drank from that pussy!"

"What do you think she's going to do?"

"We're just going to have to wait and see."

"This is so exciting. I can't wait to tap that ass."

"Neither can I, but for now, all we have is each other."

"Good…'cause I'll fuck the shit out of you in those woods!"

ဆာ

The news spread through the village like a virus in daycare. "The King is dead! His Majesty has collapsed!"

"Oh, shit!" Suma said excitedly.

"Calm down," Diva snapped. "Publicly, you should feel remorse. Don't talk about it, don't speculate, and don't ask questions. Keep to yourself. I'll do the same. Now, just between us, I think the Namma is a *bad* bitch! I mean that in every sense of the word."

ဆာ

The community mourned for almost two weeks before the courier approached Suma and Diva at work with a stack of sealed envelopes. "It's a directive from the Namma. You must read it at once. It's only for women but I'd like to know what it says."

Diva shook her head "no" and the courier ran off. She unfolded the letter and read it aloud.

*We have performed the final rites as well as the reading of the will of His Royal Highness, through which we learned that for economic reasons, he wishes for the Annual Sweet Nectar Festival to go on. However, during this period of mourning, no man is permitted to handle his wife. To honor his command, every woman in this jurisdiction, who is of legal age, married and unmarried, must appear at the royal gates on the date and time printed below. Additional instructions will follow.*

"This is bullshit!" said Diva. "She hasn't called for us!"

"And?"

"She's calling all women to give up *their* nectar but will take the money. In other words, she has become our pimp!"

"I'd like to think the Namma is more honorable than that."

"We have no reason whatsoever to believe that. Not one reason at all."

&#8366;&#8450;

The men were protesting in the streets. Marching and rioting like disadvantaged groups on the continent. The big day had finally arrived and they were angry at the letter they received, forcing them to contribute to the festival they were excluded from. Suspicions and accusations about the King's death ran rampant. Some thought it was poison, others "a heart attack from stress," and some believed it was suicide or murder. There was also the issue of who would take the throne since the King had no brothers or sons, which was a motive. Each man believed himself to be worthy.

Suma and Diva stood in line behind thousands of women who had heard about the event. Like usual, they ran out of parking and sexual tensions were high, but this time, the men cleaned, and served food instead of them.

Diva was fuming. She and Suma had been the first ones to arrive, yet every time they got close, the Namma ordered them to the end of the line. They had been waiting for four days.

"She's fucking with us. Am I wrong to expect special privileges?" Diva asked.

"No, because she wouldn't be doing this if it wasn't for us."

When there were no more women, it was their turn. The Namma held her finger to her lips. Quietly led them to her extravagant chambers, away from where she had been with the commoners. She lay back on the Continental king-sized bed, draped with red velvet covers, and spread her legs for them to enjoy.

Suma dug in first, navigating her tongue slowly over her clitoris, making her moan. Brushing her lips against the clit, sucking hard, then soft, licking her inner and outer labia, and sticking her finger in her saturated hole.

Diva was on the Goddess' breasts. Teasing and sucking her nipples. Tongue kissing her and licking her navel.

"Scrumptious," Suma said, to which, the Namma shuddered and came. When it was Diva's turn to drink, the Namma sat on her face, allowing her to stick her tongue deep inside. Suma rubbed the Namma's clit as she fucked Diva's face. The sound and sensation of the women making love sent the Namma's body into glorious convulsions again, almost immediately.

"I stopped myself from cumming with the other women so I'm extremely worked up. Now, let me please you," she said, telling each woman to lie back.

She sucked and licked each nipple, rubbed their firm asses, and fingered their pussies expertly. Before long, she had made each orgasm and was drinking the nectar from their twats. Her mouth was sticky and wet with cum and her breath smelled like womanhood. It was the happiest she had been since being on the boat with her man discovering this land.

Orgasm after orgasm, the women enjoyed one another's bodies, not caring what part belonged to whom. Exhausted and entwined, they basked in the scent of their sexual pleasure. Diva asked the Namma why they were continually sent to the back of the line.

"It's cliché to say I wanted to save the best for last so I'll just tell you about the new legend. 'Men who drink the Namma's Nectar will die mysteriously and the cause will never be discovered but women will have prosperity and everlasting life, just as the ancient scrolls predict.'"

"What ancient scrolls?" Suma asked.

"These," she said, pulling a stack of papers out of her nightstand that had obviously been printed in her office. "I just have to find a way to make them look old."

The women snickered deviously. Diva shook her head and said, "I knew it! But what's that got to do with making us wait?"

"Ladies, I know you're Goddesses, and in a sense, the legend is true. I wanted prosperity and long life by drinking Sweet Nectar from you two, and I decided that once you came, I never wanted you to leave. Welcome home, Nammas! You're royalty."

೮೦೦೪

*Tigress Healy is one of many pseudonyms for this flourishing writer. Originally from New York, she now resides in Georgia with her family. She is currently working on several erotica and cultural fiction projects. She can be reached at tigresshealy@yahoo.com.*

# coast to coast
## GRANT FAHNAH

During a longer pause than usual before the mirror, Azalia studied the different ways that she could move her head to hide her double chin. Scars from teenaged acne were slowly fading from her mahogany skin. She sighed and pulled back from the mirror, turning to the right to observe her curves from a side view, she noticed that there seemed to be less distinction between her butt and her thighs. Leaving the bathroom, she reminisced about the days when toned deltoids did not lend themselves to skin flapping under the arms, to a time when Lauren wanted her with such hot passion that they could not sit in the same room without touching each other. Those days seemed to fade away, leaving Azalia feeling utterly unattractive and completely undesired.

৪৩০৪

During her final year of college, Lauren attended every home game of the women's basketball and women's soccer teams; rain or shine she was there in the stands cheering on her team, displaying a front of school spirit. She always sat away from the others, on the opposing team side or the corner of the bleachers where no one would bother her and she could just focus on the game, or rather focus on the players. Their bestial arm and leg muscles rippling as they moved swiftly through the game haunted her dreams of caressing, touching, rubbing, kissing and holding these women, ebony skin interlocking with her golden-almond flesh. Evenings spent at the games allowed Lauren to escape from reality and plunge into a fantasy world where these women ravished her, aggressing until she completely subsided. Rendered helpless, Lauren would come over and over again at the whim of her athletic goddesses. The truth was she rarely came at all, and when she did it was usually her own doing.

After the games, she would go home to the bed that she shared with her partner. She climbed into bed, desperately trying not to arouse her, not to wake her, not to touch her or be touched by her. She often wondered if she was ever sexually attracted to her partner, who did not have the smooth brown skin, toned muscles, the beauty or the grace that the women she lusted after had. Small things about her partner made her fall in love; the way her fingers plucked the guitar, the fullness of her lips, her locks when she let them down, the endless gaze of her breathtaking brown eyes. But after three years together these things became mundane, slowly they seemed to lose interest in one another, and Lauren actively lusted after other women. She never did anything with most of these women. She didn't even make eye contact with them, let alone do anything sexual with them, though she probably would have under the right circumstances and with a huge confidence boost.

She had cheated on her partner two times over the three years, but only one time counted. The first time, the one that doesn't count, was before they were officially together. She had sympathy sex with her ex-boyfriend, who pathetically lusted after her though she was no longer interested. But the sex had been good; probably the best part of their relationship. She felt bad for him so she went for it one last time, thinking it was fair game because *technically* she was single. Her partner never really got over that; there was constant bitterness and resentment, which is why she didn't tell her partner about the time she cheated—the one that counts.

In an effort to branch out of their current social circle for New Year's Eve one year, they decided to split up and go out with their own groups of respective friends. Lauren decided to go to a house party with a group of literature graduate students on the other side of town. A sophisticated, older bunch of white intellectual dykes, she was somewhat fascinated by them but not physically attracted to anyone in particular; she chose to go out with them, thinking she was safe and would not be tempted by their bland appearances and personalities. Awkward conversations abounding, Lauren drank steadily, hoping to ease the tension in the room. A dozen gin and tonics later she came to with an older, blonde woman on top of her and a very long acrylic fingernail stroking her clit. This fingernail was an unpleasant awakening to the fact that this extra-nuptial affair was not going to be pleasurable, and in the end not worth it. Eyes open, fixated on the white ceiling, suddenly Lauren was way too sober to be in this position; she didn't even know how she got to that point anyway. She called a cab and put the blonde woman in it before her partner got home at seven a.m. to find her fast asleep. Her partner must have seen the red thong underwear on the bedroom floor, but they never spoke about it—ever.

Throughout their senior year of college, people wondered

what the two of them were going to do after graduation. They both planned to attend graduate programs on opposite coasts and it was kind of obvious to those around them that they didn't really like each other that much. No one really understood why they were in a relationship now, nor why they would want to try to make it last. Yet, everyone knew that they would attempt to stay together. What were they so afraid of?

Lauren went to the Bay Area to study marine biology. Azalia headed to New York to study journalism. They agreed to stay together, but to see other people—an "open" relationship. The only rules were no falling in love and no talking about the people you hook up with. Other than these rules, they had no other game plan for their new open relationship adventure, nor future plans to end the long distance aspect of their relationship. Azalia, wanting a fresh start in New York and cognizant of the fact that her apartment was on the seventh floor of an elevator-less building, only brought with her two suitcases from the apartment that the two of them had made home over the past few years. Lauren hitched a U-Haul trailer to her forest-green Tacoma, shoving all but the contents of Azalia's suitcases into the back of the truck and the trailer. She and her snake, Max, made the trip to California via the 101. She devoured a carton of cigarettes, many four-packs of Starbucks espresso in cans, all the while belting out days' worth of Ani DiFranco songs.

When Lauren got to San Francisco, she did not waste any time and immediately set out to discover the vast lesbian community. Her first night, she was at a club and by one in the morning, she was on her way home with a Mexican-American boi-dyke by her side, a woman that the average straight person would think to be male at first glance. This fit, toned brown body was just want Lauren wanted.

Lauren barely knew where she lived. As they walked in, she had to excuse the boxes everywhere, the unmade bed, the empty refrigerator and her chaotic life, but the boi-dyke didn't seem to notice as she was already sucking on Lauren's neck like lions eating their prey. Before the neck attack, Lauren had a pretty good buzz going, but after a few minutes of neck gnawing she was kind of tired and really uninterested in this girl. Hmmmmm, how to get rid of her… Lauren thought of plans to get rid of the girl while she proceeded to suck on her neck. She could show the girl her snake and that might scare her away. She could act like she's schizophrenic, start screaming, tell her she's tired, or having her period. While Lauren was busy thinking about how to get rid of this girl, the girl had unbuttoned Lauren's shirt and was now unzipping her pants. Lauren was up against the kitchen island. The girl lifted her up on to the cold countertop and sat her on the edge, slipping Lauren's jeans off and tightly gripping her thighs. Lauren was no longer plotting to get rid of this girl. She stared down at her thighs, this girl's hands gripping them in a way that was on the cusp of passion and pain. She leaned back on her arms as the girl's warm tongue plunged into her. The girl's flickering tongue glided up and down her clit, slowly at first, and a small puddle of Lauren's wetness and the girl's saliva collected on the cold, marble countertop. They moved quickly from the kitchen counter to the bedroom floor.

Do people really do that? She didn't even know this girl's name and the girl went down on her. Maybe things *are* more progressive on the West Coast? Lauren, not yet adjusted to West Coast time, still in her plaid boxer shorts and faded yellow T-shirt pajamas, was up with the sun, cleaning the bathroom and starting to unpack. The noises of unpacking roused last night's guest.

"Hey," the girl said, one arm on the doorframe. She looked intently at Lauren.

"Hey," Lauren replied awkwardly; she was obviously nervous.

They stood in the doorway, looking everywhere but at each other for what seemed like an eternity. Lauren now knew that yes, people really do "this," and this girl was one of "those" people who did "this." Lauren had finally fulfilled her fantasy of being whisked away by a hot-bodied, dominating woman.

"So, I gotta go in to work this afternoon, but maybe I'll see you around?" the girl said as she buckled her belt.

Car keys in hand, she gave Lauren a bit of a smirk, kissed her on the forehead, and walked out the front door in her boi-dyke way. Lauren, who really had never experienced anything like this, was actually speechless. She stood in the bathroom, 409 in hand, not knowing whether or not to feel content and satisfied, or angry and used. She ran to the living room window and, separating the Venetian blinds with her fingers, she peered out at her fleeting friend. As the girl got into her black Accord, she paused. Her dark sunglasses covered her eyes, so Lauren couldn't tell where she was looking. She then pulled down her shades and looked right at Lauren, again throwing her that same smirk before she got into her car and drove off.

Sitting in her bare living room, she pulled the yellow gloves off of her hands and sat reflecting on last night's turn of events. Feeling puzzled, yet somehow accomplished and fulfilled, she was smiling contentedly when her phone rang. She paused for a moment, staring at the name "Azalia" on her caller ID. The smile disappeared from her face and she answered the phone with a vacant, "Hello?"

"Hey, babe, how *are* you?"

"Good. How are you?" Lauren answered in a monotone voice.

"I'm okay, but I miss you so much. It's so hard out here. I mean, I don't really have any friends and the few people I have met all seem to be crazy or too busy to hang out," Azalia opened up.

"I'm sorry, that sucks," Lauren replied, genuinely feeling sorry for Azalia. She began to feel guilty about last night's events.

"I did go out last night. I went to this queer poetry reading and I met some people there, but they kinda seem like they're not lookin' for friends right now, ya know?"

Azalia kept talking, while Lauren responded with one-liner "Um-hmms" and "That sucks." Her mind wandered. For the first time, she wondered what Azalia's life would be like in New York.

Azalia, unlike Lauren, was not of the legal drinking age, which seriously inhibited her ability to do anything social with other college graduates. This also made it nearly impossible to easily meet other lesbians in New York. Before Azalia never would have dated outside of her race, it was black women that turned her on; particularly Lauren. No one else did quite the same thing for her. Azalia tried to think of creative ways to meet lesbians. She went to black lesbian spoken word readings, she volunteered at the LGBT youth center, and she perused all of the city's free papers and internet listings for any queer activities. But, no matter how many of these events she attended, she could not seem to meet anyone.

Azalia looked at the time on her MacBook: 10:23. She was in on a Friday night yet again; she had no plans for the night or for the rest of the weekend.

"Damn it!" Azalia knew that if she kept this up, she would

never meet anyone. Feeling a deep depression coming on, Azalia decided to do something to get herself out of this rut. She logged on to Craigslist New York City, entered the women for women section, and started to peruse the ads. Azalia read three or four ads before landing on "Thick, beautiful, woman of color." When she opened the post, the first thing she noticed was the picture at the bottom. There she saw the most beautiful black booty she had ever seen. She studied the picture, trying to figure out if it was a real photo or not. She decided that it was. Compelled by the tingling warmth between her legs, she responded to the ad.

An hour later, her clothes were strewn all about her Upper West Side studio, and she was walking out the door in her "fuck me" jeans, a push-up bra, and a low-cut red shirt. Her unfettered confidence was whipped out of her and a wave of cool clamminess came over her as she entered the Clit Club. With her brow furrowed, she shifted awkwardly in the doorway as she felt all eyes on her. Smileless faces turned and glanced for only a brief moment before they turned back to their present company. The music reemerged and Azalia's heart started to beat again as she reached for her phone to text her mysterious big-bootied woman. As she was typing—*I'm here wearing red shirt, where are you*—a low voice inquired, "Are you Azalia?"

She looked up to find before her a woman who would surpass her expectations of a whimsical internet encounter. Azalia studied the way that her perfectly smooth, charcoal skin was caressed by an orange dreadlock that had purposely been let loose from the rest of her locks wrapped atop her head.

Azalia looked into her brown eyes and smiled. "Yes, I am. It's actually pronounced *Aza-leeeah*; it's not like the flowers. Nice to meet you, Tamiah." She extended her hand for Tamiah to shake it. Tamiah looked at Azalia's hand, then up at her face. She paused for a minute and, with arms wide open, embraced Azalia with the first hug she had experienced since she moved to New York.

"You look like you needed that," Tamiah said as she led them to two stools at the bar.

As Azalia followed Tamiah through the crowd, she stared in awe at the multicolored Afro-hawks, funky glasses, Nikes in colors she had never even imagined, and outrageously hip clothing from teal flapper dresses, and poufy, tutu-like skirts, to full on zoot suits and overpriced vintage T-shirts. Feeling lightheaded, she took her seat at the bar next to Tamiah.

Tamiah looked at her. "Are you feeling alright?" She leaned in and touched Azalia's right leg.

Azalia looked at Tamiah's hand on her leg and paused before looking up and replying, "I'm much better now," as she flashed a flirtatious glance and bit her lower lip. She could not believe herself. Where was this coming from?! Just seconds ago, she felt queasy from the oozing coolness coming from the room, and she had somehow sequestered a huge amount of confidence, careening head on into Tamiah's not-so-subtle sexual advances.

"What's your drink?" Tamiah asked as she leaned over the bar to get the bartender's attention.

"I'll have an L.I.T."

"A what?" Tamiah looked confused.

"A Long Island Iced Tea," Azalia responded, perplexed by Tamiah's lack of familiarity with the drink.

"I never heard it called that before. I'm from Long Island. We just call it an 'Iced Tea' there." She smiled, not taking her eyes off of Azalia.

"So tell me about you," Tamiah inquired.

"Well, what do you want to know?" Azalia replied flirtatiously.

"Where you from? What are you doing here? What do you do for fun? All of that mess."

"Well, I'm originally from the South Side of Chicago. I moved here after college." She paused. "Actually, I haven't even been in New York City a month. I'm still living out of my suitcase, but, um, I came out here to go to school."

"Oh, yeah! That's great; a sistah with brains. I like that. What are you studying?"

"I'm going to CUNY for my masters in journalism."

"Masters, damn. That's all right." Tamiah nodded in approval as she threw her head back, downing her shot of Jack Daniels.

Azalia didn't ask Tamiah anything about herself, not because she wasn't interested; she just didn't think to. She was not very well-versed in blind date etiquette. Somehow, their conversation flowed well into the night, without even noticing the emptiness in the room. They found themselves sitting at the same bar-stools as the lights flashed on hours later. They were genuinely surprised to find that they had closed down the bar. As Tamiah flashed her signature to close her tab, she turned and looked at Azalia. With her vulnerable, yet commanding eyes, she asked where they were going from there. As they hopped off of their bar-stools, Azalia looped her arm through Tamiah's, looked up into her eyes, and in a whisper-like, low-toned voice, said, "Take me home with you."

෩෪

Azalia sat at the dining room table, nervously looking around while Tamiah rolled a joint. Too nervous to let herself go, Azalia knew that once the smoke hit her, she could unwind and fully embrace the night. As Tamiah pulled from the joint, she held the smoke in her mouth, signaling for Azalia to move onto her lap. Tamiah turned to her, slowly moving toward her. As their lips touched, they paused for a moment before the anticipated release. Smoking the joint down, they spent moments lingering in the lip-touching moments of tension before releasing into each other's thick-lipped, warm-tongued, passionate kisses.

The two of them were soon lost in each other, lying on their sides on Tamiah's bed. They slowly undressed each other; kissing, touching, and licking each curve as it was revealed. As her tongue flitted Azalia's nipple, Tamiah looked up toward her, and from the tortured expression on her open-mouthed face, Tamiah knew that she was completely content and ready to be taken to the next level. Azalia's chest moved up and down with her rapid breathing as Tamiah moved down her stomach, kissing past her belly to the top of her underwear.

Tamiah slowly moved her right hand up Azalia's inner thigh, lingering at the top before moving back down and up again. She pulled Azalia's underwear off of her and, with her warm tongue, moved back up Azalia's left thigh. Hovering over her wet pussy, Tamiah breathed in Azalia's smell. Tamiah moved up toward Azalia's neck, pausing to lick between her breasts. Tamiah softly kissed her neck and paused to look Azalia in the eyes. Azalia closed her mouth and looked back at Tamiah before they kissed again, harder now than ever before. Tamiah's fingers slipped past Azalia's throbbing clit into her soft, warm wetness. Tamiah held the small of Azalia's back as she writhed in ecstasy. Tamiah's other hand plunged into her, then repeated soft yet deep penetration, juxtaposed with groan-inducing moments of clitoral caresses. Vibrant colors passed before Azalia's closed eyes as her mind stopped and pure and utter pleasure transcended.

Feeling Azalia tense up inside, Tamiah pushed inside her with greater intensity. She lifted Azalia's breasts to her mouth and gently bit on her nipples as Azalia climaxed and, with a deep guttural moan, her body collapsed in Tamiah's arms. Tamiah kissed Azalia on her sweaty forehead and, without exchanging words, they embraced.

As Tamiah and Azalia lay there holding each other, body parts intermingled in similar ways to the poster of two white lesbians that hung above Tamiah's bed. Azalia could not help but think of India.Arie's lyrics—*brown skin, I can't tell where yours begins, I can't tell where mine ends.* As she lay there contentedly thinking about how good Tamiah's skin felt against hers, on the floor across the room, just below audible volume, inside the pocket of her jacket, her buzzing cell phone read, "Lauren."

ℰℂℛ

*Growing up in the cold dark winters of Wisconsin, Grant turned to writing as a source for reconciliation of the good things in life. Grant writes lesbian erotica as a process of release and hopes that those who read the work will also feel somehow lifted. This is Grant's first publication of erotica, and hopefully not the last. Grant currently lives and works in Southern California.*

# gray's anatomy
## FREAQUENCY

The instant the bat made contact with the flying base-ball, the cracking sound slid through the sliver of an opening of Soledad's window and woke her up. Her eyes were barely open when she heard the sound of glass breaking, causing her to jump out of the bed. She ran to the nearest window. Her head was pounding and she was overwhelmed by the feeling of a diesel truck running her over and over again. A quick self-pat revealed that a wifebeater was covering her DD's and bikinis were barely covering her ample behind. The beater and bikini were good signs, an indication that she had not slept with any strangers the night before. Instead, the cement-like throb of her scalp meant she had indeed drunk too much alcohol.

Soledad's only concern was her house, which had not made contact with the ball. But, across the street was old man Kennedy's brand-new Escalade. The shiny exterior heightened the fact that there was no longer a back window. The streets were as barren as a desert as he jetted from his house and out onto his front porch. He raised his fist and kicked a dirt hole into the perfectly manicured lawn.

Soledad closed the blinds and didn't envy the perpetrators for one moment. She had endured more than a few encounters with the tall, middle-aged widower, mostly when his daughter came home from college during the holidays. His little princess, Cynthia, was a borderline nymph but looked as shy as a church mouse.

The thought of Cyndy drew her back to the pain that had overtaken her head. Soledad dragged herself to the kitchen and pushed open cabinets full of samples from the drug companies. Although she wasn't big on taking medications, she had learned to simply bring home the loaded gift bags she received from pharmaceutical representatives at work.

Her fingers shuffled through the pile and landed on a small box of Tylenol with codeine but she threw those back in and retrieved some Motrin. Barely able to walk, she opened the refrigerator door and left it wide open. Using the little bit of strength that she was able to muster, she grabbed the orange juice container and gulped down four—maybe six—pills.

It took every moment of the long and excruciating twenty minutes before her head could move without the thrust of pool balls bashing against her skull. She headed for the shower and the streams of water against her face and chest felt soothing. Her hands ran down her chest and she cupped her breast while her other hand slid between her thighs. Barely grazing her clit, she shivered and tucked her middle finger deep inside. With each thrust her nipples grew harder, resurrecting in her mind the feel of Cyndy's body wrapped around her own physique.

Initially, the daydream was laced with the soft flesh of Cyndy's medium-sized breasts nestled against her back, as Little Miss Princess pasted electrified kisses all along her neck and shoulder. What really drove Soledad crazy was the sensation of Cyndy's pelvic hairs rubbing against her behind while her hands gently kneaded her belly and thighs. Cyndy always liked the role of being a tease, so Soledad would grab her hands and spin her around so they could make eye-to-eye contact.

Just then Soledad was snatched out of wishful thinking and back into the throes of reality, by the sound of someone knocking at the door.

Soledad slammed her hands against the wall, mumbling unrecognizable obscenities under her breath. She wrapped the towel tightly around her curvaceous body and pulled on a thin robe. Every third step was met with a slightly less intense clash inside her skull. Soon the repercussions of over-drinking would subside, or so she hoped. Soledad struggled to look through the peephole.

Intending to yell, she barely squeaked out, "Who is it?"

She could tell that her voice was barely audible so she cleared her throat and belted it out again. "Who is it?"

His voice sounded more like a plea than his usual command. "It's Kennedy."

She opened the door. "Come on in." Soledad cracked a slight smile and waved in a welcoming way.

Mr. Kennedy didn't look at Soledad but marched directly into her house like an invited guest.

"Did you hear that noise outside?" he asked.

Soledad could see where Cynthia got her chiseled facial bone structure and the slightly Asian-looking eyes.

"Naw, I mean, yeah, I heard something a bit ago...but I was sleep. It woke me up."

Mr. Kennedy was on the couch by then, moving Oprah magazines to the side that should have been on the coffee table.

"Well, they hit my car."

The expression on his face startled Soledad. He had always seemed tough and brash but appeared vulnerable at the moment.

"By the time I got to the window, no one was on the street. Sorry about your car," she added.

Soledad tried to reflect sympathy in her voice but the hangover still pounded through her head. Mr. Kennedy scanned the contents of the house, glanced at the door and then seemed to be peeking into the kitchen, like he was searching for something in particular.

"You've got a nice place."

"Thanks."

Mr. Kennedy looked at the robe she was wearing and then placed the magazines back in their original place on the coffee table, like he was trying to help her organize.

Rising to stand, his stature seemed almost too muscular for a man his age. "I just came by to find out if you saw anything."

Soledad shook her head as he turned to let himself out the door. "I bet it was probably some kids." He took one last look around and slammed the door behind him.

Soledad had moved into the Garden Heights neighborhood about five years prior, when she had started medical school. The house had been empty for a few years, since the death of her uncle. Her grandmother, his beneficiary, didn't have the heart to sell it. Soledad offered to rent the house and her parents offered to buy it. But, to the surprise of everyone, her grandmother surprised her and signed over the deed. She had always seemed distant and emotionally detached from Soledad but insisted that it was a gift for graduating from college and undertaking medical school.

Garden Heights was a middle- to upper-class community

comprised mostly of African Americans and located near the University of Michigan. Soledad had grown up in the heart of Detroit and the university town constrasted greatly from the inner city. Unlike where she had grown up, it was substantially harder to find a liquor store; not that she needed them.

Liquor stores were few and far between and, unlike an inner city, nestled in some unsuspecting places on the outskirts of town. Also, mostly everything closed around nine, with the exception of the posh restaurants and theaters. The town was centered around the campus and felt abandoned in the summer but overpopulated during the regular school year.

Soledad had been in medical school and living in the house for a few months before she finally decided to attend her first party. Upon leaving her house, she closed up the garage and decided to ride her motorcycle, a sparkling purple GT 750 Ducati.

But before she could start the engine, a woman ran toward her and yelled, "Those wheels are nice. I thought you were a dude for a sec but it's all good."

Cyndy sashayed around the bike, staring straight into Soledad's eyes. She stood about five-five and disguised her slim figure with a large, shiny, patent-leather black belt that complemented her blue chiffon blouse and straight khaki skirt. But what truly caught Soledad's attention were her green bedroom eyes. They looked sexy against her perfect milk chocolate, smooth skin, and brown wavy hair with auburn highlights.

"Can I ride, chickadee?" Her smile was confident and Soledad wondered if she knew what she was doing.

Soledad laughed, put her hand out, and introduced herself. When Cyndy held her hand longer than usual, it was clear she knew exactly what she was doing but Soledad couldn't push past her church girl exterior. She declined to take Cyndy on a ride and was met with a long face.

Cyndy pointed to the house directly across the street; indicating that it was where she lived. Cyndy was a straight, no-chaser kind of girl, so she pulled a pen from her pocket and wrote her phone number inside the palm of Soledad's hand. Soledad played it cool. A kiss was planted on Soledad's cheek and, within seconds, Cyndy turned and switched her small hips as she strutted toward her house.

Soledad revved her motor and glided at a slow pace out of her driveway, then stopped in front of the curb where Cyndy now stood. She flipped up the visor on her helmet and winked at Cyndy.

Cyndy looked her up and down as she licked her full lips and puckered them, feigning a kiss. Before Soledad could settle into the tingling between her legs, her eyes couldn't help but focus on the face of an angry man standing at the front door. Soledad was nobody's fool and recognized the territorial protective look of a man who was either her father, or boyfriend. Soledad cranked the engine full throttle and sped off.

Soledad left the party early. Her first thought was to call Cyndy but the thought of the old man followed right behind it. Soledad coasted into her driveway. The neighborhood was dead quiet and the house across the street was completely dark. Just as Soledad was opening her door, there was a slight tap on her shoulder. Startled, she jumped and nearly fell off the small porch. Cyndy jumped back in response but caught the falling Soledad.

With a slight chuckle, she said, "I'm sorry. I didn't mean to scare you."

Soledad composed herself and started to laugh from the pit of her stomach. Cyndy joined in and the two wiped away tears that resulted from the long laughter. Soledad fumbled with her keys and the moment the door was closed, the two locked lips. Cyndy slithered her tongue from Soledad's earlobe to her clothed nipple.

Her gaze caught Soledad's eyes rolling to the back of her head as her body went limp. The two unfastened, unzipped and unbuttoned at the speed of lightning until they were completely nude. Soledad wrapped her hands around Cyndy's firm behind and hoisted her up around her waist. Cyndy became the damsel in distress as Soledad smothered her face within Cyndy's chest and carried her upstairs to the bedroom.

The snake-like motion of Cyndy's tongue landed between Soledad's thighs. The flickering sensation got a rise out of her clit, which grew rounder and firmer. Cyndy's tongue-lashing intensified as she lapped up every last drop of moisture from the head of her mound to the eyelet of her anus. Soledad's back arched, pushing every bit of being onto Cyndy's face.

"You like that, don't you?" Cyndy announced as she pulled Soledad's hips tighter and tighter.

"Fuck me," Soledad whispered, hoping it was just a thought and not audible words. But when Cyndy's fingers penetrated with a rhythmic motion while her mouth gently suctioned the flesh of her chubby clit, Soledad suspended disbelief and released an orgasm that nearly drowned Cyndy's face and hands.

"That's right, girl. Give it, *Mami*. That's what I'm here for. Yeah, I like that."

Soledad felt a sense of comfort and frustration. She attempted to pull away from Cyndy but her grip was locked and her hand was nearly fully inside. This would be the first time Soledad had let a woman fist her and, with each circular motion, she experienced her vaginal walls receiving the small balled hand of her new lover. Her orgasm subsided with spikes of energy driving her nearer and nearer to the next moment of ecstasy.

Screaming at a pitch she thought was only capable of girly girls, Soledad was shocked at the explosion of excitement she felt in every cell of her body, including the edges of her finger-tips. Cyndy's hand was nestled deep inside her womanhood as orgasmic rays pulsated through her body and provoked minia-ture convulsions. Sweat poured from her flesh like water. They were both surprised when a jetstream of cum peaked at a height of about two feet.

"Dayum, baby. I didn't know you were a squirter."

Cyndy leaned back to enjoy the sight and Soledad was slightly embarrassed but too excited to let it show.

Soledad's body lay flat and lifeless. Cyndy brought a warm washcloth from the bathroom and patted the sweat from Soledad's forehead and neck. Their eyes met again; they searched for more answers, hoping to define their connection. Soledad smiled at the stranger and started to wonder when the sunlight would vanish from their interaction, but then stopped herself. This time she would not go there; this time she would enjoy with an ounce of hope.

Cyndy finished drying off the rest of Soledad's body and lay next to her. Soledad's muscular arms drew her closer as the two held each other. Before the sound of morning birds, the two had tossed the sheets of sexual bliss several more times.

Soledad caught a nap before she had to go to the medical school and woke to an empty bed with a small note that read:

*We must do this again and again and again.*

A generous smile swept her face and a steady throb evolved within her vagina.

ৱৎ

S oledad backed her Mercedes out of the driveway and just as she reached the street, she could see the man from Cyndy's house pulling his trashcan to the curb. In an instant, his simple gesture reminded her of two things. She had forgotten to put out her own trashcan and, despite a really wonderful night of fulfilling sex, she still didn't know the exact nature of his relationship to Cyndy. With the car now in drive, she inched her car past the mystery man. He was waving but his face was void of emotion. Soledad lifted her hand, flickered her fingers, and sped off.

The following evening, Cyndy and Soledad agree to meet at a lesbian-owned café. The place was quaint with lots of woman art, gently used couches that lined the north wall, and wood tables and chairs that had been painted a lilac staining tint. With a maximum capacity of fifty, the place was half full and the crowd was mostly engaged in the poetry reading. Soledad walked in to find Cyndy mingling with a group of women at the small bar located next to the entrance. Cyndy introduced Soledad and then the two took up seats at a small reserved table.

The corner table was near a window and was partitioned off from the area where the poetry crowd was gathered. Soledad complimented Cyndy on her outfit. It was tight-fitting, sexy, and the complete opposite of the church garb she had donned the day before.

Soledad's voice was stern but not harsh as she asked, "So who's the guy at your house?"

"Oh, so, you don't do straight girls?" Cyndy teased.

"No, of course I do. What does that have to do with my question?"

Cyndy could sense Soledad's frustration. "My father, but he doesn't know about me."

Soledad looked at Cyndy. "Well, he scares the hell out of me."

Cyndy considered that and gazed out of the window.

"Deacon Raymond Kennedy is harmless."

Both women grinned and the sing-song of Cyndy's voice comforted Soledad. She found herself looking at Cyndy and assessing their sexual acts. The two did not match. Soledad touched Cyndy's hand, and they both submitted to a mutual gaze. The silence was a bit unsettling, or perhaps it was a plea for peace.

"Let's go back to my place," Soledad's voiced as more of a question than a suggestion.

Instead of responding, Cyndy pulled her closer for a kiss and the two left.

Once in the car, Soledad leaned her head toward Cyndy and stared. Then she grabbed Cyndy's breast with one hand and unzipped her tight leather pants with the other one. The two kissed like their lives depended on it. Cyndy helped with the pants while Soledad became full of the flesh from her breast. The sucking of her nipples summoned a moan from Cyndy, who was licking Soledad's ears. A loud noise caused them to stop and look around.

Soledad was on the verge of panic and refastened the buttons on Cyndy's shirt. "Let's go home."

"I like the sound of that," Cyndy responded sweetly.

Various thoughts started to flood Soledad's brain, but she

was intent on keeping the lure of "dyke drama" at bay. Soledad placed her hand against her nose, and then placed her fingers in her mouth, resulting in Cyndy's breathing becoming labored. Cyndy tucked her fingers into her panties and masturbated. Soledad was driving and caught a glimpse.

Soledad said, "Give 'em to me. Feed me."

Cyndy pulled her hand out and laid her fingers on Soledad's lips. She used her tongue to draw Cyndy's fingers into her mouth. She devoured every bit of her sex juices and licked all the crevices between her fingers. Soledad decided to pull into an empty parking lot of a shopping mall.

Soledad turned Cyndy's body toward her and pushed the seat back. Her fully twisted body was bent forward but she could barely get her tongue to reach Cyndy's pussy. Quick moves laced with frustration and then they landed in the backseat where she was able to maneuver a little better. Soledad's hot tongue had a slow motion but Cyndy's gyrating hips suggested the speed was ideal. Soledad suckled her clit and munched on the lips that lay wet, yet gorging with blood that rushed to that point. Her tongue pounded into Cyndy's wet hole. The thrusting incited Cyndy to place her hand on the back of Soledad's head; she loved being tongue fucked.

Soledad used her lips and teeth to draw more sex juices and swallowed every drip. Cyndy's orgasm was accompanied by loud, short pants and nasty curse words. At the height of Cyndy's climax, her thighs squished Soledad's head. Luckily for Soledad, it was harmless and she was still able to breathe. She moved her tongue further back for a rimming job. Cyndy begged Soledad to "stop" and "don't stop." A sexual confusion ignited excitedly.

Soledad ran her tongue from clit to ass a dozen times or more.

Cyndy's hips jumped as her legs fanned back and forth, beating against the car and Soledad's head. She was intent on pulling the cum from Cyndy's pussy as she continued her thorough sucking of the clit, followed by a tongue fuck in her vagina and ass. Cyndy could hardly contain herself; her uncontrolled motions were a dance of pushing and pulling. Her body twitched uncontrollably and she shouted church phrases of joy that included, "Oh, my God" and "Help me, Jesus." Soledad's strong arms and body blanketed Cyndy as she descended from her multiple orgasms. The car was warmer than a hot day in the desert and the windows had a one-inch layer of fog. A short time passed before they finally left the parking lot.

Once they arrived at Soledad's place, they cooked dinner in the nude and shared their sexual fantasies. Cyndy confessed to wanting to be fucked with a dildo. Soledad eagerly pulled a medium-sized black cock from her closet and fucked her for nearly an hour on the stairs. Soledad's stamina was tested as Cyndy yearned for more and more. They took their fuckfest onto the enclosed back patio. Tall windows revealed the beautiful night sky and allowed the swirl of cool air to invade the room.

The two ended up exhausted from their fuckathon as Soledad laid out on the floor and Cyndy reclined on a small chair, nearly asleep.

"You know what you look like?"

Soledad was surprised to hear the sound of a voice and raised her head to make sure Cyndy was speaking.

"Who?" Soledad replied with a bit of laughter in her voice.

"The guy on the medical book. Your body is so perfect. What's that book called?"

Soledad didn't want to think about anything medical and shrugged her shoulders.

"You know what it is. It has the same name as that new doctor show on TV." Cyndy's tone was insistent now, as she hit her palm against her head, trying to remember.

The room was silent, with stars gleaming against the naked brown bodies of the two women. The sound of a passing train in the distance was an indication that more time had elapsed than they thought. Soledad sat up against the couch; she could view the beauty of Cyndy's sweet face. Cyndy was trying to stay awake and gave Soledad a little hand wave. Soledad recognized the enjoyment she sensed when spending time with the woman. It was the first time she had experienced that deep-seated feeling of desire and love. Soledad decided she would not be pessimistic. Instead, she would use the power of positive thoughts. She would always try to be the best.

"Gray's Anatomy." Cyndy's eyes opened and she pushed herself to a upright sitting position. With outstretched hands, she motioned for Soledad to come to her.

"Yes, baby, that's exactly what I was talking about. The famous doctor was Henry Gray with an 'A' but the show is about Meredith Grey with an 'E'."

Soledad felt a sense of accomplishment. She did not understand how the two went together, but it didn't matter. Removing the harness from her waist, Soledad crawled on top of Cyndy and cuddled next to her in the chair.

Soledad could see the moon waning, but the sunlight in the sky could not possibly compare to the sunshine in her arms. She was tired but felt it necessary to place continual tender kisses on this gorgeous woman's face, neck, and lips. This woman—now deep in slumber—was her lover.

෨○ල

Soledad and Cyndy dated for two years before the Peace Corps in Africa and a college on the West Coast tore them apart. The distance meant holidays and school breaks were the only time they spent together. During those times, Soledad befriended old man Kennedy and kept in closer contact with him than Cyndy. Throughout the years, she never actually disclosed the nature of her relationship with Cyndy to him, but somewhere deep inside Soledad knew that he understood and was all right with it.

ଚ୍ଚ

*FreaQuency is a native of Ann Arbor, Michigan, a community activist-writer, poet, playwright, filmmaker and mother of three teenagers. Her work has appeared in* Shenandoah, Callaloo, Harrington Lesbian Fiction Quarterly, Lodestar Quarterly, San Gabriel Valley Poetry Quarterly, *and a few anthologies. She is currently finishing a collection of erotica and has started writing a novel. Website: comingoutblack.com*

# the meeting
## NALEDI LARATO

**W**hat does it mean to desire someone so much that you feel it in the depths of your being? I never thought I could desire someone so much that I would ever consider sharing them with another; until I met Kaye. Our meeting was destined. Two women desiring to meet a soul mate; someone who could capture your intellect and be fierce, and someone who was sensual such that the depth of your being was set on fire just by peeking a glimpse of her body, or hearing the sound of her voice.

By chance, I never expected to meet Kaye at a racial social justice institute. More specifically, I never intended to encounter any white person that I would want to date; let alone sleep with. I had made a political decision over twenty years ago not to date white, or do "vanilla" as it is called by black queer folk. Rather, I expected to be surrounded by people of color; activists charting out the next attack on the "white privileged." Instead what I encountered was a coppertone white woman engaging me about her trip to California and how she was gay. I did not disclose my sexual orientation at the time. Black women don't "put our business out in the streets;" in particular to white people we don't know. Nevertheless, I engaged Kaye in conversation until the institute began. I attempted to signify to Kaye that I was "gay friendly" by sharing that gay pride was going on in Los Angeles. That elicited a smile.

Kaye had a roommate who had requested a single room while my roommate had not arrived yet. Kaye asked if she could be my roommate and I gladly accepted. Once again, Kaye engaged me in conversation, so I inquired about what she did as a career. She was an applied anthropologist and adjunct faculty member at a nearby university. I laughed and shared with her that my undergraduate degree was in physical anthropology; that I had an affinity for anthropologists. I noticed that Kaye's black DKNY glasses contrasted with her copper skin and beautiful, highlighted curly hair. As she was putting up her belongings, I noticed various tattoos and body art on her torso. Kaye enjoyed wearing hip-hugging pants and short shirts that provided glimpses of her art. I wondered about the symbols and how alluring they were on her skin.

As the institute progressed, Kaye and I spent more time passing notes between us rather than paying attention to the lecturers. Our non-verbal conversations ran the spectrum from academic issues, to we haven't defined structural racism, to my conception of the white privileged that corresponded to her conception of structural racism. She eventually asked me about interracial dating. I shared with her that I had made a political decision not to date white. I also asked her what type of individuals she was attracted to. We definitely were interested in each other but were testing the waters.

In our room at night, our conversations ranged from sharing about our dating experiences, sexual orientation, and emotional dilemmas as intellectual/sexual beings. Although the light was very dim, I could see the contours of Kaye's nipples in her tee.

I attempted not to stare but I was aroused by the sensual allure of Kaye's beautiful body and erect nipples. At one point, she was cold and wanted to jump into my bed. I did not respond; perhaps I didn't know how to respond. It had been over five years since I had been in a relationship; let alone had sex. I was ambivalent about engaging in an interracial affair. Although Kaye was Italian American, an ethnic group I had always had empathy for, I was unsure about dating someone "white." My politics, being African centered, were in question. My mantra had always been, "Couldn't I find a beautiful African woman/ man to mirror my greatness?" Now I was attracted to someone white and considering a relationship.

Nevertheless, Kaye and I continued our foray into getting to know each other better. The day finally came when our discussion at the institute focused on our backgrounds and racial conscious-ness. Kaye shared with the group that somewhere in her lineage there had been mixture with Africans and that she wasn't sure how to identify herself. She certainly saw herself as being white but was confused about what it meant to have African heritage. Unfortunately, the moderator was not sensitive and said to Kaye in jest, "I always knew you were a 'person of color.'"

When I encountered Kaye later in the evening she was visibly upset; pacing back and forth. I immediately asked her if I could walk with her. She was upset about her personal disclosure and felt violated. As we proceeded, the conversation turned toward us. I felt a warm feeling creeping into my body as I walked next to Kaye. I was hoping that she didn't realize my attraction toward her and my nervousness about strong sexual feelings. We'd reached a fork in the road; I brought it to her attention. She asked me if she could hug me and I said, "Yes."

Not only did we hug but we began to kiss. As we kissed, I

gently rubbed the contours of her butt. We continued walking and talking until Kaye directed me toward a more intimate location, then backed me up against a wall, groping my behind and rubbing her pelvis against mine. Needless to say, I dampened with excitement at the thought of rubbing another woman's pussy and, in particular, engaging in public sex. We walked a little bit more; holding hands until we reached the party.

As I was about to leave the party, I informed Kaye that I would be waiting for her. When Kaye arrived in the room, she immediately jumped into my bed. We began groping each other's body, not really kissing—a sign that this was all about "fucking" and not intimacy. While Kaye rubbed her hard clit on my thigh, she slid her long, strong fingers into my wet vagina that was waiting to be entered. I grabbed her from behind and wanted to enter her; except that she was on the "rag." We spent the night enjoying each other's bodies.

## interlude — "they're all going to know" "fast forward"

Kaye drove me home from the institute, both of us sharing our life histories and shocked to find out the similarities between our families and personal abuse histories. We shared that we had done "the work" that had provided the emotional healing necessary to have healthy intimate relationships. We vowed not to re-create the same abuse patterns in this relationship. We also vowed not to let societal norms about race destroy our emerging bond.

The next morning I made passionate love to Kaye's body. I

awoke, rubbing on Kaye's wide but firm behind, examining her body art that gracefully followed the curves of her body. From the dragonfly sucking nectar from the flower located on her left shoulder, to the green iguana circling her right hip, to the winding rose on the opposite hip, to the Ohm sign at the base of her spine, to the red and green snake on her right ankle, and finally the sun sign on her left lower abdomen. I was intoxicated by her. As our clits found each other, rubbing in slow motion, my spirit began to feel at one with hers. Her tongue pushed ever so deeply into my mouth, and our tongues intertwined moving in motion with our clits, and the sound of our juices mixing. That was the moment I realized that I could fall passionately in love with someone "white." No longer fixated on color but on the feelings of making love to a woman, a woman who matched my sexual desires, with no boundaries.

We eventually explored penetration with a dildo. Although rubbing against a woman's clit is exhilarating, entering a woman with a strap-on dildo elicits a different type of excitement; one of raw power. Penetration engenders domination and power over someone else's body. I penetrated Kaye's pussy as if she or "it" was mine. I wanted to let her know that she was mine so I fucked her pussy until she came. I could feel Kaye becoming more excited, which in turn made me more excited. I no longer relied on physical sensation, but immersed myself into Kaye's energy field. I became in tune with Kaye's spiritual, emotional, sensual, and physical energy.

Kaye and I engaged in love making and fucking every week for two months. I remember the first time Kaye allowed me to "eat her pussy." While she always pleasured me with one hand, or both hands since she was ambidextrous, her tongue was golden. Kaye would cradle me in her arms first, stroking my clit, making me wet. She would then glide lightly down between my legs, placing her tongue on my clit. She would stroke my labia, then insert her forefinger into my wet, soft and gushing pussy. I would moan and whisper, "Kaye, I'm going to cum."

She would stick her tongue deeply inside me, tasting my juices until I came into her mouth. I loved the feeling of her long fingers entering me; I wanted her to enter me with a dildo and become one with my body. Glancing down in between groans and ecstasy, I would see her curly highlighted hair in between my legs. I would grab her head with my thighs while I climaxed, wanting to push her tongue deeper and deeper into my wet, moist and throbbing vagina.

## the first — doing vanilla

There's a myth that eating black pussy is different than eating white pussy. Kaye's pussy had no color, in my mind. I was just eating someone's pussy that I was in love/lust with. I remember the first time I asked Kaye to let me go down on her. She hadn't been able to allow herself to emotionally make herself vulnerable with most of her past lovers. As a result, Kaye never experienced deep orgasms; ones that come from making oneself completely defenseless by trusting your partner. I was so into Kaye that all I wanted to do was to make her feel safe and to enjoy making love with me. I slowly eked my way down Kaye's body and slipped my head between her thighs; thighs that had waited an eternity to be kissed and sucked, on my way to her succulent red mound. I slowly licked, sucked and plunged my tongue deep into her vagina. I felt her body respond to my caresses as I felt her warm juices ooze into my mouth. Her taste was barely noticeable but her wetness, oh, her wetness, told me that her spirit was in rapture. Following the motions of her body, and the increasing swelling of her clit and labia and thrusts of her body, I worked her into orgasm and stopped. She pushed my head back in between her thighs as my tongue dove deeply into her wet pussy, ever so deep, tasting, wanting to lick and suck every last drop of her juices. As Kaye exploded into orgasm, my spirit merged into one with her spirit and for a split second our energy merged.

## s/m and other kinky sex

It began in jest, me sharing my handcuffs with Kaye in her bedroom. I lightly clamped them onto her wrists; ensuring that I didn't hurt her. I was always very gentle with Kaye—embracing my feminine energy. She remarked in jest that they were real handcuffs. She attempted to escape but realized that they were indeed real and that she could not escape.

I quietly uttered, "You don't really know me, do you?"

Kaye's normally cocky attitude turned into a perplexed look as her face flushed. She attempted to put her legs through her arms but I gently guided her to the bed and laid her on her back. She could not reach her arms through her legs. Rather, her ass was now "high in the sky" on her back. I held her down, taunting her face-to-face.

"You know what I could do to you on your back?"

I desired to take her right there, in handcuffs, rubbing my

clit against hers. She responded by groaning and rubbing me back. Is this rape or the desire to dominate another being who wants to be raped?

## solitude

While touching her the other evening, I briefly paused and rubbed Kaye with my finger.

"Don't stop, please." Her request was like a whisper.

While Kaye exhibited a wildness and fierceness about herself, at that moment I knew Kaye's spirit. She was shy and hesitant about asking for what she deserved, to be loved for who she was and to be treated gently.

Kaye and I continued our journey—learning each other's bodies, desires, and fantasies. One of my favorite joys was strapping on Long John Silver and taking Kaye from behind. With an audience of four cats, Kaye and I tussled on her study floor, her on all fours with her ass in my face and me grabbing her shoulders and guiding the long silicon dick, complete with balls, strapped on with a leather harness into her wide, wet and inviting pussy. Kaye began to groan as I grabbed her hips and pushed her butt into my pelvis. Enthralled by the sheer force and power of entering another woman from behind, simply peering at her body excited me. Kaye kept asking to be "fucked" and I eagerly responded with each thrust. I felt Kay's wetness dripping onto my thigh.

# the meeting

ஐૠ

*Naledi Larato is a native Los Angelena, a rarity in the state of California. She has always had an intellectual and activist interest in how collectives of people make sense of their world and organize themselves. Subsequently, her intellectual interest spans indigenous spiritual healing systems, identity, gender, and sexuality, of Afro-descendent people. She holds a doctorate degree in public administration from the University of Southern California and master and bachelor degrees in public health and anthropology from the University of California, Los Angeles. She has lived abroad in several African countries, and traveled to South America, and Europe. Naledi considers herself to be a global citizen and her desire is to set foot on every continent. During her leisure time she enjoys eating, reading, photography, international travel, yoga, cycling, and rock climbing.*

# never say never again
## SHATIRA

I stood at her door, nervous as hell. I couldn't believe I was actually there, and was very tempted to turn around, jump back in my car, and ride back across town. I would call her, or email her as soon I got home to tell her that I got a flat tire or, more truthfully, apologize for changing my mind. I was sure she would be upset, since I had already changed my mind more than a few times before. It was by my doing that we hadn't met in person yet, and I was sure she was growing more impatient by the day.

I had been standing at her door for at least three minutes before I made up my mind to turn around and go home. As much as I wanted to, there was no way that I could go through with it. I didn't realize that she had been peering at me through the peephole, so as I turned my back to descend her steps, I jumped as I heard the heavy wooden door open. I stopped in my tracks, almost afraid to turn around.

"Oh no, sista, you're here now. I got you. You may as well turn around; although I do like the back view."

Her throaty, yet sultry voice sent a tingle up my spine. I turned around and faced the devastatingly sexy Aretha. Her crimson painted lips were curled into a sensuous smile, and I knew there was no way I could deny myself of her any longer than I already had.

Aretha stood to the side of the doorway and beckoned me in. I took a large breath and mounted her stairs. She made a low whistle as I took tense steps past her.

Closing the door quickly, she turned to face me. I smiled at her as I removed my coat. Aretha reached out to help me, moving so close to me that I could smell the intoxicating scent of Cool Water for women; my favorite. It felt odd, being this close to a woman, but I liked it. Even though I was fully dressed in a short sleeve cotton T-shirt and a denim skirt, I suddenly felt naked as her eyes roved over my body. She grinned approvingly and turned to hang my coat.

I had met Aretha on an online forum dedicated to black women. On the site, women of color from all over the world shared tips on dating, sex, beauty, and other matters pertinent to our community. There was also a place to post poetry and short stories. I posted a few poems and received plenty of warm feedback. Aretha's was the warmest. She emailed me and told me how deep it was, and how much she enjoyed reading it. I checked her profile, and realized that we lived in the same city. I emailed her back to thank her for the kind words, and a friendship was forged.

We spoke for a few weeks via instant messages and emails before exchanging pictures. She was a beautiful woman, with coffee-colored skin just a few shades darker than mine, and sepia eyes that shined like fire in all of her pictures. Her smile was alluring and mischievous, as if she had a secret that she wanted you to plead with her to reveal. She was curvy but toned, with a nice ass, and had the best set of breasts—besides my own—that I had ever seen.

We began innocently enough, but after a while things began changing. I had saved all the erotic pictures Aretha had sent me, and many nights I had stared at her pictures, rubbing my breasts, imagining what it would feel like to graze them against hers, or to cover her nipples with my mouth. I would lie in my bed, naked, and whisper her name, wishing that somehow she could come and extinguish the fire burning between my thighs for her sexy ass. I dreamed about her spreading my "big pretty legs" and massaging my thick clit with her fingers while tongue kissing me. She had told me she was only into women, and as a person who secretly wondered what it would be like to become intimate with a woman, this intrigued me.

Aretha was the first person whom I had ever shared my secret desires for women with in my entire life. I had always claimed to be "strictly dickly," but deep inside I had never ruled out the possibility of physically being with a woman. It was strange, but in the short time I had been conversing with Aretha, I felt comfortable with her; like we were old girlfriends. I kept postponing meeting up with her, but my curiosity eventually got the best of me, and led me to the woman's door.

"Let me make us a couple of drinks. Make yourself comfortable and have a seat in the living room."

She flashed that sexy grin of hers and headed toward her kitchen. I walked into the spacious living room and took a seat on the black leather sofa.

It was late in the evening, so because of the quietness of the house, I could hear crickets harmonizing outside. The room was dimly lit with candles scented like jasmine. I could tell she was trying to set a mood.

"I didn't turn on any music because I wanted to know what you were in the mood for," Aretha said as she entered the living room with two glasses filled with ice and a clear liquid, along with a bottle of expensive vodka.

"It doesn't matter," I answered nonchalantly.

Secretly, I hoped she would turn on something sensuous and romantic, some "panty soaking music," as my ex-boyfriend liked to call it. As she stopped at the coffee table directly in front of me and bent down to set the beverages on it, her ample breasts jiggled, and I got a clear view down her light-blue V-necked top. My mouth watered at the caramel mounds of flesh that were not constrained by a bra.

Aretha walked over to a stereo system mounted on the wall and pressed the play button. As if she had read my mind, the room was instantly filled with the sounds of R. Kelly's *12 Play* album. I stirred in my pants a little. This was the number one "panty soaking" album for me. By the time he had crooned his way to twelve, I was usually naked; no matter where I was.

She walked back over to the couch and took a seat next to me. She was sitting so close that I could smell her minty fresh breath. Surprisingly, I was getting less uncomfortable with the situation. She passed my drink. I sipped slowly as she stared at me, seductively stirring her drink with a slender finger and then slurping the liquid off as if she was orally pleasing a man. I watched her without words for a few moments.

"So, my dear..." She finally broke my trance. "Now that I have you here, what shall I do with you?"

I wanted to tell her to do whatever made her happy. My center was throbbing to be touched, the same way I felt whenever I was turned on by a member of the opposite sex. All I wanted to do was tear my clothes off and press my body against hers, but I was too afraid to speak, so I shrugged a response. She smiled knowingly and set her drink on the table.

Aretha leaned in and kissed my mouth. I parted my lips and she slowly eased her wet tongue inside. I held my breath at first, but soon my tongue was entwined with hers. Her hands grazed my shoulders, while mine remained in my lap, afraid to touch her. It was as if she would disappear if I touched her, like my ultimate fantasy would be over, and I would wake up lying in my bed with my hands in my panties, alone.

Aretha was an aggressive woman; if she wanted to be touched, she was going to be touched. Thus she forcefully took my hands and guided them along her firm thighs. We were wearing almost identical short denim skirts, so our knees touched as we continued to kiss. I felt my temperature rising, and my nipples hardening.

Aretha broke from the embrace and gently pushed me down onto the couch. Silently, she lifted my legs and removed my strappy, high-heeled sandals. Setting one of my legs on the top of the couch, she pulled my silky purple panties aside, revealing my pulsating flower. I closed my eyes as she slid her fingers into my wetness.

"You like the way I stroke that pussy, baby?"

I moaned as she rubbed my swollen clitoris with two fingers. I sighed in response and spread my legs wider. My inhibitions were gone, and there was no turning back. I totally surrendered myself to this gorgeous woman. I sank deeper into the couch and spread my legs wider, inviting her to go deeper.

"That's right, baby, get comfortable," she encouraged me.

I opened my eyes and raised my hips as she slid my panties off. She quickly unbuttoned and unzipped my skirt and pulled it off. Then she stood and pulled her top over her head; her exquisite dark breasts flopping out. My mouth began watering at the sight of her pretty black nipples. I watched as she removed her skirt, revealing that she wasn't wearing panties, and that she had shaven, just as she promised. She kept her eyes fixated on me while she stepped out of the skirt.

Sitting back on the couch, she leaned down to kiss me again, and I could feel her breasts grazing my shirt. I took my hands from my sides and began caressing them. They weren't firm, but they were soft and smooth. She stopped kissing me long enough to remove my shirt. I was wearing a bra that unhooked from the front, so she undid the latch with her teeth. She rested her naked body on top of mine and we kissed passionately for what seemed like hours. I loved the feel of her warm supple skin against mine, the scent of her perfume, and prayed she wouldn't budge. Our hands roamed each other's bodies as if we were looking for something misplaced. I squeezed her tight ass and she moaned in ecstasy. I realized that I had found her weak spot, a place she had refused to tell me about, only taunting that I had to come over and discover it for myself.

After we grew tired of kissing, she stood and led me to her bedroom, which she called "Sappho's Paradise." In the middle of the spacious room was a queen-sized bed covered with a black satin comforter, and what seemed like a dozen pillows. The walls were adorned with images of beautiful black women locked in various sexual positions. Aretha climbed on the bed first, and patted the spot beside her.

She motioned for me to lie on my back, so I obliged. She kissed my lips, and then began to blaze a path down my body, stopping at my navel. She left a trail of fire at each stop, and I felt as if I were going to explode. She sucked on my neck, which I had told her was my sensitive spot. I raised my hands over my head as she palmed my breasts. Aretha flicked her tongue against one nipple at first, before pressing my breasts together, and taking them both into her mouth. I whimpered in pleasure when she stuck her tongue into my belly button, her hands moving to my waist. After dwelling there, she stopped and looked up at me.

She grinned at me. "You want me to taste the cat, don't you?"

I weakly nodded yes. Aretha laughed a little as she hovered over my clit. I looked down as she stuck out her surprisingly long tongue and lapped over the flesh. I was speechless as I watched her taste me as only men had before but, inside, I was screaming *Yes! Yes! It feels just as good as I knew it would!*

She devoured my pussy with a fierceness that only excited me more. I ran my fingers through her long straight hair as she spread my lips wider and went further inside of me. There was no other place I wanted to be. I boldly asked how it tasted, and her muffled response sounded as if she was feasting on the nectar of the gods. I grinded my hot pussy on her face while she nibbled and sucked.

Feeling myself beginning to climax, I cried out in pleasure and bucked faster. She began rubbing my clit fiercely, and eating me faster. In an instant, I gave one last yelp and felt my hot juices spilling onto her face. She lifted her head, and came close to my face. I had never been so turned on by my own scent. I leaned closer to her and kissed my taste from her face. I sucked on her lips, retrieving some of my own juices.

Feeling quite bold, and desperate to return her favors, I laid her on her back and began suckling at her breasts. Big nipples always excited me when I saw them in porno movies, so hers did something for me as well. I suckled at them as if they contained my sole source of nourishment, and she whined in delight.

I was impressed at myself for not being shy anymore. I spread her legs, and kissed the insides of her thighs.

"That's right, baby," she purred. "Make Mama feel good."

I was more than willing to oblige.

I rubbed her thighs as I leaned into her freshly shaven love. Her clit was bigger than mine, and pierced, something that both startled and alarmed me. I didn't exactly know what I was doing, so I imitated her motions. I stuck my tongue out, and flicked my tongue against her clit. She tensed up, and then relaxed. I spread her lips and began licking away at the delicate flesh, just the way men had done to mine before. I knew I was doing a good job, by the way she tugged at my hair and lifted her legs. She had me in a locked position, but I didn't mind. I was enjoying having a mouth full of her sweet pussy. I slurped on her sweetness for a while until she began to quiver. Sensing her orgasm, I squeezed her nipples, and sucked hard on her fat clit. She locked me in tighter and yelped as she drenched me with her fluids. We were both drained.

As her tremors subsided, I moved next to her on the bed. Our naked bodies gelled like a single entity, and we were silent. The last track on *12 Play* could be heard faintly from the living room, and our breathing was heavy.

I didn't know what to say to her. I was shocked at myself, but thoughts of what had just transpired aroused me. Aretha was looking at me with a big smile on her face.

"See? I knew I just had to get you over here."

I grinned and reached out to feel her breasts all over again. This was definitely something I had to have more of, and would never try to deny myself of ever again.

80C3

*Shatira is in her mid-twenties and was born and raised in Northeast Ohio. She started writing poetry and stories as a child, and moved into erotic fiction during college. She is currently working on a poetry book and an erotic collection of short stories tentatively titled,* Forbidden Flavors. *She enjoys traveling, shopping, and classic Black movies. Shatira can be reached via MySpace at myspace.com/shatira83.*

# toesies
## LYNN LAKE

I buzzed Laila's desk for the fourth time in the last half-hour. And after five long damn rings, the girl finally picked up. An hour late back from lunch. "I want to see you in my office immediately," I stated.

"All right, Jasmine," she replied.

Then she took five more minutes to make her sweet-ass way across the tiny office before finally knocking on my door.

"Come in!" I yelled, keeping my eyes on some paperwork. "Sit down."

The petite, auburn-haired princess with the huge hazel eyes walked across the carpet and sat down in one of the chairs in front of my desk. She was a seemingly shy, demure little thing— until you got to know her; or more appropriately, she got to know you.

"Raif Jensen from CanTech Construction called while you were out," I intoned, looking up. "Apparently, he still hasn't received the revised draft of the Happyland Care Home blue-prints, and he's not very...happy."

I pursed my lips, chilled my eyes, glaring at the girl. She looked back at me, all passive innocence and sweetness, perched on the edge of the chair with her tiny hands folded in her lap.

"There're only two changes to incorporate into that plan—why's it taking you so long?"

She shrugged her small shoulders under the soft, pink sweater she was wearing. "It just is, I guess."

I gritted my teeth and clasped my hands tighter on top of the desk. My budding architectural firm's reputation was on the line. "Well, that's totally unaccept—"

I choked on my angry words. Because Laila had leaned back in her chair and crossed her legs, bringing her right leg and her right foot up into my field of vision. The girl's slender lower limbs were clad in sheer white stockings, her small feet in a pair of pink, three-inch-heeled, open-toed pumps, the toes on her right foot winking a clear, glossy finish under their silk wrappings, big toe flashing a silver ring.

I gasped. "I...I want those...blue...blueprints completed and sent over to..."

Laila's foot was bobbing up and down, half as fast as my heart was beating, her plump-topped brown toes wiggling, waving at me.

"I know what you want, Jasmine," she said, strumming her toes on the angled leather platform of her shoe. "What you *really* want."

I glanced up into her sparkling, mischievous eyes, catching the smirk on her wet, juicy lips. Then my laser gaze was back down on her dangling foot again, my mouth open and lips trembling, tongue unable to rationally respond, eyes blinded to business. I'd never seen a prettier pair of peds, more perfectly formed toes, than when Laila had first strolled into the firm, and into my heart.

Her fingers left the hem of her short, white skirt and walked over her rounded knee, down her silk-clothed shins. She slid her slim fingers around her slim ankle, then onto her heel. And I gasped again, as she pushed the shiny, patent leather pump off the back of her foot with a subdued pop I could've heard from a hundred yards away. My neck burned, the heat rising up to my face, down to my pussy.

The show-off shoe yawned down, exposing a curved, cup-pable heel, some of the girl's breathtaking arch, the band around the bottom of her toes, the only thing keeping the erotic footwear airborne. I could hear my pussy pulse in the quiet of the stuffy room, the juices flowing and mixing, the thumping in my chest warning me that my heart was about to burst. Did burst, when Laila tilted her foot, tip down, and let the sexy shoe slide right off her ped. It plummeted down to the carpet, along with my jaw.

Only a thin layer of silk now lay between her foot, her toes, and me.

She abruptly swung her leg around and propped her foot up on the pedestal of my desk, and my lungs collapsed, my fingers strangling one another. Laila arched the delicately constructed size-six ped, pointing her painted toes directly at me.

I flung myself at them, springing up and seizing the angel foot, sending my chair roller-crashing into the wall behind. I grabbed onto Laila's foot at the heel and arch and yanked it forward, shooting the girl down in her chair as I brought the exquisite ped up to my flushed face. It was warm and soft and smooth and sensuous, all graceful curves and rounded eroticism, the five little hourglass piggies all-in-a-row so utterly adorable, delectable.

I was damn well out of control, and knew it. And didn't care.

Sculpted lady-feet will make this blue-eyed, ice-nigga melt anytime, and slender, suckable toes with pedicured tips will set this "sole sister" on fire. Don't know why, don't care why. It's as instinctual as the need to eat, an awesome, all-consuming hunger that compels me to scoop up tapered, toe-crowned peds and make sweet, mad love to them, no matter what the cost.

"On your knees, bitch!" Laila hissed, unveiling the cost.

She yanked her foot free, the slim, silken ped sliding out of my grasping hands, toes slipping agonizingly through my outstretched fingers. Then I was on my knees, and Laila was seated in my leather executive chair, both her beautifully contoured feet bare to the stocking on the floor. "Toe the line, foot-slut!" she commanded.

I dropped down onto all-fours and bent my head down until my chin touched the carpet, nose hovering over the top of Laila's right foot. I thanked the foot gods that be that I'd had sense enough to put my long hair up that morning, so there was nothing to get in the way of my visual and oral ped appreciation. Laila riffled her toes in their flexible silk encasement, and I caught the breeze, the heady, musky scent of her foot. Then I shot my thick tongue out and licked her big toe.

She jumped, her foot-digits smacking me in the mouth. I ran my tongue across the bridge of her toes, back again. Then I tongued the quintet of edible piggies on her left foot, then her right again, moving my head back and forth, tongue out and licking, painting those delicious foot appendages.

"Suck my toes!" Laila hissed, tilting her feet up on their heels.

Before she'd even gotten all the words out, I'd gotten all the toes in, opening up my mouth and inhaling half of her right foot. I gorged on her ped, taking it almost to the heel. Then I slowly pulled back, lips sliding over and under her wicked arch, tongue wet-cushioning her tender sole, mouth milking the rounded ball of her foot. Until I reached her toes, and I sealed my lips tight, locking the foot-digits in the wet-hot cauldron of my mouth, slashing my tongue back and forth across their puffy bottoms.

Laila groaned, and I mouthed three-quarters of her other foot. I sucked hard and long and wet on it, nibbling those luscious toes almost right off her ped, sinking my teeth into their rich plumpness. Back and forth I went, down on my hands and knees at my subordinate's beautiful feet, head bobbing, fingernails clawing into the carpet, making urgent love to Laila's feet and toes with my mouth and tongue.

"You…you want them naked, don't you, toadie?" she rasped, chest heaving, mouth hanging open. The girl had never gotten fully used to the ferocity of my toe lust.

I looked up at her, mouth full of foot, and nodded. But she had to jerk her ped back to get me to let go of it, the darling toes gliding out of my greedy mouth glistening with my hot spit.

She fumbled under her skirt, unfastening her garter straps, as I pushed up off the floor and onto my knees again. I sat on my heels, bum bouncing impatiently like a bitch wagging its tail, overexcited to get a treat.

Laila slid off her stockings, until at last her ballerina legs gleamed ebony bare in front of me, balanced on the tips of their nude, pointed toes. "Show me your pussy," she ordered.

I leapt to my knees and unhooked my skirt, letting the garment drop, revealing my plain white panties with the personal wet spot upfront. I pulled them to the side, showing off black pubes heavy with moisture, my slit dripping with want.

Laila looked at my hot spot, into my feverish eyes devouring her posed peds on the carpet. "You want to suck on my naked toes, don't you?" she taunted.

I nodded eagerly.

Finally, she lifted a leg and folded it out to almost its full, limber length. Then she brushed my quivering lips with the trimmed tips of her saucy toes. My body and pussy went molten. And when she toe-tickled my mouth a second time, I grabbed onto her foot-digits with my teeth and swallowed the tip of her ped, filling my mouth with heated brown skin.

"Damn!" Laila groaned, slumping down in her chair.

I grasped her ankle and urgently sucked on her wicked, wiggling toes, cheeks billowing and throat working, my head spinning and my body burning. I couldn't get enough toe, tugging on all five at once, then pulling up her left leg and jamming her feet together and cramming all ten into my mouth, excitedly sucking on the matched set.

Then I mouthed each foot-appendage individually, swirling my tongue all around the little fat-headed digits, in between them, up and down the delightful rows. And just as I was biting into the silver ring on Laila's right big toe, she shook her other foot free and touched it to my pussy.

And I flat-out exploded.

Orgasm flamed up inside me and swept through my body, rocking me back on my heels. I shuddered out of control on the end of Laila's feet, seared through and through by fiery ecstasy. But not once did I drop those exquisite foot-digits out of my whimpering mouth, desperately sucking on them even as I blazed with toe-triggered orgasm.

Laila took just as long as she wanted on the CanTech blueprint revisions; there was no pussyfooting around that fact.

A week later, the ped-blessed princess decided to take a three-hour shopping tour in lieu of a construction trailer meeting at the Happyland project site. I'd just gotten off the phone with an apoplectic Raif Jensen when she sauntered into my office, shopping bags hanging off her arms.

"This is the last straw, Laila!" I announced convincingly, nervously noting that the bags were labeled "Shoe Fly Girls," "Hollywood Stocking," and "Pedi-Curator."

"Is it?" the little toe-vixen asked.

She plopped down in a chair with a sigh and stretched out her red-stockinged legs, giving me a good, gaped-mouth view of the tiny red bows that decorated the lacy tops of her sexy leg garments, the red, open-toed, outrageously blade-heeled plat-form shoes that sexily displayed her silky, scarlet-tipped toes.

"I...well..." The conviction drained out of my voice as the blood rushed from my head to my pussy, as I stared at those gorgeously platformed peds.

Laila yawned like a kitten, then lifted her luxurious legs and plunked the funky heels down on top of my desk. She crossed her legs, the whisper of silk a full-throated scream for attention to me. The tangy scent of shoe leather and foot perspiration permeated the air, smothering my good senses.

"Shopping's sure hard on a girl's feet," Laila murmured. "But that pedicure helped. Why don't you check it out, Jasmine?"

I was already working her shoes off, my fingers twitching with the desire to toy with her toes—throat dry and tongue swollen with the hunger for her foot-tips—when Alessandra strutted into the office.

"So, this is what passes for work in America?" the tall, raven-haired woman asked, raising an imperious eyebrow at my hands full of feet.

Laila's shoes kicked out of my hands; clunked down on the floor.

"Oh, I forgot to tell you, Laila," I said. "This is the new owner of the firm—Alessandra Oliveira de Souza. I've, uh, sold out to some foreign interests."

Laila was up on her feet. "N…nice to meet you, Ms. Oliveira…de Souza," she groveled.

Alessandra regarded the girl with a critical eye, hands on her hips, long blue-stockinged legs spread and flowing luxuriant out of a short, darker-blue skirt. "This is the one you told me about, huh, Jasmine?"

I nodded.

"I hear you are quite the little foot-tease, Laila," Alessandra said. "What do you think of my feet—and legs?"

We both gazed at Alessandra's slender, shining stems, our eyes traveling down in tandem, down to her spike-heeled, blue suede shoes, the tapered tips of her nose-diving peds peeking out at the ends.

"Um, they're, um, very…pretty," Laila mumbled, hanging her head in submission.

"Show me how pretty."

Laila glanced at me. I gave her a tightlipped smile, my finger-nails chewing into the desktop. Then she walked over and dropped to her knees in front of Alessandra, as she'd brought me to my knees so many times before. She reached out and grasped Alessandra's calves in her hot little hands.

Alessandra's elegant lower limbs trembled, as Laila squeezed and rubbed her muscled calves, ran hands up and down nylon-wrapped shins, encircled and caressed slim, tendon-taut ankles.

"There is a new boss in this town," Alessandra informed the girl rhetorically. "And she says you are going to obey Jasmine from now on. As Jasmine obeys me." She beckoned me forward with a finger.

I joined Laila down on the carpet, each of us taking a curvaceous leg. We fondled those velvety-smooth, heavenly sculpted limbs, cupping and squeezing the clenched calves, rubbing the soft, vulnerable backs of the knees, kneading the thicker flesh of the firm, full thighs.

"Take off my shoes," the statuesque leg-goddess demanded, her black eyes burning down at us mere mortal worshippers.

Laila fumbled with the straps on the slut-heel, while I had my foot blazing bare to the stocking in no time. I bent my head down and nuzzled the slick ped, inhaling the intoxicating aroma of leather and spice and everything naughty.

Then I licked Alessandra's foot, running my wet tongue up from the toes and over the arch and around the ankle. Her leg quivered; her foot jumping. I did it again, and again, clotting her stocking with saliva. Before slashing my tongue over her exquisitely long toes, back and forth, like a concert pianist running her fingers up and down the shiny keys of a grand piano, the crescendo in my smoldering pussy building and building.

And while I tongue-lashed Alessandra's toes, leg-fetisher Laila grasped her around the ankle and licked up and down the back of our boss's lower limbs, swirling her tongue in and around the sensitive underside of the knee. Alessandra gasped, her knees buckling.

Then she was out of our loving hands and tongues and striding around my desk. She sat down in my chair, enthroning herself, legs draping over the edge, feet off her legs. Laila and I hastily kneed over to her. "Take off my stockings, show me your pussies," she ordered.

We pushed our hands under her skirt and took hold of her stocking tops. I quickly popped her garter clips open and slid the nylon leg dressing off and away, then anxiously picked up her bare foot and crammed my mouth full of sparkly, blue-tipped toes.

Her legs were bronze, her feet golden, her toes scrumptiously plump at the top. And as I licked and sucked on the outstretched foot-digits, I watched the leg-struck Laila expose Alessandra's other stem, her hands shaking with reverence as she slowly disrobed the gleaming limb.

"I told you girls… sh…show me your pussies," Alessandra reminded us, her voice breaking like her underlings' will. She wetted her lips, her fingers choking the chair's armrests.

Laila cradled Alessandra's shining leg in her hands and held it up like a sweet-ass trophy for display. Then she kissed its smooth, warm surface, stuck out her pink tongue and licked the burnished skin, sunk her teeth into the bare, fleshy thigh. As I sucked on one lovely toe after another, Alessandra's toe-nails bit into my tongue with excitement.

She finally had to shake the both of us off her lean-muscled limbs before we finally complied with her repeated demand. We hiked up our skirts and plunked our butts down on the carpet, spreading our legs. Laila tore her lacy red panties apart, exposing a dewy, clean-shaven slit while I pulled my frilly pink panties to one side, exhibiting pubes nasty with moisture. Alessandra nodded her approval, then extended her glamorous legs and gently touched our soaking soft spots with the tips of her toes.

"God!" I gasped.

"Shit!" Laila yelped.

Alessandra brushed her toes over our needful pussies, big toe touching my clit and sparking an arc of sexual electricity that streaked all the way through me, setting me to shimmering. We grabbed onto Alessandra's erotically constructed ankles, almost pulling her right out of her chair, frantically rubbing her feet, her toes, over our burning pussies. She watched, wide-eyed and open-mouthed, as the two sistas on the ends of her limbs desperately got themselves off on her feet.

"Goddamn!" Laila cried, shutting her eyes and biting her lip. Her body shook, legs vibrating on the floor, as she footed herself to gushing orgasm.

I drove Alessandra's big toe into my slit and plowed her other toes up against my clitty, triggering my own spectacular orgasm. "God, yes!" I wailed, toed over the edge. A wall of wet heat surged up from my buzzing button and suffused my quivering body, drowning me in ecstasy.

Alessandra sat there and gaped at us, blown away by the foot frenzy, her glorious legs trembling in rhythm to our wild orgasms.

ഇൻ

"Thanks again for all your help, 'Ms. Oliveira de Souza,'" I congratulated my straight, but always adventurous, friend later that night. "I know it must've been kind of…freaky and all for you, but you did a great acting job—almost right to the end." I grinned. "I won't be having any problems with little toe-tease Laila from now on."

Alessandra Johnson stared at me, her eyes burning strangely, her face flushed and shiny with perspiration, her breathing rapid and shallow.

"Um, are you all—"

"On your knees, bitch!" she hissed.

"What!? Wh…what's gotten into you?" I babbled, dropping unconsciously to my knees in front of my friend's long, stockinged limbs, her dangerously slanted-down peds with those squeezed-tight, sweetly edible toes.

"Toe the line, foot-slut!" Alessandra commanded, a changed woman.

ॐ

*Lake's writing credits include "Hustler Fantasies," "Leg Sex," "18eighteen," "Desire," "On Our Backs," "Desdmona.com," "Feminine Zone," and stories in the anthologies* Truckers, After Midnight, Sex & Seduction, Sex & Submission, Five Minute Fantasies, Spank Me, Ultimate Sins, Seriously Sexy, *and* The Mammoth Book of Lesbian Erotica.

# not tonight
## M.B. LEVINE

Nina was tired of her husband. The coolness and the lack of intimacy that had become the foundation of their relationship wore her head and heart out. She wanted more: More passion, more closeness; more sex. As it stood, Eric would reach for her once, maybe twice a month. Somehow, it was enough for him. If Nina reached for him, he would go frigid; complain of stress and fatigue, citing some old football injury or a hard day at his job as an accountant. Eric would walk around the house content, while Nina continued to stew in her frustration. It wasn't that sex with her husband was unsatisfying. Eric was a skilled lover. The way he touched her, how he used his tongue—Nina didn't have a complaint about his technique. The thing was, getting it so good so infrequently only made her want more. The same way using her vibrator made her want to jump on the first man she saw.

She'd made a decision after their last session. Even though she came, Nina had been so preoccupied with the number of weeks that had passed prior to that episode and the number of weeks that would probably pass before the next one, she was not able to lose herself. She came, but she wasn't satisfied. So she decided to cut him off. No more ass for Eric, no matter how much she wanted it. Her vibrator would have to do the job.

About three weeks had passed when Nina realized Eric's pattern had been to get some close to the end of each month, like it was the rite of passage to the turning of the calendar. She remained firm in her decision, even imagined the power she would feel when he reached for her and she pushed his hand away. He would be puzzled because she had never in their ten years of marriage denied him. It would be great. Only thing was, Nina was horny as hell. Even using the vibrator and the dildo she had recently acquired alone and together with her hands in her SUV going to and coming from work, and with the shower head twice a day, Nina was close to raping her husband. If she didn't get some real sex soon she was going to break when his hand grabbed her hip by the end of the week.

During her endless masturbation sessions, Nina noticed that her fantasies had become dominated by sex with women and were getting her off harder than any thoughts of being with men ever had. The more she thought about being with a woman, the more her body yearned for breasts, hips, and a cunt under her hands, smoothed by her lips, moistened by her curious tongue. Nina became so fixated with the images, she made another decision: She had to get her hands on a woman. Otherwise, she'd be fucking Eric by Thursday. And she already had a woman in mind.

Rene had lived next door to Nina for only two months. She was a single woman who left for work early and sometimes came in rather late. But mostly she kept reasonable hours, getting home at around four every afternoon. Nina's schedule at the mid-sized advertising firm where she was the art director was flexible, allowing her to go in early for a few hours and work from home in the afternoons so she could be there when her eight- and ten-year-old daughters got off the schoolbus. Nina met Rene during one of her daily afternoon walks around the neighborhood. At their first meeting, Rene revealed that buying the house was her rebound move after ending a five-year relationship with her girlfriend, Teresa. When Nina asked why they'd broken up, Rene said she needed open communication and regular sex. Teresa wasn't giving her that. When the two parted so that Rene could go in and shower off the remains of her interior painting job, Nina finished her walk with a hot, wet pussy.

Rene was attractive. The same height as Nina, around five-six, but slimmer, more toned. Her skin was butterscotch and she wore her long, bone-straight hair pulled in a tight ponytail for work. A few weeks later, after several conversations with her tired, paint-splattered neighbor, Nina saw Rene leaving her house dressed in a cute, flowing sundress, her long, light-brown hair hanging loose to the middle of her back, her pretty face brightened by a trace of blush and lipstick. After Rene drove off, Nina checked on her daughters who were in the family room watching videos, then locked herself in the bathroom with her vibrator. Even though the girls were there, she didn't make herself rush through it. She licked the tip of the pink dick, then rubbed the head over her dark nipples and slowly down her slightly rounded stomach before stopping at her throbbing clit. She smoothed the vibrating tip around her clit until she moaned deep and the ache became almost painful. When she slid the vibrator into her slick twat, first to the base of the head, then halfway down the shaft, she bit hard on her bottom lip to stop the scream she desperately wanted to unleash. Nina ground her hips and when she got down to the end of the seven-inch tool, she held onto the edge of the tub as she lost herself in the orgasm.

"I'm going for my walk!" Nina yelled the words in the direction of the family room the next afternoon. Eric had come home early after leaving work for a dentist appointment and was spending time with the girls.

"Bye, Mommy!" her daughters yelled back in unison. Nina waited for Eric to respond, but he said nothing.

She abandoned her plan to take one quick lap around the neighborhood (four short of her usual) and instead made a bee-line to Rene's house when she saw that the pickup was in the driveway. During their talks in the afternoons, Nina had shared with Rene the problems in her marriage and Rene had extended an open invitation for Nina to come over and talk whenever the need arose. When Nina knocked on Rene's door, she was ready with a story of being ignored, disrespected, and unsatisfied.

"Hey, girl." Rene's smile made her face, clear of the splotches of paint Nina was used to seeing, bright and pretty. She was beautiful. Suddenly, Nina grew shy. She wasn't a particularly self-conscious woman, but standing in Rene's doorway with a plan of seduction she had been crafting for the last couple of days, she wondered if Rene would even want to be with her. Doubt started to push through and Nina found herself unable to move.

"Are you okay?" Rene's smile disappeared and was replaced with concern. "Come in, Nina. You look like you need to talk."

Rene took hold of Nina's hand and pulled her into the house. Inside, Nina forced herself to breathe and worked on convincing the negative voice in her head that she could make her fantasy happen. She had to. Eric's silence when she left the house meant he would be coming for her soon. The closer he got to acting out his desire, the ruder he was; like it was her fault he needed the physical release.

"What's wrong, Nina?" Rene's hand was on her neighbor's shoulder, squeezing gently, but firmly enough to cause a warming between Nina's legs. Her doubt slipped away as she looked into Rene's dark eyes. Her full lips were begging for a kiss and Nina was burning to oblige. "Come sit down."

Nina allowed herself to be led to the couch in the living room. She sat first and watched Rene pull her rob tighter around her slim hips and what looked like an exceptionally firm ass.

"I just got out of the shower, so please excuse my attire." Rene's hair was damp and her skin still glowed with moisture. She turned her body so that she faced Nina. Rene held Nina's slightly trembling hand in both of hers and waited.

Nina felt frozen from the waist up. Her mouth wouldn't work and her eyes were stuck on Rene's face. She couldn't stop staring. Between her legs, the fire was spreading. The women looked deeply into each other's eyes. Nina felt the heat rise up her body and noticed that Rene's checks were flushed.

"You're beautiful, Nina. Do you know that? Does he tell you?" Rene rubbed one hand up over Nina's bare arms. Her eyes languished over the dark skin she loved. She had never been with a woman lighter than a caramel candied apple.

"You're the beautiful one. I love your face. Your body is fantastic." Nina still couldn't move her eyes, but she found herself moving closer to Rene and reaching out to cup the apple of Rene's left cheek. "You're exquisite."

"How do you know? You haven't seen me yet."

Rene pulled away from Nina and stood. She slowly untied

the belt and pulled the robe from her body while staring into Nina's eyes. Nina's gaze moved across Rene's body, gliding over her full breasts, down her muscled abdomen, to her neatly groomed pussy, and well-toned thighs. From the light pink-colored toes, Nina's eyes bounced back up Rene's body to her eyes. Rene's smile added to their glow.

"Now what do you think?"

Nina moved to the edge of the couch. Her eyes were full of Rene's luscious body. Her mind whirled with the reality that her fantasy was coming true as her body exchanged heat with the stunning woman standing in front of her.

"Come here." Rene's smile grew broader as she walked slowly over to Nina. When she stopped, Nina opened her legs and beckoned Rene to come closer with an enticing glance. Rene moved into the space between Nina's legs. She was trembling and her breath became deep and heavy. Nina used her fingertips to run the length of Rene's thighs from her knees up to where they met in the middle. Rene sighed when a thumb grazed her hardening clit. She shut her eyes tight when Nina's lips caressed the front of her thighs, her hips, and her soft nest of public hair. Nina reached behind and grabbed Rene's ass, pulling her closer as she unleashed her tongue to seek out the origin of the scent that was filling her nose. She sucked Rene's clit into her mouth, rolled it around on her tongue; held on to Rene's writhing body. Nina lifted one hand to cup a breast while she continued to explore the throbbing organ in her mouth. Rene moaned from the pit of her spirit. She filled her hands with Nina's curly, shoulder-length hair while grinding her hips into her new lover's mouth.

Nina had forgotten all of her fantasies. She was acting on

instinct and responding to the affirmation of Rene's moans. She sucked her clit, fondled her breast and ass until the need to go deeper overwhelmed her. Rene continued to moan even after Nina pulled away from her. She was barely aware of being moved and then helped to the couch where Nina encouraged her to lie down. Before the pleasure of Nina's tongue could clear fully from Rene's mind, Nina was on the other end of the couch on all fours, her head between Rene's legs. When Nina's tongue entered her, Rene let out a scream, her legs trembled, and she reached again to fill her hands with Nina's thick mane. They found their rhythm. Nina's tongue darted in and out of Rene's cunt, her lips sucked and licked while her hands clung to the firm, gyrating ass. The scream released as Rene reached orgasm and took up all of the space in Nina's head. When she looked up, Nina sucked the finger she had plunged in Rene's twat into her mouth and smiled.

"You are exquisite. I knew it."

Rene smiled back and seemed to instantly recover. "Your turn." She pulled herself up and stood. Then she got Nina to her feet. "Let me help you."

Slowly, she pulled the tank top over Nina's head. As she moved down her body to untie the string on Nina's sweatpants, Rene made a point of moving her hands over Nina's heavy breasts and round stomach. As she bent down on her knees to pull down the sweats, she stuck her tongue in Nina's navel, kissed her stomach, and ran her tongue over the cotton panties where Nina's pussy was warm and wet.

After Nina stepped out of her pants, Rene reached for the panties, pulled them slowly down and off. As she stood up, she fingered Nina's clit, then sucked her neck as Nina threw her head back. Once the bra was discarded, Rene licked and sucked each dark nipple, lingering as Nina's breath caught in her throat and was then released in a long moan.

"Lie down on the couch, I'll be right back." Rene disappeared into the back of the house. Nina played with her slick twat while she waited, her desire so powerful she was almost in pain. She opened her eyes when she heard Rene reenter the room. Standing over her with a beautiful, mischievous smile, Rene held a dildo in each hand.

"One for now and one for later." Rene placed the long, double-headed dildo on the coffee table, the other eight-inch purple dick she held in her hand as she knelt on the floor next to Rene.

She kissed Nina. It was long and deep; breathtaking. Nina had to open her eyes to be sure she wasn't dreaming. Next, Rene's tongue slid down her throat and rediscovered her breasts. As she teased Nina with her tongue, Rene circled her clit with the head of the dildo, covering it with Nina's slickness. Nina faded into the ecstasy that was building in her pelvis. She moaned and whispered pleas for Rene to fill her with the purple cock as her hips lifted into the air in search of penetration. Rene moved at her own pace, licking her way down Nina's body, teasingly putting the head into her hot pussy for one or two thrusts and then abruptly removing it to resume circling.

Nina was begging to be fucked, screaming the words as she clutched at her lover's hair. With Nina's clit in her mouth, Rene sucked and rolled her tongue, then pushed the dildo into her twat to the base. Nina bucked her hips, delirious from the sucking of her clit and the firm fucking of her pussy simultaneously. She came wildly, thrusting and screaming, tearing at the pillows on the overstuffed couch, her legs spread wide accepting all Rene offered.

Rene placed soft kisses on the inside of Nina's thighs as she listened to her breathing slow and normalize. She rubbed her stomach as she waited for Nina to tell her she was ready to move on.

"That was so good." Nina pushed the words out in between efforts to catch her breath.

"Are you okay? Do you want something to drink?" Rene looked into Nina's dark eyes which were focused on her.

Nina smiled and ran her fingers lightly over Rene's face. "I just want more of you."

Rene returned the smile and got to her feet. She picked up the double-headed dong from the table at the end of the couch, then offered Nina her hand.

"Let's go to bed."

In the bedroom, the couple exchanged more breathtaking kisses while holding and caressing each other. They touched all over as if for the first time. After they made their way to the bed, Nina stretched out on her back and Rene straddled her. Nina took advantage of the position and traced Rene's nipples with her hungry tongue and filled her hands with Rene's full ass. As she moaned over the attention Nina was lavishing over her, Rene slipped two, then three fingers inside Nina. Before tongues and hands and fingers could bring them to explosion again, Rene pulled away and reached for the double-headed dildo she'd left on the nightstand. She smiled down at Nina, who was stroking her clit with one hand and massaging her breasts with the other.

"Turn on your side."

Nina obliged without hesitation, positioning herself so that her thick, smooth ass was facing Rene. She smiled over her shoulder as she watched Rene slide into place behind her. Rene lifted her right leg and slowly guided one end of the dildo into her cunt. She ran moist fingers over Nina's hip and across her ass before gently easing the other end of the rubber dick into Nina's hot pussy. Nina moaned as she backed her ass into Rene's crotch. Again, the couple found their rhythm. Rene held onto Nina's hip as she met her bucking ass with her thrusting pelvis. The women fucked vigorously, each focused on the building sensations in their bodies and the sensual sounds of lust deposited into the room.

They erupted in unison. Rene wrapped an arm around Nina as the waves rolled over her; Nina clutched the arm, embracing her as she screamed through her own climax.

Resolution came slowly. As heart rates came down, the women clung to each other: entwining legs and arms and kissing deeply with exploring tongues. While they talked softly to each other, Nina realized the sun was going down and she needed to get back home. Reluctantly, after several attempts, they parted and returned to the living room to retrieve their clothes. At the door, the couple shared a long, deep kiss and made plans for their next meeting. Nina smiled to herself as she walked back to her house: Rene was her new workout routine.

She slipped into the house, ran upstairs quickly, and showered before coming back down to cook dinner. After the meal she spent some time with her girls and then tucked them into bed. When the last story was read and the last good-night kiss placed on soft cheeks, Nina realized how tired she was and climbed into her own bed. Twenty minutes after burying her head in her pillow, Nina felt Eric reach for her. She let his warm hand linger for a few minutes; allowed his fingers to trace the line of her hip. Then, when he clutched at her flesh and moved down to pull up her short nightgown, Nina lifted his hand and placed it on the bed behind her.

"Not tonight, hon. I'm really tired from my walk." Nina's smile lingered as she drifted off to sleep.

ഇൗരു

*M. B. Levine is a writer and book reviewer. She has written reviews for Midwest Book Review, ForeWord Reviews, and Independent Professional Book Reviewers. Levine is the author of two novels,* Splendid *and* Problems in Living. *Her third novel,* Woman Free, *was published by Cacofithes Publishing House in the spring of 2008.*

# in the heat of the night
## CHUCK FELLOWS

Snapping my cell phone shut, I swore quietly. Work was really getting on my nerves lately. Why did they always have an emergency when I had important plans? Sierra was not going to like it when I told her that I needed to leave before the weekend; instead of early Monday morning. She had been planning on a weekend at home for just the two of us. Maybe the last one this summer before she went back to work in the fall. I turned and saw her and it was obvious she already knew. She had guessed already, or maybe she had heard the conversation. Liquid brown eyes looked into my own gray ones and a single wet track slid down Sierra's left cheek. Whoever said, "Parting is such sweet sorrow," was a damn fool. I know from personal experience. So does Sierra. This job took me away more than it was ever meant to.

"Oh no, Shelly. Not this weekend. Please tell me you don't have to go early." Sierra's voice broke. She poked her head between my arm and chest, and in the process placed her creamy brown cleavage right at my fingertips.

"I'm not leaving until tomorrow, baby, so we still have all night. I need to be in Toronto by mid-afternoon." Sierra's bottom lip pushed out, the pout still adorable twenty-five years after I first saw it from across the dance floor in college. I slid my palm along her cheek and brushed the tear away with my thumb. I pulled her face toward mine, intending a tender kiss, but decided at the last second to rub noses instead. Unfortunately, I pulled her a little too close and we bumped hard, her dreads swinging around and slapping my ears.

"Damn," I said, rubbing my nose and then my ears, and my nose again. Sierra looked at me as if I were crazy.

"What the hell was that?" The surprise cleared the last of the tears from her eyes. "Thought you'd knock me out and have your way with me all night?"

There was that moment when it could have gone either way. But it soon passed and, before long, we were both giggling like teenaged schoolgirls. I couldn't help myself. I pounced on her, pinning her to the sofa with my body.

"Shel!" She breathed heavily under the weight of me. "Get off!"

She was right, of course. It was far too warm for wrestling on this fine summer evening. But I didn't move right away. Sierra's fist thumped my shoulder in protest. I thought about it for maybe a second, but then thought better of it.

Now, it is true I'm bigger than Sierra, but when she wants to fight back, I know better than to try and hold my own. I raised myself up on my arms, looking at the beautiful woman below me. We are quite the pair, this woman and me. She is gorgeous with shoulder-length dreads and long, pink nails. Whoever said butch/femme was passé must have been kidding. Either that or they had never seen us together. I'm older by many years, but come on—I'm not that old. I lean wildly to the butch side, but have all the same body bits under my shirt and tie that she has under her dress and lacy things. And it was those lacy things and the wonders they tantalizingly hid that were my goal all of the sudden. After all, we only had tonight before I had to leave.

Sierra's hands pressed upward, trying to lift my bulk off of her. Her knees pushing against me to relieve the pressure of my body on hers had spread my own legs apart so one was between her thighs and the other foot was resting on the floor just to the side of the coffee table. That worked somewhat to my advantage, since it gave me a leverage to use against her. When I discovered the struggling had made her dress slide up, I moved my knee upward, closer to the heat and heart of her silk panties. I lifted myself higher off of her with my arms, while lowering my head to kiss her wrist.

"Don't fight me, baby. I want to kiss you."

Sierra's hands dropped to her chest and I gently kissed the back of her slender hands, concentrating on each in its turn, making the dusky skin damp with my own sudden desire.

"Okay, Shelly. I'll be good and quiet for you." The fan whirled away in the other room.

"Good, yes. But I hope you aren't very quiet, Sierra. I'm gonna need some noises to remember while I'm away."

Her hands slid around my waist and, when I frowned, she lowered them to her sides. I wanted her and I really wasn't going to prevent her from distracting me for a while; maybe hours; could be all night. I would sleep on my flight in the morning.

My smile widened and within seconds, so did hers. I pressed my knee higher and her eyes fluttered closed, the thick black lashes resting on her cheek. I kissed her nose this time, gently brushing my lips across the silky brown skin and wishing I never had to leave her side or her bed ever again. For the life of me, I couldn't figure out how she stayed all cool and collected on such a summer's night. Sierra opened her dark eyes and looked up at me as a plan formed in my head. I'd love to be able to keep her up all night, and if that wasn't going to be possible, at least tire her out and make sure she could feel me inside her for a couple of days, at least.

I slid to the floor, landing right between Sierra's knees. Her summery flowered dress had ridden up and, if I were only lower, I would have been able to see her panties. But there was plenty of leg for me to work with. I ran my hands down from her knees to ankles, feeling legs softer than my own furry ones ever were. Slowly, my hands trailed back up. I kissed each knee slowly and gently. Sierra threaded her fingers through my hair, her touch electrifying my clit. With my hands resting on her lower thighs, I started kissing and licking my way north to the Promised Land. Sierra giggled as I pulled her legs apart just a bit more. I could see her panties now. Cherry red with more flowers. Small, dark-brown ringlets peeking out from under the elastic. I could smell her excitement, too. The scent of her making my mouth and cunt respond eagerly. As I kissed higher and higher on her thighs, Sierra pulled the dress up over her stomach to make sure that I could easily reach my goal. And reach it, I did! Using teeth now, I nipped and pulled on the silk panties now soaked with sweet cunt juices. The way Sierra smelled was making my own cunt flood with excitement. I moaned deeply with my mouth nestled between her lips. I couldn't quite feel her clit, but I knew when I found it by the soft mewing noises Sierra suddenly started making.

"I want these panties off." I reached for her hand as I sat back on my feet. Sierra pulled herself up, smoothing her dress down with her free hand as she did so. "Oh, no. Don't cover up again!"

Sierra smiled and lifted the whole thing over her head, leaving a rounded expanse of dark-brown skin between cherry red panties and a matching lacy bra that barely contained her beautiful breasts.

Well, I thought, if she was going that far, I wanted all of her. I jumped up, grabbed her hand and headed for our bedroom, pulling her along behind me. Once there, I turned to face her, took her in my arms, and kissed her softly on the lips. I unhooked the back of her bra, releasing her breasts, the dark-brown nipples puckering immediately. I leaned over and took one of the hard buds in my mouth while tugging her panties down around her ankles. Sierra stepped neatly out of them as I switched to her other nipple. Oh, the scent of her pussy now seemed to fill the small room and I didn't want to wait any longer.

Backing Sierra up to the bed, I pushed her back onto it and made sure to wedge myself between her knees. Her legs fell open and the tight, soft, downy curls framed an exquisite dusky interior, complete with a tiny pink clit peeking out at me. A trickle of wet spilled out and ran down the crack of Sierra's ass as I admired her spread out before me. That did it. I had her scoot back on the bed. I climbed on the bed between her parted thighs and pressed the length of my body against hers. Still not enough, though. I jumped up and quickly stripped down to nakedness myself. Now, as I lay on top of Sierra, I could feel her soft skin against my own.

My kisses started on her lips, my teeth briefly taking hold of her bottom lip before traveling down her neck. First one side and then the other, as I lowered myself down her body. My breathing had gotten ragged and I noticed Sierra was holding hers, then moaning and holding again. I reached her nipples, solid nubs of dark brown that fit perfectly between my lips. Moving from side to side, my own full breasts pressed against her stomach and I could feel the fine hairs on her belly. Sierra moaned louder when I took a last nibble of her right tit, using my teeth. I sunk lower.

Soft, round belly kisses over and over again. The wet of Sierra's cunt was now coating my right breast as I worked from side to side, lower and lower, and closer to my goal. I shifted and my own hardened nipple brushed against her clit. I pushed two fingers deep inside her cunt as I took a mouthful of dark brown curls between my teeth and tugged. Sierra's clit was right in front of me, but still I did not make my way there. Instead I kissed her nether lips and pulled on tight curls while I worked my fingers in and out. She was so open there was room for more and I slid another finger inside. Fucking her slowly, I could see her clit grow with her excitement and now the pink bud was pushing out from under its dusky hood. Sierra opened up even more, the inner pinks of her cunt glistening with every slow withdrawal. A fourth finger added, with my thumb folded over and still she opened. I touched her clit with my other thumb, gently circling. But it was too much and Sierra's cunt started to close on my fingers. Her thighs pressed in against me, threatening to push me away from her body. I went back to kissing. Up and down her inner thigh, as far as I could reach, while still fucking her. She relaxed and started to open again. I turned my hand, curled my fingers and watched the whole thing disappear inside my lover. With a breathless voice, I announced, "I'm all the way in you, baby. Feel me fill you with my love."

Sierra gasped and tried to see for herself, but her round belly was in the way. So she reached down, felt my forearm and made a small noise. From my vantage point, I thought I could see a single tear spill over and run down her cheek.

"Are you okay, Sierra?" I asked quietly, afraid I was hurting her and knowing there wasn't any way I could get up to hold her any time soon.

"I'm okay, Shelly. Just a bit overwhelmed. I'm gonna feel this for days. Will you make me come?"

She bit her lower lip and closed her eyes as I lowered my mouth on her clit, licking carefully with my tongue, trying not to put too much pressure there. But it didn't really matter. Almost immediately Sierra's pussy clenched around my wrist, released and clenched again. Soft, warm juices flowed over and out as I kissed her pink rosebud. I moved back and forth slowly, feeling Sierra come for me. I smiled, knowing the night had only just begun.

Within minutes, Sierra's cunt opened again and I pulled my hand out carefully. I climbed up to hold her in my arms, kissing her, and felt my own hard clit pulsing with need. But not yet. There was still most of the night left to go. And there was no way I was going to waste any of it. We talked and kissed; cuddled and kissed some more. Sierra told me a joke that she had heard earlier and we both laughed at the silliness of it. My fingers caressed Sierra's cheek and neck as she recovered from having me fill her with my fist. Our sweaty bodies cooled with the evening air. Before long, Sierra's fingers found my nipples and I snuck my tongue between her lips. I wasn't ready to be distracted yet. Our tongues touched and the spark grew. Kissing Sierra deeper, I moaned as I envisioned her opening for me again. I wanted to take her again. Make her come again before I let her have her way with me.

Sierra's dusky-brown skin glistened with sweat. I couldn't help myself. My tongue followed the curve of her body, from jutting hip to rounded breast, licking the salty droplets as I went. The night, thankfully, crawled on. I was in no hurry to sleep until I was quite sure we had both had our fill. And I wasn't even close.

Sierra giggled as I slid my body over hers, gliding in the heat of the August night, our bodies drenched with the humidity of our lovemaking and our hearts flooded with the lust of lovers rediscovering each other's bodies. She giggled again, as my hip caught the top sheet and my own sweat fastened to it. The sheet rose with me as my mouth traveled down to her breasts, my hands resting on either side of her hips. I kicked the sheet off the already magnificently tangled bed.

"What are you laughing about, My Love?" I lifted my head from kissing her soft belly, marveling at the dark line of hairs traveling downward. The fine lines at the corners of Sierra's dark eyes crinkled and she smiled in the way that simultaneously made my heart melt and my cunt flood. She said nothing, but beneath me I felt her strong legs fall open, the scent of her excitement rising to my nostrils. With both hands cupping my face, she pushed me down toward her pussy.

I eagerly began once more, my tongue gently licking her still swollen clit.

ଽଓ

*Chuck Fellows lives in Western Massachusetts. Other stories can be found in* Pinned Down By Pronouns, Rode Hard Put Away Wet, Best Lesbian Erotica 2006, Hard Road Easy Riding, Lipstick on Her Collar, Best Lesbian Bondage Erotica *and in the online journal,* Suspect Thoughts. *Many other short erotic snippets can be found in the inboxes of various friends and lovers.*

# bad behavior
## TERESA NOELLE ROBERTS

I blame the damn bridesmaid's dress for my bad behavior that night, the damn bridesmaid's dress and the fact that my very, very straight best friend (that would be Ellen) decided to hold her wedding in a glorious oceanfront inn.

And it was definitely bad behavior, even though it didn't turn out as bad as it might have, as it probably should have, if you believe in karma or cosmic payback.

Then again, the dress, the fact I was willing to wear that hideous dress as an act of love and friendship, might have given me enough good karma to balance the bad.

I always said I'd do anything for Ellen. I'd just been thinking more along the lines of entering a burning building or rescuing her from terrorists, not wearing a frilly peach-colored thing— I'm sure there's a better way to describe it, but "thing" sums it up for me. Too many ruffles, too many buttons, just too much. I'd begged to wear a tux. She said no, and no amount of whimpering would get her to relent, but she did concede that I could change into something more me during the reception.

It was the kind of dress even a femme couldn't get out of on her own, let alone all-thumbs, tomboy me, and at the time, it seemed like a good idea to ask one of the other bridesmaids for a hand. I should have grabbed one of the girls that I knew from college, but they were all dancing up a storm by then, and the only one I could find was the gorgeous, brown-skinned, almond-eyed one whose name I wasn't even sure of, Shari or Cheryl or something like that. The one who actually looked good in peach satin frills, like some diva from the Jazz Age, getting ready to sing at the Apollo.

The one with the obvious engagement ring, a band of gold and white fire on her slim brown finger.

I was thinking bridesmaid solidarity or something like that. I swear; I didn't have an ulterior motive.

Not that ulterior motives hadn't crossed my mind. The combination of adorably unnatural burgundy hair, velvety milk-chocolate skin, and a heady perfume that I'd noticed even during the rehearsal dinner had certainly gotten my attention.

Then I saw the ring and dropped that notion like a hot coal. I'm not exactly the queen of monogamy—okay, I've pretty much made a career out of being the secondary girlfriend or some-time playmate of every poly or commitment-shy queer woman in the area—but I do have a simple ground rule: I don't do cheating. Not always so easy to follow in practice, but sticking to the clearly single (or the dateable-as-a-set, although that offers its own challenges) spares a woman a world of grief.

So, yeah, when I caught her popping into her room as I was heading back toward mine, I might have had a naughty thought or two, but no actual intention other than the stated one: to get out of the dress from Hades and into the super-elegant and actually comfortable man-tailored pantsuit I'd gotten for the reception.

"Just get it started," I said, realizing, too late, of course, that the dress wasn't the kind to stay put well unbuttoned, and my suit was two rooms away. "Or maybe we'd better get to my room because my other clothes…"

But as Shari-or-Cheryl went to unbutton the zillion little buttons at the back of my bodice, she made a strange noise. Then she started nibbling on the back of my neck, murmuring something about the softness of my skin. I should have stopped her, at least asked a few critical questions, but before I could manage, her hands snaked around my waist, started playing with my breasts—in tits-on-a-shelf mode thanks to the dress and apparently self-consciously sensitive me—and my brain shut down.

She kicked the door shut.

The next thing I knew, Shari-or-Cheryl and I were rolling around on the double bed in her room, kissing like a couple of breathless kids. Her kisses tasted of champagne and cognac and, lightly, of menthol cigarettes. Between kisses, she kept saying things along the line of, "I've never done anything like this before," but she kissed like she'd been kissing girls for years. She rubbed against me like a cat, begged me nonverbally for more. Her hands went everywhere, leaving little trails of flame behind them. (Unfortunately they didn't burn off the dress.)

A straight girl was trying to get her hands under my skirt with speed that was boggling me—and I'm not exactly the shy type.

That went to my head and my clit in equal measure.

Remember the lame joke about the Winnebago? I figured mine was going to be waiting in the parking lot with a big rainbow-striped bow on it, because this woman wanted me. Wanted me badly enough that even if I hadn't been attracted to her beauty, her sensuality, I'd have been turned on a little bit by her sheer determined lust.

I didn't have the patience to deal with her bodice. The buttons

and my own urgency were defeating me. I tugged in exaspera-
tion, trying to pull it down off her shoulders—it was cut so it
seemed to stay in place through magic anyway. It tore under
my impatient hands. Her eyes widened, but she didn't object.
Her breasts were as beautiful as I expected, small and firm and
perfect. "I've never ..." she said, but it broke off into a moan as
I started to suckle.

Delicious breasts that molded right to my hands. She even
tasted good, faintly spicy, faintly sweaty, with an undertone of
tobacco that I normally wouldn't have liked but did on her.

She clenched her hand on mine, giving me a good look at her
engagement ring— not a huge rock, but still, a definite rock.

One of my three functional brain cells chimed an alarm at
that point, but I hit the snooze on it. Hadn't I always wanted to
be a learning experience for an adventurous straight woman?

Well, yes and no. That was always one of my top-ten fantasies,
but one I'd never acted on—and I'd had chances before—
because it just sounded like trouble. Combine it, though, with
spontaneous almost-anonymous sex in some romantic setting
(another top-ten hit) and I was doomed.

And settings didn't get much more romantic than this one. I
could hear waves crashing, hear thunder over the sea. The bed
was huge and cushy and had a green velvet duvet. The air smelled
of ozone and salt and some herbal-floral potpourri and her perfume, even more lavish now that we were all tangled up together.
The scent of her arousal, sharp and hot and spicy, drowned it
all out, and that was with her still lost in yards of hideous peach
satin.

I couldn't figure out how to get the dress the rest of the way
off, so I gave a mighty tug like they do in the movies. It didn't
work—they must use strategically designed clothes to get that

effect in the movies, or maybe with a few drinks in me, I'm a bigger klutz than I ever realized—so I just flipped up the skirt.

Her underwear wasn't pretty. It was plain cotton hipsters, Hanes or the like, white, functional, modest. It surprised me— I'd have figured a hot, feminine straight girl, on a dress-up occasion, would have on something fanciful and lacy. I decided I liked it, though. It seemed to prove she hadn't planned to pick up someone tonight, that she'd been overwhelmed by lust, just like I had. No forethought. Not a scheming adulteress, just someone who had adultery fall into her lap.

I frightened myself by gushing hot moisture when I thought of her as an adulteress. Most of the time, I'm all about being an ethical slut. I've turned down a lot of sexy women because there was something shady about the situation. And maybe those years of being the polyamoury poster child came back to haunt me, because the sheer sordidness of the situation made it seem hotter.

I dived between her legs, losing myself in her scent, her heat, and a pile of fabric.

She made vaguely embarrassed noises that stopped when I began to lick her through the cotton. She was already wet enough so that I could suck out her juices, filtering them through the soft white knit. Even her juices were spicy.

When I peeled the panties off of her, revealing her swollen, deep-purple lips, her erect clit, she almost protested. She got as far as, "I'm a little…" Then I licked, and she buried her fingers in my hair, and if she still had doubts, they got lost under moans and giggles and squirming.

First one finger, then two, then three. Her pussy walls sucked me in, clasped around me. I wished for the lube that was back in my room so I could give her more, for a dildo (also in my room, because you never know who you might meet, even at a thoroughly hetero, thoroughly vanilla wedding) so I could fuck her. Then I realized she probably got fucked plenty and might appreciate the oral attention. (I don't want to say guys skimp in that department, because really I wouldn't know, but I've read a few issues of *Cosmopolitan* while waiting for some girlfriend or another and I get the impression that some guys—maybe too many of them—do.)

She took forever to come, but she seemed to be enjoying the journey so the fact it was slow was fine with me. I was enjoying myself mightily, the smoky salty flavor, her squirms and moans, the texture of a new girl. When she did come, it was a silent clench, her little hands driving into my shoulders, her slender body bucking under me. *Lovely*, I thought. *Delicious*.

Then she started crying. Big, silent tears, not a melodramatic scene that felt forced, and that made it worse because it made a *Real Problem*, not a way to cop attention or duck the responsibility for what happened.

Great. She was hurting somehow, probably all torn up and confused because of what she'd done, and it was my own damn fault for breaking my own basic rules: no straight women, no women with partners.

My first impulse was to run, but I was the experienced one here, the one who should be doing the comforting. Running would have been wrong, and I'd already been wrong more than enough tonight.

"Hey," I said, putting my hand on the delicate line of her shoulder, shivering despite myself at the contrast between my black-coffee skin and her milk-chocolate coloring. "Want to talk?"

"Want to lick you," she said, still crying, and tried to roll me over.

But she was still hampered by skirts and it didn't work quite right, which, I figured, was all for the best. My pussy disagreed. I told it to shut up, that listening to it had already gotten me into enough trouble.

"Uh-uh. Talk first. Crying and sex don't mix."

"I've never..." she said.

"I know. And it must be weird."

She shook her head. "No, it isn't. I never have before, but I've wanted to. Always. And it felt like coming home and that's why I'm crying. I don't really know you—frankly, I'm not even too clear on your name..."

"Tonya," I said, not wanting to admit I was a little foggy on hers, too.

"And that still felt more right than ten years of what I thought was pretty damn good sex with guys."

Oh my God. Yeah, the Lesbian Conversion Patrol was delivering that Winnebago now. A lavender one with a special built-in cabinet for storing the sex toys.

I wanted to send it back.

"Isn't that going to be a problem for...?" I pointed at the ring. The diamond caught the light and winked at me accusingly.

She laughed through her tears. "Funny, in that special sense of funny that means really kind of awful. The night before we were supposed to be flying here, I had one Margarita too many and started talking to Frank—that would be my *ex-fiancé*—about all sorts of things, including the fantasies about women. And it turns out my formerly beloved is a lot more conservative than I realized. Things kind of went downhill from there, into the kind of fight you just can't stay engaged after. And I tried to throw the ring at him because no man is going to get away with calling me some of the names he used—but the damn thing won't come off." She tugged at it in demonstration. "I figured it was a sign, that maybe we could work things out. Only now I think it's more of a sign that I've been eating too much comfort food lately because deep down, I knew it was a mistake to marry him."

I felt much, much better. Not that I should have gone there, thinking what I'd thought, making the obvious assumption about the ring—but it sounded like instead of screwing up someone's future, I might have been pointing her in the right direction. Women? Maybe, maybe not. That was for her to decide. Away from that Frank character? Definitely a plan.

Realizing that let me admit that the night was still young and I was still very, very horny.

"You know what's a sign?" I said, smiling in what I hoped was an evil way. "That I have extra-slippery silicone lube back in my room. I bet we can get that damn ring off you in no time!"

"Will the lube work on my dress, too?" she asked. "Because I feel like I've got a lot of catching up to do and it's going to work a lot better naked."

We never did make it back down to the reception. But eventually we called room service for champagne and some huge shrimp cocktails.

And housekeeping for a pair of scissors.

௸ఞ

*Teresa Noelle Roberts writes erotica, romance, and speculative fiction, both under her own name and as part of the writing team known as Sophie Mouette. Her erotica has appeared in* Succulent: Chocolate Flava 2, The Mammoth Book of Lesbian Erotica, Best Women's Erotica 2004, 2005 *and* 2007, Lipstick on Her Collar, Fishnetmag.com, *and many other publications, and she writes erotic romance for* Phaze. *When not writing, Teresa can be found belly dancing, cooking, or enjoying the beach.*

# it's all the same
## ELYSE CARINE

"Every time I get ready to go shopping, you tell me 'It's okay, Boo, get what you want,' but when I get home and you see the receipts, there's some issue. Can you please make up your mind?"

Julissa was becoming quite flustered and could feel her almond skin begin to change color. She had recently gone to an African-American hair-braiding boutique in lower Manhattan for microbraids against her better judgment. The last time that she had gotten microbraids, she had lost quite a bit of her thick shoulder-length mane, and the "no edges" look was not becoming to her mate, and quite below her own satisfaction ratings. She had chosen "African-American" this time because the American portion of the name apparently translated into—we care about your actual hair and will ensure that we don't snap it off at the root, tie it in knots, pull it out of your head, or yank it so tightly that you will have little bumps all over your scalp because we know that you want your hair to grow and be healthy. This was obviously not the case at the African hair braiding "salons." She had chosen light-brown and blonde twenty-inch human hair to accent her own light-brown "I change with the season" locks.

"Boo, I am not saying that it's a problem. I am simply saying that you spend far too much money on trivial shit. Shit that you know you don't need, shit that you know you don't use, shit that's just shit. You could be spending it on things that we could use around here, like oh, I don't know, FOOD maybe."

Clarisse knew even as she let the words escape her lips that Julissa had not, and would not pick up a frying pan. She was simply too cute to cook. Clarisse was a large woman, lovingly named for her maternal grandmother...though she preferred to simply be called "Reese." She was nearly six feet tall, and very broad. She reminded you of a slightly smaller George Foreman. George of the new days, not the old statuesque muscle-bound God, the newer statuesque damn-he-a-big-grillin'-fool-type George. She had short, natural hair that was currently platinum blonde and screamed, "HEY, LOOK AT ME, I'M NOT ONLY GAY, BUT I'M A DYKE," though she claimed to be oblivious to that fact. She had put on about twenty pounds since she and Julissa had officially become a couple two years ago, even though they had dated for four. She couldn't decide if it was because she was comfortable being in a relationship, or if it was the stress of trying to find new ways to keep the attention of the fine-ass Black and Italian woman that she lovingly referred to as "Boo."

"Whatever, Ma, you always say the same thing, but these candles were on sale, and you don't complain when I light them and do my special dance for you."

Julissa placed her hands on her ample hips and began to slowly grind toward Clarisse, never breaking eye contact. The way that her hips swayed reminded Clarisse of a Caribbean sea gently swaying to a warm evening breeze. She couldn't take her eyes off of her. Julissa continued to sway, and began to turn around so that Reese could get a good look at what was to come. Her honey and brown sugar braids gently caressed her perfectly round derriere in a way that reminded Reese of the reason that she truly did not care that this woman had her damn near broke. Julissa still maintained eye contact…when Reese wasn't longingly glancing down at her ass.

*How does she do it?* Reese thought.

Julissa backed up closer to Reese now, closed her eyes, and leaned the back of her head onto Reese's right shoulder. She moved her left arm around Reese's neck and rubbed her right thigh with the other. She never stopped grinding. It was as though she had a Caribbean rhythm in her head, something Bob Marley or perhaps Shabba Ranks. Now, she added little pulses with her back to the sensual grind.

"Baby, they were only a hundred dollars for the set…and I only bought three…you know how I love to bathe by candle-light…"

Julissa cooed barely loud enough for Reese to make out the words, not that it mattered now. If she'd had a dick, it would be throbbing by now, and a drop of love would be glistening at the tip. Alas, she did not; therefore the silk boxers that Julissa had purchased for her last birthday had become very moist and sticky.

"Could you help me?" Julissa pleaded like a schoolgirl confused by a difficult lesson, motioning toward the leather pea-sized button at the base of her neck that held closed the Mizrahi mini-dress that Julissa had brought home last week. Once Reese unbuttoned the button, it was as if that was all that was holding the dress together. Julissa grinded her way out of the dress like she were calling upon the gods of love to rain down upon her and bless her body with endless pleasures. Reese did just that. She began to slowly place soft wet kisses on her neck and caressed her shoulders gently, yet with the firmness of a love that thought that she might escape if she didn't.

A soft moan escaped Julissa's lips as she began to feel the wetness between her thighs. She couldn't help but to reach for the warmth and brought it back to Reese's lips. Reese gladly received the juices from her partner's fore and middle fingers with an intensity and passion that made Julissa feel like she would explode. Julissa arched her back and inhaled as if she were taking in her last breath. Reese moved her hands from Julissa's shoulders to her soft, supple breasts that seemed to respond to her touch. Reese couldn't even bring herself to think about the fact that Julissa had left the house braless again. She firmly cupped the breasts that filled her hands and gently spilled over a bit with intensity. She pinched the perky nipples that were centered on Julissa's perfect breasts with an authority that caused Julissa to cry out in painful passion.

Reese spun her around and took Julissa's face into her hands, planting a kiss in her mouth that was breathtaking. Reese's tongue seemed to search Julissa's mouth for some long lost treasure that she had been seeking since the dawn of time. Julissa knew that Reese did not enjoy being pleasured, but she couldn't help herself. She began to grope for Reese's breasts and was met by severe resistance. Reese grabbed her by the arms and threw her to the leather sofa. She landed in a sitting position with her feet dangling toward the floor. Reese pinned Julissa's arms above her head with one hand and spread her thighs with the other. When she felt that Julissa understood her desires, she knelt down on the floor in front of her, and moved her hands to bend Julissa's knees onto her shoulders. Reese stared deep into the almond-shaped hazel eyes of this beautiful, curvaceous woman that she had come to love, and couldn't believe that she was all hers to do as she pleased. She bent her face down to Julissa's thighs and caressed them with her tongue and hands simultaneously. She began to grip Julissa's thighs with such passion that Julissa thought she would scream, but she didn't; she only moaned with more and more intensity as she enjoyed the pain. Reese moved her hands to grip the place where Julissa's hips and thighs met. She moved Julissa closer to her face. That only meant one thing. Julissa braced herself for the pleasure.

Reese forced her thick, hot tongue into Julissa with massive force. She moved her tongue up and down and around and around. She caressed the clitoris without reservation. She was relentless in her quest to taste Julissa's thick, milky release. She gently sucked and sucked; licked and licked; sucked and licked; licked and sucked.

"Oh God," Julissa moaned. "It feels so good, Ma... fuck me." Reese moved her left hand down toward Julissa's light-brown forest and gently inserted her forefinger into her pulsating middle. Julissa cried out with pleasure. Reese continued to suck and flick Julissa's clitoris with a vengeance. She knew that Julissa liked it rough, so as she thrust her finger into Julissa's hot pussy, she switched from one, to two, to three fingers...thrusting, and licking, and sucking...and licking, and thrusting and sucking. Julissa was now screaming out with pleasure and began to push Reese's head deeper and deeper into her wetness. Reese knew that her Boo was close, so she reached up with her free hand and pinched Julissa's nipple hard and refused to let go as Julissa screamed with ecstasy. Her hot, wet pussy clamped down hard on Reese's fingers and her pelvis thrust forward hard and long. Oh, the juices began to flow. Reese loved the fact that Julissa came like a man...not that she would know firsthand how a man would come, but she'd seen it on videos. Reese opened her mouth and took in all of Julissa's creamy fluids as she enjoyed the look of satisfaction on her lover's face. At that moment, Reese knew that she would never let Julissa go, no matter what. Besides, the candles were kind of cute.

℘℘

As she rode the train to work once again because her love was too tired from partying all night to get up and drive her in, Reese thought about the day before and how much she loved the little woman that brought on her migraines at least once a week. As her express train into the city flew through local stops on its regular route, she reflected upon all the good times that they had. For each stop that she passed, the reflection of the inexplicable love that they made filled her thoughts. She reminisced about the trips that they'd taken. Vegas, San Francisco, the Caribbean cruise. She relished in the private jokes that they shared, the laundry room at her parents' apartment building, the white party that they'd attended in South Beach last summer, and the Jacuzzi at that little knock-off motel out on Route 1 because they just couldn't wait. There were way too many to conjure up now, and there was certainly no purpose in getting herself all worked up on the way to work without Julissa there to satiate her desires. The good times far outweighed the bad...didn't they? There were countless times that she'd waited up for Miss Thang to appear, and she didn't...

always calling from one of her girls' houses saying that she'd fallen asleep...or something to that effect. There was also the fact that this girl spent money like it grew on trees. Reese didn't even want to think about her credit rating right now. Julissa was irresponsible, spoiled rotten, and selfish...hence this morning's train ride. Just then, a huge smile came across Reese's face, the kind that would crack your lips if they weren't properly moisturized.

"But she's all mine," she said to no one in particular.

The man seated next to her reading his paper looked up at her for a moment, quizzically, then looked back at the day's news.

&#8253;&#8278;

As Julissa rolled over in her and Reese's plush king-sized bed, her sleepy eyes read the alarm clock. *It can't be 10:45*, she thought. She reached over next to her and saw that she was alone.

"Damn."

She was still feeling groggy as she sat up and tried to focus. She reached over to the nightstand for the remote and clicked on the television. Cartoons, of course. That's how she started every day. She began to stand up, but ended back on the bed again.

"Whew!" She laughed out loud.

Her second attempt at standing was much more successful, but still wobbly. She recalled numerous Martinis of random flavors... some of which she could still taste now. Funny enough, they were not as good now as when they went down. On her way to the master bathroom, she held each wall with resilience. As she sat on the bowl, she gazed up at the marble walls and deep Jacuzzi that she'd purchased last month. She clicked on the television above it and caught a piece of *Maury*. She giggled at these silly women with their cheating men. How long ago that was for her. She'd met Reese at a rough time in her life. Four years ago, she'd been juggling about five or six deadbeat dudes, and had nothing really going for her but her good looks and determination. She had considered going back to school for nursing, but who had the time? She was working at an upscale boutique in the city, but only part time. Her afternoons were filled with naps, her evenings filled with dates, and her weekends filled with partying with her girls or more dates.

She knew that her mother was sick of her mooching, she reminded her daily, but please. What else are parents for? She knew that she'd move in her own time, and see? *See what happens when you are patient?* she thought. Here she was, twenty-nine years old, with her own townhouse in a fabulous suburb of northern New Jersey, a gorgeous BMW 745 at her disposal, credit cards, cash, and all of the additional accoutrements that come with a successful businesswoman who is head over heels in love with her. It had been so natural for her to allow Reese to love her. She was big, strong, intelligent, and most of all sexy. She made Julissa feel like a real woman. Reese made her realize that all of the men that she had been dealing with were actually boys posing as men. The majority of them only talked the talk. They mostly had the three Bs: bad credit, baby-mama drama, and worst of all, bad dick. Some of them had been burned in the past, like poor old Maurice. He'd gone through it with his ex-fiancée. Oh, what a trick that broad was. *But why did he have to take it out on me?* Julissa thought. *I didn't sleep with his best friend from college.*

He was so demanding and untrusting. He wanted to know every move that she made...be it to the store, or to the bathroom. Julissa had gotten so used to him asking, she'd begun to just blurt out what she was doing before she'd even done it. Her friends thought she was crazy. Then there was Paul, who had been burned by his crazy-assed baby-muva who took him to court for just about everything he had. He was so cheap, you could almost hear him squeak when he moved. Who had time for that?

Reese was different, she'd been so open, so caring, so loving. Julissa had never even considered being with a woman before, but technically, in her mind, she wasn't. Reese was more of a man than any man that she knew, with the exception of her father, who was probably the only person on earth that would give her as much if not more than Reese. She was strong, business-minded, and tough. Reese also had very masculine features, but she was still able to exude an air of femininity when the situation called for it. Her business partners respected her, her family and friends adored her, and what seemed to be every gay woman on the planet wanted to be with her.

Julissa stayed on her toes...at least in her mind she did. She knew that she had Reese wrapped around her little finger. It had taken her two years of serious dating to get with this woman, and now, she wasn't going anywhere. This woman had shown her things that she'd never seen before, she'd helped her clear up her credit that had been a wreck ever since that first AMEX card back when she was eighteen, she'd taken her places she'd never been, nor thought of going. There was no one that could come in between them, and Julissa knew that.

Just as she stood over her Whitehaus crystal vessel sink that changed colors with the water temperature, about to brush her teeth, she heard what sounded like Reese's cell phone ring. She must have forgotten it that morning when she left for work. Julissa went into the dressing room where most of Reese's things were and searched for the ringing Treo. As she got closer, the ring got louder. *Ah, her man-bag,* Julissa thought and giggled to herself. She picked up the bag and fished out the phone. The name *Carmen* flashed across the screen as Julissa pressed the answer button.

"Hello?"

She was met by a click on the other end. *Now who the hell is Carmen?* Julissa thought as the message waiting indicator came on. She couldn't resist. The message played.

*"Hey, it's Carmen. Wondering if I can see you again. I had such a wonderful time last night. I'm so glad you finally caved in and let me take you out. Call me later when you have the chance. Besos amor."*

Julissa must have played the message at least five times. *Besos amor? This person must have the wrong number. She could not possibly be leaving a message for* MY *woman talking about what a wonderful night she had. Reese was at home last night when she called, just like she always is.*

A hundred thoughts raced through Julissa's head. Was Reese seeing someone else? What did this Spanish floozie look like? Probably fucking Jennifer fucking Lopez. What was happening? She didn't know if she should call the number back or confront Reese with it. She never expected this from Reese. With those other niggas, this was a daily occurrence, some bitch calling because of this, that, or the other thing, but the last four years had been other-woman-drama-free. Was it possible that this was happening? Julissa suddenly felt dizzy and lightheaded.

She ran back into the bathroom to vomit, but nothing came up except more leftover cocktails. She was still gripping Reese's phone when it rang again. This time, the name read *Maxine*. Both times, the numbers were private, or "secret" as the screen read, only the names came up. What the fuck? Julissa couldn't bring herself to answer the phone. She left it on the vanity next to the sink and went back into the bedroom. Thinking back, Clarisse had NEVER left her phone at home…or anywhere for that matter. It was her right arm. *Have I really been this stupid?* Julissa thought.

"All this time, I've been faithful and true, and this bitch is no better than all the other niggas I've dealt with."

She could feel the warm tears run down the side of her face and onto the pillow on which she laid her head. She held her stomach and rocked from side to side, as if she had ulcers. That's what the pain felt like. She had made a promise to Clarisse the first time that they'd made love. If she ever found out that she cheated, there would be no questions asked.

ଚ୍ଚଠା

This had been unequivocally the worst day of the year for Reese. Even though she'd taken the express train this morning, she was two hours late because some inconsiderate jerk had decided to end it all during the morning rush hour. Her secretary was having issues with her kid, and had to leave early. The deal that she had with Hit Street Records had fallen through because their CFO was under investigation for tax evasion and embezzlement. Her brother had called and said that he and his wife were getting a divorce, and now, her

Louis Vuitton briefcase handle had broken as she was coming up the stairs to the townhouse.

"Boo...I've had the worst day...I need a hug!" she yelled up the stairs to apparently no one.

"Where you at, Ma?" Reese yelled down toward the laundry room. But there was no answer.

The car was in the garage, the keys were on the table in the foyer. Wait, why would Julissa's keys be on the table if she wasn't here? Reese left her briefcase, or what was left of it downstairs with her trench coat and walked toward the bedroom. Everything was perfect; the housekeeper must have come by that day. She went into the master bath and found her Treo on the vanity along with a yellow sticky note that simply read:

*Carmen and Maxine called.*

Shit!

଼ଓଓ

*Elyse Carine is a 34-is-the-new-24-year-old aspiring novelist currently residing in Central New Jersey with her fiancé and two beautiful daughters, 13 and 1... Don't ask.*

# a woman
## D.L. KELLEY

I have never been with a woman.

But there was something about her; some magnetic force that captivated my gaze. My eyes never averted in her presence, but instead, completely took her in. She dragged my eyes behind her around the room as she flirted with couples and touched other women. I grew hot with embarrassment and curiosity, but she never left my sight.

In college I'd found myself attracted to my roommate. I think she knew. She was no nudist, but she seemed to take pleasure in baring all her assets in our closet-sized dorm room. She was a petite, light-skinned girl, with long brown hair and green eyes, perky ample breasts and a proportionate backside. Always in makeup and high heels, always *done*, she was my polar opposite. We never ran in the same circles because she was so outgoing and seemed to thrive on the attention lavished upon her in any setting. I was a loner; never the "it" girl in the room and always the wallflower.

Just as I was tonight. I remained the only person in the room with my black mask over half of my face, and all of my clothing still on.

Maybe I didn't want to be noticed. That would explain why

I continually came to La Lounge Couples Club on Saturday nights, the only night when single females were allowed inside alone, sat in the very back, at the very far end of the bar, sipping my very plain club soda, watching as everyone else participated in their own freedom.

That's what was so attractive about *her*. She was so free. I craved for her to sprinkle on me just a pinch of her spirit of abandon, but I couldn't dare put myself in that situation with her.

I watched the way her teeth gleamed through thick, plum-stained lips as she grinned and chatted about the taboo so casually with other partygoers in attendance. I watched the way her eyes sparkled when she connected on some secret level with another woman, and sometimes that woman's man, and began to stroke her hands on their exposed body parts. Her long, slender brown fingers raked this person's neck and that person's thigh, weaving into and out of their intertwined limbs, as if she was searching for treasure. I watched her breasts gently sway to the rhythm of her step. Unknowingly, I licked my lips as I imagined the sweetness of her melons in my mouth. I watched her so intently, that I didn't realize she'd locked her eyes on me. And she was coming over.

She didn't saunter. She didn't exert any effort, really, to create sex as she moved slowly across the room. But there wasn't an eye in the room that was not fixated on the length of her chocolate legs, the graceful rock of her round hips, the alter-nating rise and fall of her plump cheeks. To say her presence exuded sex did her no justice. She could have easily been fully clothed in a suit and slacks, but that body still could have seared through the buttons and seams, reached out and grabbed the attention of all those around her. To say she was beautifully molded was a sad understatement.

I began sweating, on both my brow and between my thighs. My hand fumbled to find my drink in front of me at the bar, and I knocked the glass over into my lap.

"Shit."

Her hand was suddenly covering my own and I instinctively dropped the napkin I'd grabbed to dab at the mess on my navy blue slacks. My breath was frozen in my chest. I couldn't lift my head to look at her. I couldn't allow myself to be lost in her, not this close. From across the room, where she couldn't see what she did to me, yes.

But she was so close. I felt compelled to look at her, to let her see me.

She said, "Don't worry about it. It's club soda. It won't stain, sweetheart." Her voice was husky, sexy. Her breath was sweet with a hint of mint. She cooled my face as she spoke to me, so close that our noses almost touched. Her skin was smooth and glowing in deep bronze under the club lights. She didn't speak loud, but I heard her just as clearly as if she was yelling through a megaphone. The sound of the music, the moans and cries of other guests' ecstasy all began to fade. I heard only her breathing now. I inhaled her deep, the high taking hold of me, reeling me toward her, into her arms.

But I did not move.

I have never been with a woman.

"You're here every week. You always sit right here, in the back. You always wear your mask...your clothes..." Her tongue was pretty, deliberately finding each syllable and carefully placing them together to give to me like a string of pearls. I wanted to kiss her thoughts before they became her words. I wanted her to feel me in her head, the way I felt her.

But I only nodded a simple yes and my leg began to shake. I

could not believe she'd noticed me all that time. My cheeks grew warm under her gaze, but I was blushing from humiliation.

"You're here every week watching us...me. Do you like to watch, and nothing more?" she asked, staring me up and down, gently disrobing me with her eyes and taking into account everything I'd always tried to hide. I felt uncomfortable with her directness, but an arousal sparked a flame inside me and now replaced the dim flicker that kept my center warm. I felt a throbbing, a nagging, an aching at the apex of my legs. I wanted to spread them open so she could ease my pain.

But I only softy answered, "I don't know."

Her hand was on my thigh now. I was so sure she could feel the heat rising through my slacks, smell the anxiety and desire. I thought I heard her ask me if I was scared, but by then I didn't know what either of us was saying. I couldn't focus straight. Her hand was moving up my thigh, to my zipper.

I have never been with a woman.

She was pulling my zipper down, tasting my neck with her pretty tongue, snaking her hand up inside my blouse, over and into my bra. She moved with a certain swiftness, but her touches were slow and measured. Her hand was so warm on my chest, cupping my small B-cup breasts, bringing them to life. I felt my nipples lifting themselves from their downward gaze. The fire inside me was now a rippling wave flowing through me, heaving in response to her every touch.

Her hand was in my pants now. I tensed. The sensation of her warm skin touching mine was a completely new experience.

"I have never been with a woman," I found the voice to say to her.

"I know, sweetie," she answered. Her eyes said she'd be gentle, but my body wanted to feel her wrath. I wanted her hands to play me like a guitar, strumming all kinds of beautiful chords from deep inside me. I wanted her to find my voice and create in me beautiful music to swing my hips to; just like hers. I wanted to reach octaves above my shallow self-inflictions, my lacking confidence and nervous self-consciousness.

Her index and middle fingers walked over my unshaven mound, treading through the brush on a careful hunt for my inner beast. I screamed, *RELEASE ME*, through lips that had no tongue. I tasted her fingers where I had no mouth.

She found me, crouched, shivering from fear and expectation, a tiny, hard pearl, pulsing volumes of unspoken verses through its vibration. The pads of her fingertips were silky smooth as she rubbed an unfamiliar wetness against my clitoris.

I sighed.

Her tongue traveled southward to meet her hand in my blouse, and each inch covered glistencd with the sweet minty dew of her kisses. I felt like a brand-new morning.

I moaned.

She bared her teeth in a satisfied grin. Her eyes were big and warm, inviting me to relax. I wanted so badly to give in to her, to the atmosphere surrounding us, pressing down on us. But I couldn't.

I have never been with a woman.

There were people watching us. Women and men touched themselves and each other in ways I was never able to touch even myself. I was wide-eyed with shock, embarrassment and shame. My eyes fought to stay open, but some invisible force kept pushing them closed. *Relax*, it told me. *Let them see you.*

I stood up, not by any power of my own, but by that same

invisible force. In my upright position, I felt like I was floating, held aloft by the gaze of so many wanting eyes. She peeled my top from my torso. I slid my navy flats from my feet and lifted my legs out of my slacks. She smiled at my harlot red lace panties and matching bra, a secret I'd kept for so long beneath my daily, mundane black or navy slacks and thick white blouses, then slowly removed each piece as well. She took her time reveling in my nakedness. Her hands moved over my body as if she was molding me into some beautiful piece of pottery. I wanted to reach out and touch her just the same, but I stood with lifeless limbs at my sides and a vibrancy only waiting to burst from within me. I could feel the tingling at my fingertips. I could feel the nerves in my skin jumping up to meet her touches. But I was cemented in my stance.

When her hand returned to my own, she spoke again:

*Touch.*

*Your.*

*Self.*

The delay between the movement of her mouth and the words reaching my ears felt like decades. I wasn't quite sure I understood, but I felt my fingertips suddenly moisten and warm. I felt a pressure against my walls, as my own two fingers pressed inside me and climbed deeper. I ran my tongue over my top lip, bit the bottom. Her hand wrapped around my wrist, guiding my movement. She helped me stroke up and down, in and out. Her other hand mirrored my every move, sliding her fingers into and out of her own moistness. Her toothy smile ceased as she licked her lips.

I watched as her tongue unwrapped words for me in the same manner she'd carefully unwrapped my body. My ears waited for her spoken symphony to silence the cacophony of wild thoughts running across my mind.

*Taste.*

*Your.*

*Self.*

Slowly, she brought my hand up between our faces and, instinctively, we began to lick the juices from it. The pads of my fingertips had wrinkled from their dive and the texture tickled my tongue. She sucked my middle finger into her mouth first, then allowed me to do the same to my index finger. I marveled at my own sweetness; the smell, the warmth, the flavor of myself that I never knew. It made me hungry for something more. I wondered if she tasted as sweet.

I have never been with a woman.

But something penetrated me at my core; a sharp, interminable *something* that shook me free from my own self-set boundaries. As if suspended in some out-of-body experience, I witnessed myself entering her most private region with the same fingers of mine that she'd led in my self-discovery. I kept my eyes open long enough to watch hers close. That satisfied grin washed over her ever-seductive face. I slid into and out of her with ease. My motion was slow. I wanted to feel every dip and hill of bare terrain, and she let me have my expedition. I could feel her slick walls collapse onto me, trap me in her dark cave, then loosen the hold so my fingers could match her muscles throb for throb. She squeezed. Released. Squeezed. I pressed into her. I was wanted. I felt needed.

Slowly, I painted her landscape with my tongue, in long strokes and short strokes. The colors of our delicious passion merged with my unfamiliar excitement till my mouth's palate dripped in new tints and hues of ecstasy. We were a master-piece.

My mouth covered her body from head to toe, tasting each carnal response she offered. I answered her with a quickened pace walking along her walls.

*Lay.*

*Down.*

She descended upon me, straddling my hips with hers. I could feel the weight of her body bending the bristles of my thatch. The hairs returned to me, prickling my sensitive skin.

She pressed her mouth to mine in a deep kiss, tangling our tongues into knots; exploring my oral cavity with the same gentle voracity her fingers had earlier expressed inside of me. Her kiss was slow and sensual. Her lips were soft and plump. They warmed my own. The pressure made me want to devour her tongue and ravage her mouth like a madwoman. But I let her lead the dance between our lips.

She kissed my mask as if it was my own skin. She never reached to remove it from my face. I was eased by her respect for my personal space, although I didn't want to leave any room for any space between us. I wanted us to become one.

I have never been with a woman.

But when she pressed her tongue against the jointess that held my lips tightly together between my shaking legs, I felt a surge of electricity speed throughout my body, bursting in every blood vessel. I was suddenly sweating again, but this time from some heat radiating within me; a warmth that swelled with each gesture of her tongue.

She licked and sucked my bud with her pretty mouth. I couldn't help but watch her soft, wet lips disappear into my bush before my eyes rolled back into my head and my lids slid closed. I felt my lips part, welcoming her invasion, then close again around her tongue. She sipped from my stream, made her way up and down the banks on each side, stopping for several moments at a time to play her tongue against my hood. Her delicate fingers gently pulled back the skin and exposed my clitoris, to which she applied soft kisses and enveloped it in her twisted tongue as if she was trying to protect it.

My moans grew louder, matching the din of the crowd that had thickened around us and the music that now seemed very far away.

She beckoned, "Come here," with two fingers inside me, and the surge of energy returned immediately. My body trembled, heated, and pressure mounted from deep within. She'd called and sent for the peak of my pleasure and it came…I came. Crashing down hard around her, it came. Creamy, wet, warm, it came, slipping through my lips, glazing my hair, and landing in her open, waiting mouth. I could not move, but my body heaved. I could not think, but every conceivable and inconceivable sensation ran through my mind as I tried to make sense of what I was feeling.

Slowly I gathered myself and though my high never subsided, I felt myself slipping down to earth again. I could feel her hands still on me. I could smell the sweetness of her skin, how she tasted. I could hear her breathing and feel her body on top of mine, her nipples pressing into me. Her mouth was on my neck. My cheek. And finally, lightly, she kissed me on my forehead.

Her hand swept slowly over my face and rested with the tips of her fingers beneath my black mask, then moved up to stroke my hair. She kissed my closed eyes and I began again dreaming about my taste on her lips, and hers on mine.

*Open.*

*Your.*

*Eyes.*

There was only blackness. I saw nothing. I blinked a few times, then removed the silk mask from my eyes, wiping sweat across my forehead in the process.

No different from any other Sunday morning, I found my exhausted body tangled in my bed sheets, wet and cold. My clothing from the night before was strewn across the floor. An unfamiliar dampness stained my inner thighs.

I was plagued with the same dream every Saturday night, the orchestration of my wandering hands and tossing and turning throughout the night. And just like any other Sunday morning, I found myself thinking, curiously...

I have never been with a woman.

৪১৫৩

*D.L. Kelley is the self-published author of* The Ink Came, *a short collection of romantic and erotic poetry. Besides writing, music and singing are first loves. She is a single mother of one and currently resides in Long Island, NY with her son.*

# the mile high club
## SHASHAUNA P. THOMAS

Everyone knows about love at first sight. Even those who don't believe in it. They think it's impossible. How can you love someone you don't even know? Most people chop these initial feelings up to instant attraction, infatuation, or horniness. I, myself, was one of those doubters, but when it came to finally finding Ms. Right, I knew that I loved her before I knew it was her that I loved. The best way to explain what I mean is to start at the beginning. Hello, my name is Melissa, I'm twenty-four, light-skinned, five-six, gay, and live in Denver, Colorado.

I moved to Denver two years ago, after I finally came out to my parents, friends, and the rest of my family back in New York. I'd known for a long time that I was gay, but I didn't tell my parents because I wasn't exactly sure how they would take the news. I needed them pleased with me to help pay for my tuition at Columbia. I even dated a few men in high school and slept with a few guys in college, but none satisfied me. Sure, I enjoyed the sex and had orgasms but definitely nothing to write home about. Some of them were undeniably skilled and very creative in the bedroom, but they weren't what I really truly wanted. If you have a craving for a certain food that you don't have access to, the hunger isn't sated no matter how good the food available to you is.

My parents freaked out at first and went through the usual steps of denial, anger, self-pity, and then self-doubt, as if they had done something that caused me to turn out the way that I did. Like playing too much touch football with my dad and brothers was the reason women turned me on and men didn't. My brothers and friends were understanding and supportive off the bat, but it took my parents some getting used to. While they were getting used to the daughter they never really knew, I decided to move to Denver, start a new life, and live with my old college roommate, Stacy. My best friend had been out the closet since the first day that I met her. It was through her that I learned about the gay community on campus and joined the LGBTA as a straight ally. When I came out to Stacy, she kept screaming, "I knew it! I knew it! I knew it! You've always been too fine to be straight," and acted like I said that I'd won a million dollars.

I lived with her for the first few months and then moved out on my own when I found a job, as well as a nice place to live. After living a couple of months in Denver, my parents realized how stupid they were acting and embraced my sexual orientation. Even though I chose to stay in Denver, we are actually much closer than we ever were before. So, with my friends and family all supporting me, a great job, and my own beautiful home, everything in my life was looking up. The only problem was that I was lonely. Sure, I hung out with Stacy and even went on a couple of dates with women. The few I went out with were nice but they weren't what I was looking for, and even though I wasn't physically a virgin, I had never slept with a woman before. I wanted my first time with a woman to be with the right one.

Especially since my first time with a man was *soooo* disappointing. Plus, I had had too many instances when I was aroused, left unsatisfied, and had to go home and take care of it myself. It happened so often that I tended to shy away from sexual behavior with others because I couldn't take the teasing anymore. I began living by the motto "Don't tease me if you can't please me." I couldn't exactly describe what I was looking for but I knew once I found it, I'd know.

Hanging out with Stacy was cool but I didn't do that too often when she met her girlfriend, Sharon, because I'm no third wheel. Stacy offered to set me up on blind dates with numerous girls, but I never agreed. Stacy was always wilder than me, and I was afraid of her taste in women—no pun intended. Sure, Sharon was a cool person and I loved hanging out with her, but Stacy and Sharon were in an open relationship, which was something I couldn't handle. If I wanted to be with someone who wanted to sleep with me and other women, I'd date men. The two of them were always off trying something new, which I did admire them for, but I knew I'd never do it if I wasn't with the right person. Someone I trusted completely. I also realized that I was being picky and using my work as an excuse to not get out there like I should if I truly wanted to meet someone. So when they asked me to go out with them one evening, I agreed and they both knew the perfect place to take me: The Mile High Club.

The Mile High Club was one of the hottest gay and lesbian nightspots in Denver, according to Sharon.

"And I'm not just saying that because my cousin owns the place. It's great. Trust us, you'll love it. Stacy and I go there all the time. Plus, I want you to meet my cousin, Sasha."

I knew they were trying to set me up again, but I didn't respond.

I figured even if I didn't like Sasha in that way, she would prob-ably be another cool person to hang out with. Besides, if the club was as big as they made it seem, I definitely would meet tons of eligible women.

We agreed to meet up at Stacy's and drive there together. I arrived at their place on time, wearing a sweater and snug-fitting jeans. When Stacy opened the door wearing a spandex black dress, and I saw Sharon in the back of her wearing a similar dress but in red, they shook their heads. They took me into the apartment, sat me down on Stacy's bed, and started raiding the closet for a different shirt for me to wear.

"Wait. What's wrong with what I'm wearing? Aren't we going up into the mountains?"

"True, but once we get in the club, it's going to be packed. Plus, the club has climate control so it'll feel like seventy degrees inside. We won't be outside long enough for you to be cold. You need another outfit to…show off your assets," Stacy replied, shuffling through her closet.

"I'm taller than you, Stacy. I can't fit your clothes."

"You might not be able to wear my skirts or pants, but you can kind of fit my tops."

"No, I can't. My breasts are bigger than yours."

"True, but a top loose on me should fit nice and snug on you," Stacy replied with a devilish grin, and Sharon snickered right next to her, trying to help pick a top.

"Your jeans will look fine with this little number," Sharon said as she pulled out a black halter-top with a low, revealing back and a V-dipped front. I looked at the top and knew right off the bat that they wanted me to look sluttier than I usually dressed for clubs. I went to the bathroom and changed into the top, but because of the way the top was made, I couldn't wear my bra. Even though it was a size smaller than I usually wore my tops, it did cover all the essentials and still left enough skin revealed to spark one's imagination. I came out, left my bra and sweater on Stacy's bed, let them briefly inspect me, and then we were off.

The drive to the club wasn't long because it wasn't that far up into the mountains around Denver. At first sight, the club looked like what it once was: a large, old ski lodge. From the driveway leading to the larger of two parking lots, the club looked almost as if it was tucked into the side of the snow-capped mountain. We heard the music blaring from inside. At first, I was worried it'd be dead inside since there wasn't anyone on line waiting to get in. Once we got past the doormen, and walked in, that fear flew right out the window. The huge ballroom was turned into the main dance floor of the club with two bars on each side of the floor. One side of the room was completely made of glass, which faced the side of the mountain. With the lights low, smoke machines running, and music blasting, the view was simply an added bonus. The lights from the club would play off the white snow outside the window.

I had a blast, first dancing with Stacy and Sharon, then dancing with other females in the club. I knew there were gay clubs, but I'd never been to one before; even back in New York where there were tons. The women were beautiful and some were even hot, but none especially piqued my interest. Still, I hadn't been out in a long time, so I was having a blast partying and was definitely hitting the drinks harder than usual. We were sitting down at our table, taking a break from dancing, when I noticed Stacy and Sharon were whispering to each other and looking at me.

"What are you two up to?" I asked, looking skeptically at them.

"Well…we…have something to tell you. Actually, Stacy, why

don't you tell her? She's known you longer," Sharon said before she lifted her drink to take a long, leisurely slip.

Stacy looked at me and hesitantly began. "Well…um…Mel, we've got something to tell you."

"Okay. What is it?"

"You see…this club isn't a regular club. It's more of…a fantasy club."

I started laughing because I was definitely tipsy and her statement made absolutely no sense. "What do you mean, fantasy club? It looks real enough to me."

"Yes, it really is a club, but it's not *just* a club. It's a place for gay people to come and live out their fantasies. As you know, this place used to be a ski lodge. What you don't know is that the other rooms have various uses. Some are used for specific fantasies while others are private rooms for you to live out your own fantasy with people of your choosing. You see, the reason we didn't tell you before was because we were afraid you wouldn't come."

I stopped laughing and was now in shock; trying to absorb this latest information. "So, why are you telling me now? You're not inviting me into a fantasy room with you guys, are you? I knew you two were into freaky shit but this is a whole new ball game for me."

"No, no, no. The reason we're telling you is we want to go into one of the fantasy rooms and we didn't want you to think we disappeared on you. Plus, you can go in and out of different rooms yourself as an observer. You don't have to participate and it could keep you occupied while we have a little fun."

I could tell by their faces that they expected me to have a fit, and demand they take me home, but I wasn't that upset. I was pissed that they sprang it on me, but I was having fun. I didn't want the night to end yet; plus, these fantasy rooms sounded interesting.

"What fantasy are you guys going to act out?"

"We're going to try the mile high room. It's made to look like an airplane bathroom, but a little bigger. Since we never did it in an actual plane before, we thought it might be fun," Sharon said, looking at Stacy seductively. They both got extremely horny when they drank. They promised to meet me back at our table and left.

I sat there a little while but my curiosity got the better of me, so I grabbed my drink and walked in the same direction they had gone, toward the female fantasy rooms. The fantasy rooms were divided into two hallways, one for men, and one for women. I passed through a few; one had a school theme with two girls dressed up as Catholic school girls trying to get extra credit from their female teacher. The next one was a sports theme, where a cheerleader was seducing the female head coach. The third room was the one that got my attention. At first, it was the fact that there was a huge crowd. The room was larger than the others, so more people were able to come in and watch. I looked and saw it was a torture room. The walls were painted black and there were various contraptions I'd never seen in real life. There was a young woman chained to the ceiling in the middle of the room. She, like some of the people in the audience, was wearing a mask to conceal her identity. Otherwise, she was completely naked. I was so stunned to see her restrained that I hadn't noticed another woman walk in through the crowd until she brushed up against me. When I turned around, my mouth dropped open. She was wearing black knee-high boots, leather booty shorts, leather gloves, and a leather halter-top. She had caramel skin, and her hair was pulled back in a ponytail. She had a rose tattoo on the center of her lower back that was visible only when she hunched down in front of the girl hanging from the ceiling. She smelled fruity, and even though she wasn't close to me anymore, her scent was still in my nose. Just looking at her, I began to get aroused.

The leather woman didn't say anything as she teased the restrained woman into mindlessness. First, she caressed the girl's stomach, then down her inner thighs as she kissed her way up. Once she made it to her pussy, she started with little sensual kisses and teasing little licks. As the girl continued to beg, she stood up and placed her leather-gloved hands where her lips were while whispering in her ear. Soon the girl was screaming as she came. By then, I was extremely wet and felt almost as if I was the restrained girl. The leather woman had affected me more than anyone ever had. I was so lost in my own thoughts, I hadn't realized that the crowd had begun to disband, while others released the naked girl, helping her down. I turned around to leave when I felt someone grab my arm and pull me into a corner in the room. When I turned around, I found myself face-to-face with the leather woman.

"Hello there, lovely lady. Did you enjoy the show?" she said in a near whisper. With every word, she pressed her body more into me.

"Yes…it was…very interesting. I've never seen anything like it."

"I saw you. You seemed to be really into it. Did I make you excited?" Feeling her leg separating mine, I couldn't think straight enough to speak. "Well, what's the matter? Cat got your tongue? Or does tongue got your cat?" She was rubbing her leg against the crotch of my jeans. Her little motion was causing my already wet panties to become soaked. "Since you won't tell me, I guess I'm gonna have to find out myself."

Then she took off one of her leather gloves, slipped her hand into the side of my halter-top, and started playing with my nipple. Her nipple rubbing felt so good, I was moaning before I knew it. I closed my eyes, leaned my head back on the wall, and continued to moan.

Somewhere along the way, I felt her lean her head forward and start licking and sucking my neck. Then she took her other glove off and unbuttoned the front of my jeans. Before I could say anything, I felt her hand go inside my panties. She moved her fingers in slow circular motion in time with her other hand on my nipple that was hard and sensitive. Her fingers made my body feel like it was on fire.

"Oh, you are excited. Do you like that? Huh, baby, tell me. Does that feel good?"

I couldn't say anything. I just continued to moan, this time louder. A few people heard me, looked, but then kept on their way. She continued until I had the best orgasm that I ever had. I was so wet, I felt it running down the inside of my legs.

"Oh, you're a sensitive one. I like that. Very responsive." She put her fingers to her lips and sucked my cum off. "Umm. Tasty. I hope you come back real soon. I would hate to get a taste and never have a complete meal."

With that said, she left the room.

I was shaking, and my legs felt like if I tried to move, they might give, so I buttoned my jeans but stayed leaning on the wall until I felt the shaking stop. I'd never done anything like that with a woman before, much less in public. I'd never had an orgasm like that either. I knew that I'd found her, the one I'd been looking for. The only problem was that I didn't know her name, much less who she was. Then it hit me that she might be in a relationship already and I experienced jealousy for the first time. It was definitely a night of firsts. I was again so lost in my thoughts that I didn't realize, until the last moment, that I was inches from our table, and there was someone else sitting with Stacy and Sharon.

"Hey, there you are. We were about to send out a search party for you," Stacy said as I approached and took my place next to the newcomer.

"Yeah, I went exploring and got caught-up in one of the fantasy rooms. How was your fantasy?" I asked to be polite, but I could tell by the afterglow on their faces, they had had a real good time.

"Oh, it was great! Even though we rarely repeat our fantasies, we just might do that one again in the near future. It seems so real. The sink works and there is even a sound system that sounds like the plane's engines, announcements over the loud speaker from the captain, and a flight attendant talking outside the door. It was hot."

I listened to Stacy as I turned to face the woman sitting next to me. She had beautiful brown eyes, caramel skin, and long hair worn straight down her back. She was wearing a cream wraparound dress, which showed off her beautiful breasts and her long shapely legs. I wasn't sure if it was the great orgasm I'd just had but I felt my clit jumping. I didn't think it was possible but I was getting wetter by simply being next to this chick. I didn't know who she was but I wasn't complaining about her being there, that's for damn sure.

"Hey, Mel, this is my cousin, Sasha. Sasha, this is our friend,

Melissa. She's new to the scene," Sharon said before taking another sip of her drink.

Sasha smiled and nodded my way. I returned the smile, but was really mesmerized by her full, red, kissable lips.

"Really? I hope you're enjoying my club. What do you think?" Sasha was looking at me as if she was sizing me up.

"Yes. I love it. I've never been to a club like this one but I can definitely tell it's one of a kind. What gave you the idea for the club?"

I tried to focus on my words but her nearness was making it very hard to concentrate. I wasn't sure what was happening to me. Going years searching for that one woman who affected me this way, and in one night, I'd met two. The Mile High Club was officially my favorite spot.

"Well, I always wanted to own my own club but I also wanted my club to be different from other gay clubs. I wanted to provide a place for people to meet new people and have fun, but also have a chance to get to know people better, as well as live out some of their fantasies. Everyone has fantasies but few have the means to actually act them out."

"Why The Mile High Club?"

"Well, as you know Denver is nicknamed the Mile High City. On the plane here, when I moved from California, a lovely flight attendant made me a member of the Mile High Club. I never saw her again but since that was always a fantasy of mine, I never forgot it. When I learned Denver's nickname, I felt it was a sign."

We went silent for a moment, just smiling and looking at each other. I knew she was feeling me; her eyes were telling me that she wanted to do all the things I wanted her to do. Stacy and Sharon decided to break the silence.

Clearing her throat to draw our attention, Stacy asked, "So which fantasy rooms you see?"

"The schoolroom, the locker room, and the dungeon," I responded after waving over the waiter to order another coconut rum and Coke.

Sasha picked up the questioning. "What'd you think of Black Rose's exhibition?"

Figuring she was talking about the leather woman, I was surprised she knew what happened at first, but then I remembered she was the owner and probably knew everything that went on in her club.

"I didn't know that was an exhibition. I thought it was a couple acting out their fantasy."

"Oh, no. Black Rose works here. She goes around the different fantasy rooms to make sure everything is good and everyone is having fun. Sometimes she participates in the fantasies, if there are singles or if she feels she can add to the fantasy. We have a man doing the same thing in the male fantasy rooms. Even though Black Rose does indulge in her own fantasies every once in a while, to my knowledge, she isn't in a relationship. She's definitely a free spirit, which is probably why she's good at what she does."

"And you? Are you blissfully unattached?"

I couldn't believe that I actually said that. I'm usually not that forward with what I'm thinking.

Sasha chuckled low before she replied, "Unattached, yes, but blissfully no. I'm looking for someone I can connect with, not just someone to fill my lonely nights."

By this time, Stacy and Sharon were back in their own little world. This was fine with me because I was being sucked into my own with Sasha.

We stayed at the club until closing. I was tipsy and exhausted, but still on cloud nine as I reflected on the night's events. Thoughts of Sasha and Black Rose kept running through my mind. I began fantasizing about being with them both and I masturbated until I came and fell asleep with the biggest smile on my face. Over the next three months, The Mile High Club became my second home. I went with Stacy and Sharon, and without. Each time I was in the club, I would dance and hang with Sasha in the main dance room, and when I went into the fantasy rooms, I saw Black Rose. Sometimes she'd see me, and sometimes she didn't. When she did, she'd come over and take control. She'd do different things, depending on the room that I found her in but I noticed she tended to favor the Dungeon Room. At first, I figured it was because she came off as the type that liked to be aggressive and in charge, but later I began to think that it might be because, even though it was the room that drew the biggest crowds, it was also the room where very few people stepped up to the plate. Even though it was a fantasy, people were still too shy to totally let go of their inhibitions.

The more I saw both of them, the more I grew infatuated. I couldn't seem to get enough. I'd see them at the club, then fantasize about sleeping with one or both of them, masturbate, and fall asleep with the memories. I had mixed feelings. I was dating Sasha in and out of the club, but I never saw her in the fantasy rooms. It seemed that area was Black Rose's domain. Even though I was strongly drawn to both, I began to fall in love with Sasha. Black Rose was sexy and knew what she was doing. Sasha, on the other hand, wasn't only sexy as hell; with her, I could talk about anything and everything. We'd stay on the phone for hours after we'd just left each other. I knew that I wanted her; I wanted her to be my first. To make love to her all night, wake up in her arms and make love all over again. Sasha knew I'd never been with a woman, which is why she felt it was important for us to wait. To make my first time special. Even though we both agreed, I guess she was getting tired of making out, getting hot and heavy, and then pulling back. That's probably why she set me up the first night we made love.

She invited me over to her house for a romantic home-cooked dinner. I wore a black spaghetti strap dress, and matching heels. She was wearing a brown wraparound dress, similar to the cream dress she was wearing when we first met. We had meat loaf, mashed potatoes, chilled wine, and cherry cheesecake for dessert. After dinner we slow danced in her living room to romantic music, then she led me into the bathroom where scented candles were lit everywhere. The bathtub was filled with vanilla scented oil and bubbles. Facing me, she undressed, never taking her eyes off of me, then she began to undress me. When we were completely naked, she grabbed my wrists and backed into the tub. Once in, she made me turn around so that my back was facing her and we sat down. She lathered the loofah and began to bathe me thoroughly. Soon, I felt her hand drop the loofah and start to massage my breasts and nipples as she licked and nibbled my neck. Then her right hand dropped from my breast and moved down between my legs; first moving in a circular motion on my clit, before pushing three fingers inside of me. I began to moan; my whole body tingled in waves from my toes up to my head as she moved in and out.

"Oh, Sasha...oh, please...don't stop."

She never uttered a word, but she didn't stop until I came.

I turned around and started kissing her passionately. We didn't break the kiss as she urged me to stand up. We stepped out of the tub, and she backed me up out of the bathroom and into her bedroom. Only when she pushed me down on the bed did we break the kiss. I looked briefly around the room and took in the sight. There were more scented candles everywhere, and white rose petals thrown all over the bed. She pushed me further on the bed and leaned over me. Her face was so close to mine, I could feel her breath on my face as she whispered, "Stay still, lay back and enjoy. It's going to be a long night."

With that, she kissed me deeply, her tongue diving inside my mouth. Then she kissed my cheek, my neck, and my collarbone. I closed my eyes when she moved down to my breast. She lingered there, licking around the base of my breast in a circular motion until she got to the hard peak. Then she took each nipple, one at a time, into her mouth, licking and sucking them.

She proceeded further down across my belly until she got to my pelvic bone. Skipping over my pussy, she started kissing and licking the inside of my thigh; slowly moving upward, causing my clit to throb with anticipation. Finally, she kissed my pussy lips before slowly parting them. She began with slow kisses and licks all over before she gave her undivided attention to my clit. She took long up-and-down licks on my clit before sucking it into her mouth where she alternated between sucking and lightly nibbling. I moaned and thrashed my head about. The feelings were so intense, it didn't take much manipulation for me to scream out while I came for the second time. I was lying there recuperating when she moved away from me to take something out from her drawer. She came back and once again leaned over me. She kissed me passionately as her legs made me spread mine farther apart. Then I felt it, the double-ended strap-on she'd gone to put on, as she entered me slowly. The strap-on was huge and it felt like it was stretching me from the inside out as she relentlessly moved slowly in and out. She rode me slowly for hours, hitting spots I didn't know existed. All the while, her hands and her mouth moved all over my body. She fucked me with the strap-on until we both came three more times.

I lay on the bed a little sore, completely exhausted, and for once in my life completely satisfied, when she got up and took the strap-on off. Even though I was too tired to move, I watched her with love and adoration. No one had made me feel the way she did, and she made my first time so special. I loved her and I'd never forget this night. When she turned around to take the strap-on to the bathroom where she'd clean it later, I noticed something I hadn't seen before. There, in the center on her lower back, was the same rose tattoo I had seen numerous times on Black Rose. I lay there, speechless, as the realization sank in. Sasha was Black Rose. That's the reason I never saw them together. When Sasha came back in, she could tell by the look on my face that something had happened in the short time that she'd left the room.

"What's the matter, baby?"

"You're…you're Black Rose?" I stammered, still in shock and disbelief.

Her face went from concerned to relaxed. "Yes and no."

"What?"

"Baby, I'm Sasha, the woman who loves you. However, when I'm in the fantasy rooms at the club, I'm Black Rose. Black Rose is kind of like my alter ego. Maybe when I was younger, I was Black Rose, but now I'm older and wiser. Doing all the things I do at the club isn't who I am anymore."

When she said that, it occurred to me all the times I was

looking to find Sasha in the fantasy rooms, I had never once thought to look for Black Rose in the main dance room.

"If Black Rose isn't who you are anymore, then why do you continue?"

She could sense my shock wearing off and figured it was safe to approach so she walked over to the bed and lay down next to me so she could look me in the eyes.

"I'll admit it, when I first became Black Rose, I did it because I enjoyed it, but now, I do it for the club. Black Rose helps the patrons to achieve the most pleasure out of their fantasy. Remember when I told you there was a man in the male fantasy rooms doing the same thing Black Rose does?"

"Yes."

"Well, he is my partner. Even though I own the club, and I hired him, he's more like a partner, as I usually depend on him when it comes to making sure the gay men are happy and enjoying themselves. We never have sex with the customers, unless we want to. What we do in the fantasy rooms is purely business. I can't speak for my partner, but for me it means nothing."

Even though I should've been relieved to know that she didn't care for all the women she messed with at the club, the only thing that popped into my head was all the times we'd spent together in the fantasy room. One of the reasons I'd chosen Sasha was because I wasn't sure if Black Rose was really feeling me or only doing her job by keeping a customer happy.

"So all the things we did together when you were Black Rose meant nothing?"

"No! Not at all!" She almost yelled and looked hurt. "When I first saw you in the dungeon, why do you think I took you into the corner after the exhibition?"

I didn't reply; just looked down at the sheets and shrugged.

She put her pointer finger under my chin and lifted my face so I could look her in the eyes again.

"I did that because I wanted you. I didn't know you, or know anything about you. I didn't even know you were friends with my cousin. All I knew was that, for the first time in a long time, I wanted to be intimate with someone. Not just physically, but emotionally. I wanted to give you pleasure and enjoy you giving it to me. Why do you think I kept messing with you in the fantasy rooms? Because I wanted to make your fantasy come true."

"But you have. You are my fantasy. I looked for you in the fantasy rooms but I never found you."

"Really? For a while there, I thought you were more interested in Black Rose than me. You seemed to let me go farther as her than as myself. That is part of the reason I didn't tell you at first; I wasn't sure what you wanted."

I had to chuckle at the conversation. It'd gone from me being shocked to my lover telling me she was jealous of her own alter ego.

"I admit that I found Black Rose sexy, and as her you'd done things to me that no woman had ever done. But you, as yourself, are sexy as hell and have come to mean so much more. You've touched me in places that Black Rose never could...I wanted you before I realized it was you that I wanted."

"That's all I ever wanted to hear." She laughed while she pulled me into her arms and began kissing me. "So...you're okay with this, right? You accept what I do at the club and know that it means nothing to me, right?"

"Well...I guess I can accept it on one condition," I said, playfully pulling away.

"Oh, yeah. What's that?"

"That every once in a while I get the honor of sleeping with both Sasha and Black Rose."

She looked at me, confused. "What? Why?"

Smiling, I looked her straight in the eyes. "Well, I have this fantasy of you and me in an airplane bathroom. But since you're never in the fantasy rooms, I guess Black Rose is going to have to do."

I kissed her and then we both laughed.

"I'll see what I can do."

"Now it's time for you to lay back and see what I can do."

I kissed her again on the lips as I leaned her down to lay her back on the mattress. Then I slowly began to kiss my way down.

"Oh, Melissa…you're a quick learner."

I didn't respond as I proceeded in my descent. Then I ate my first pussy and I was hooked. Sasha tasted so good that I continued until she came twice in my mouth. After I licked up every drop of cum, we made love the rest of the night, and finally fell asleep in each other's arms as the sun came up.

&DCR

*After graduating with two different BA's from Cornell University & SUNY Stony Brook, Shashauna P. Thomas returned to live where she was born and raised: Bronx, New York. Besides working hard and spending time with her family, she takes time out every day to indulge in her passion for reading and writing erotica that she hopes to publish in the near future. She believes everyone would be happier with a daily dose of spice in their lives.*

# tootsie rolls
## FELICIA D. ALBRITTON

Even after a good night's sleep, I was still a bit slow. The weather was dreary, cold, and rainy. To top it all off, the wind was blowing like crazy. It was cool, though. I was prepared for anything the day might bring. Trying not to feel rushed, I called the secretary to let her know I would be a tad bit late. I didn't have any appointments until ten.

I'm Dee Charles; a graduate of Falcon University with a BA in business administration. Public relations was my minor. I earned my broker's license in less than the required time; I'm one of the youngest agents to even have one. A car accident after college made me get off to a slow start, but I recovered quickly. Being one of the top five agents for Caswell Realty during the past quarter, the sky wasn't about to fall if I was late one morning.

I turned on Mary J. Blige's CD and blasted "Take Me As I Am" to get my day rolling. The shit, shower and powder sequence went by without a snag. Fine as I wanted to be, from the lapels of my tailored suit down to my expensive gator pumps, I always had to look in the mirror one last time before leaving my six-figure condo. The world was not ready for D. Charles.

I didn't eat my usual cereal bar so I decided to splurge and went to Burger King for some French toast sticks to go along with my caramel latte. The service was great. The fact that I had a girlfriend deterred me from giving the drive-thru employee a second look.

Well, I guess my interest in her did not have to be strong because I later found out that she had given me a steady glance. I returned to get breakfast on a regular basis, just to see this fine, well-proportioned female. Kim was a manager, having worked for the franchise since high school. After graduation, she had relocated to Greenville to study business administration at the university. Since she was experienced, it was easy for her to get the open position after relocating from Richlands.

She shared an apartment with her cousin. I got the scoop on Kim from another manager, who I occasionally associated with after hours. Nita knew that I had a way with women. She would tell me the things that Kim liked, so that I would stand a good chance of rocking her world.

Well, things had more of a lemon twist than a strawberry zing. Nita was short for Anita; she was like my partner. A recovering alcoholic, she was trying to get back on her feet with the job at Burger King. After five years of hard work, she was the store manager. Before the bottle, her drinking binge, she was the coolest. Nita would treat everybody like royalty. The women loved her and knew if they were to enter a club with Nita, they would be in VIP. When Nita was down and out, I was there for her; unlike so many others that she had once surrounded herself with. We were like boys, but girls. We had once dated the same women and compared notes; typical stuff guys do.

I got the chance to entertain Kim and join her for several evenings of pleasure. The very first night we had time to chat, she called during a heated argument between my girlfriend and me. This only added gas to the fire. I left my condo to cool off. I met Kim at her apartment complex, where the night was in an unusual glow. She approached me with a smile stretched across her face. Her words started to fumble as she asked me to walk around the lake with her.

While strolling toward the bank, she gazed in my eyes and said, "You amaze me. I could've never gotten a guy to walk with me. You agreed without even a second thought."

"Kim, I learned a long time ago that every moment in my life is as precious as the next, so I do all that I can to see a smile on another's face. Besides, it brings joy to my heart."

As we sat by the lake, the moon cast a sparkle on the water that only the warmth of silence could explain. She had already become comfortable with me. She mentioned that her cousin was dating this guy in prison, so love to her had no boundaries. I nodded with ease, and smiled. Just as I had thought, the question concerning me having a girlfriend quickly surfaced.

"So, you have a girlfriend?"

"Yes, but I also have a social life."

"What is she like?"

"Look, things are not good right now. After the argument we just had, I don't think the relationship will last."

I was totally honest with Kim; lying could ruin a friendship. It felt good, making her aware that things were not the best. I didn't want that to hinder us from being friends. She was cool with the situation and appreciated my honesty.

As our friendship progressed, I learned that she had never been with a woman. She was a tease, and someone was already fiddling with her emotions. We were becoming an item, going to clubs, dinner, and even the movies. Late-night ice cream and moments of hugging and kissing were the norm. She never hesitated to ask about hanging out but I was cautious when it came to spending my money on women. Some were addicted to the mall, and my pocket.

Christmas was around the corner and she wanted a birthstone ring; had stressed me out about it for weeks. I was in a position to make her desires vanish. I tried to make amends with my ex-girlfriend, but it was a waste of my time and hers.

ഐൽ

"Tamika, why have you been so hostile lately? Have I done something to you?"

"No, Dee, it's me. I want to be alone right now. Being here with you is a distraction from everything else I'm trying to do."

"What is it you're trying to do? I need some clarity. Why are we breaking up?"

"Dee, you're a good person, but not the right person for me."

"Tamika, I need more than that. We've invested four years in this relationship and now, you want out. That is total bullshit, but I hope you find what you're searching for."

"Dee, I love you and maybe, someday, we'll cross paths again. But, for now, I need some time to sort things out. Besides, I think God's punishing me for being with you. My best friend dies and, now, my dad."

"You don't need to be alone. I want to comfort you. You don't think we can work this out?"

"I don't want to talk about us!"

"Okay, so it's because I'm a woman? Can I at least get an

explanation as to why you act like you're angry with me all the time? Like I did something to you?"

"I don't owe you any explanation!"

Talk about a blow to the head, I had put this woman through school, given her the down payment on a new car, and this is what I received in return. I refrained from calling her a bitch since I loved her and wanted us to have a future. The shit got even worse.

The wind must have shifted because Kim's entire attitude changed toward me. I didn't have a clue why, so I asked.

"What is really going on with you, Kim?"

She blared out, "You can't keep shit, can you? Everything that we do, becomes the hot topic at work. I can't even go a day and not hear your name or something you've said."

"I don't have a clue what you're talking about. I haven't spoken to anyone on your job."

"Really? Then why is it that Nita knows everything about us?"

"You must be wearing a wire or something because I have not spoken to anyone from your job."

�──჻──

After about three days, I paid Nita a visit. She was spilling her guts before I could even ask her anything.

"Yo, man, don't get caught up in her games. It's kind of my fault. I should've told you that I tried to get with her months ago. She'd heard stories of my lavish spending in the past. When I wouldn't spend my money on her, she started playing these games to make me jealous. But, she doesn't know our history. From the first time she saw you come in Burger King with your three-piece suit on, she had to get to know you. Then, when you turned and spoke to me, I knew my chances were slim. I remember how you used to wine and dine women, and then shoplift the booty.

"She's the kind of woman that wants it all, and she lives by this. If one won't, one will. I wouldn't and you would, so she chose you. Every time you do something for her, or you go out, she rushes home and calls me to make me jealous. She tells me everything; she even told me about the tootsie rolls."

"She actually told you that she let me eat them from between her breasts?"

"No, she told me that you bought her a bouquet that was made out of them and gave it to her over dinner."

"So, she failed to mention the kinky stuff we did with the tootsie rolls after dinner?"

"Yeah, Dee, I was wondering how long it would be before her attitude changed. Look, I'm sorry. I should've told you the deal. I didn't have any idea how far she, or you, would take this thing."

"You mean to tell me, she tried to play me?"

Kim told Nita everything but she failed to tell Nita how I got her Apple Bottom jeans off in the middle of the floor while we were watching movies one night. Here's how it all went down:

ഇൗരു

K im sat on the floor and I sat on the couch across the room. Kim unbuttoned the top button of her jeans and grabbed a blanket.

"Why are you so far away from me?" I asked.

"I didn't want to cross any boundaries without permission."

"Dee, you're welcome to share my blanket."

"I'm going to be honest with you. I want to share your jeans. I promise that I'll give them back when I finish."

"Why do you want my jeans?"

"I want to try them on, to see how they fit."

"What size do you wear?"

"I wear your size."

"No, you don't. You just want me to get naked."

"You're right; I really want what's in your jeans."

I moved closer and proceeded to kiss her neck. She rolled her head away from me, acting shy. I saw her head fall back; I then began to suck gently on her neck before heading south. Her breasts welcomed me. Her nipples were so hard that if I had bit them, they would have crumbled. I began to beg for her jeans.

"Take them off for me. I'll give them back as soon as I finish. Please?"

"No. Dee, you might turn me out. Shit, you feel so damn good."

"I'll be as gentle as the creator of the word itself."

"Why does it feel so damn good, Dee? Tell me you won't tell anyone, if I do."

She was melting at each caress of my tongue. I was so caught up in the moment that I only listened for the words "okay" and "yes." I was focused on getting in her bikini underwear.

"Dee, promise you won't tell."

Never making the promise, I said, "Who would I tell? We hardly know the same people."

She slowly pulled her jeans down, so I could see her hairy, thick bush covering her jewels of passion. I took the palm of my hand and cupped her ass cheek while clearing the jeans below her knees. I pushed them the rest of the way off with my foot.

She grabbed my shoulders and whispered in my ear, "Please be gentle, like you said."

She closed her eyes and I seduced all of her body parts. Her grip on me tightened as I introduced my tongue to her clitoris. I stroked it back and forth like a kid on a park swing. I pulled and teased, pulled and teased, sucked and pleased until I literally buried my face in her pussy. I took my time, consuming each moan. She sank her nails in the back of my ears, her legs locked with a slight tremble.

Clenching her teeth, she whispered, "I'm cumming."

When all motion stopped, I crawled to kiss her nose and caressed the side of the face. As I cuddled with her, I grabbed her jeans with my right hand.

"As I promised, here are your jeans."

All she could say was, "Thank you. When do you want them again?"

ℰℭ

"Dee, you mean to tell me you ate that ass out?" Nita asked.

"Yeah, and I fucked her, too. Her pussy is so damn juicy! You should've seen her when I hit it from the back, yo!"

"But she acted so innocent, Dee."

"Nita, let's play this chick, man. Do you have feelings for her?"

"I think a lot of her but I've only gotten as far as a kiss and a finger fuck."

"Okay, let's do this."

"Cool, I'll invite her out and, like always, she'll turn me down and then you ask her the same night. I'll be at the club with another girl and I'll brush my friend off on you. In turn, you get missing for about ten minutes."

"Sweet! I'll even get the new agent from the office to chill with us. I think she likes me. I want to see Kim's reaction and let her know that she was played, like the sucker she took me for."

෧෧෨

Our plan worked out for the both of us. Kim was mad because she thought that I was disrespecting her.

"Why are you acting like you came here alone?"

"I'm not; I just didn't want anything to get back to your job, about us being together tonight."

I didn't even pay her way in the club and only danced with her twice. One of my dance partners, Trina, really got me pumped and decided she would freak me on the dance floor. I called her my Poodle. Kim was really pissed-off the entire ride home and didn't even want to kiss me after a night of her own medicine. Nita ended up taking both her friend and the new agent home.

Back to my poodle Trina. She was sexy, smoothly cool, and intelligent. She had so many people fooled because she was the District Attorney for Pitt County. Her after-hour activities did not lurk in the same category as her day job. Her sex was so powerful that one would think that they were having an asthma attack during a night of passion with her in full gear. Trina was the double-breasted-wearing DA by day and freak by night. The woman had her shit together. Trina was like my extinguisher. In case of a fire, she would definitely be the one to call.

After Kim found out that she got played, she decided to kiss up to me.

"I forgive you for the little stunt you played at the club. I really want us to be together."

"You have to be straightforward with me, Kim. Besides, we

can only be friends right now. I just got out of a relationship."

"What about the way we made love?"

"Boo, we just had some damn good sex."

ℰℭ

For Christmas, I bought her the ring. Soon it was back and forth, back and forth with the games. Then, I simply got tired. She had bragged about the ring to everyone, like she forced me to buy the damn thing. Since she liked playing games, I decided to keep the ball in my court and score.

It happened to be a nice day. You know, the pneumonia weather cold for four days, then hot as hell the next two or three. I called my cousin to get my bike out of his garage. After picking it up, I rode to Kim's apartment to retrieve my ring. She had this thing for bikes; the sound of a motorcycle made her horny. She acted like she was so hurt, thinking she had creamed another sucker, but didn't know she was getting sucked. I told her if we fucked one more time, I'd consider letting her keep the ring.

"Come into my bedroom and we'll see."

I was a horny mess. She undressed me and led me in the shower.

"What's in the backpack?"

"Just some treats for you."

She gave me a bath and I returned the favor.

I couldn't wait until we returned to her bedroom, so I removed one of my best treats for her—a nine-inch dildo—and slid it inside her. Her mouth opened wide and her eyes bucked with amazement. I lifted her onto the bath counter, and she leaned into the mirror. We both made faces; like this would be the last time we would ever fuck. With each stroke, I tried to go deeper. Her pussy was wetter than ever; it made a sloshing sound. Before she could get that first nut, I turned her over and rode her ass like a wild bull. She had cum running down her legs. She was slumped over the counter but when she got up, there was this possessed look in her eyes. We both reached a climactic state of exhaustion.

We returned to her bedroom and lay on the bed. When she fell asleep, I got up, put on my clothes, and left the box on the bed beside her. It was empty.

I saw her off and on, not speaking as though she didn't exist. I later found out that she had a manager's position at the newly opened market, six miles from my condo. I visited often, to get food and nutritious snacks; not even giving her a second look.

One evening, I did some shopping just before dark. I entered the lane next to Kim's. As I waited for the cashier to ring me up, she handed me a note that read:

*I have watched you come in and out of this market, and you're always alone, but the items that you purchase are for two. Who are you entertaining these days?*

I looked back and smiled as I left the market. After putting my bags in the car, and reached to open the driver's side door, she tapped my shoulder. "Give me another chance to totally explain myself."

I gave her the number to my message line. "Call me later."

Before I could get home, she had already called twice. I didn't return her calls for two days. When I finally decided to call, I was interrupted, and had to cut our conversation short.

It was good to know she realized that she had destroyed what could have been a true friendship. We could've gotten to know each other on a different level but she wanted to keep it on the player level. Players play and gamers game. If you ever get your booty shoplifted, then you lose. There is no coming back from that with a real player.

Months went by and we talked briefly about what happened. She was very apologetic about her childish actions. I informed her that true friends are few and hard to come by. They are like tootsie rolls. Once you eat them, they are gone. Then all you do is remember what they were like. Something like what happens with relationships. I wonder whatever happened to Tamika.

The moral to this story is gold diggers can only dig so deep until they bury themselves. It is wise to cherish the goodness and kindness of the free-hearted individuals that walk this earth.

ജയ

*Felicia D. Albritton is a native of Snow Hill, North Carolina. God gave her the gift of writing. What you just read is one of the many testimonies she has to share. Each experience teaches a lesson about life, love and how God can change your life.*

# the flipper
## ZANE

As a child, no one would have ever thought that I would grow up to be known as "The Flipper." I certainly was not a dolphin, and I did not do carnival tricks. In fact, I was a quiet little girl, lost in the hustle and bustle of New York City. My parents both worked like their lives depended on it. Then again, most of our lives depend on work so, in retrospect, they were perfectly normal. My father worked three jobs. He drove a taxi, worked at a dry cleaner and did handyman work. My mother was a waitress at a delicatessen and a housekeeper at a seedy motel. Even though they put in so many hours, they still tried to shower love on me and my three siblings whenever an opportunity presented itself.

My older sister, Rosanna, was the "stand-in" matriarch of the family. It was her job to make sure that my two brothers and I got up and got dressed, ate breakfast, and arrived to school on time. She was seven years older than her next younger sibling and truly had the world placed upon her shoulders. As soon as she graduated from high school, she made a mad dash to get the hell out of NYC. She hopped a train to Atlanta—a place she had always dreamed about visiting—and never came back.

Both of my parents were livid, feeling that she had deserted us, and her responsibility. Now that I am grown, I understand why Rosanna left. She was overwhelmed by being our "stand-in" mother and never was able to have a life of her own; she was too busy taking care of our needs. Now she is much happier. We talk from time to time. She is married with two kids and at least now she is taking care of her own responsibilities and not someone else's.

My two brothers turned out like night and day, despite the fact that they were inseparable as children. Marco became a priest; Ricardo a drug dealer. They live within five blocks of each other but they might as well be a million miles apart. Every now and then, they cross each other's path on the street and give a quick head nod or a half-felt handshake. Marco has obviously sworn off sexual gratification; Ricardo has six baby mommas and counting.

Everyone except Rosanna has a problem with how I live my life. She probably does not mind because she has her own issues to worry about. They all have their own issues but the others still waste no time trying to judge me. Even Ricardo has the audacity to make lewd comments and he literally kills people for a living, one small plastic bag at a time. Nothing steals life faster than drugs; not even cancer.

Back to me, they call me Flipper. I could have been many things because I have always been brilliant. That may seem egotistical of me to put it that way, but it is true. My IQ is 148—140 or over means you are a certifiable genius. I enjoyed school but because it was never challenging, my mind wandered to other places; mostly up the legs and skirts of the other girls in the class. Yes, I am a lesbian; always have been. My mother even tried to set me up on dates with boys; even though she was terrified of me losing my virginity or, heaven forbid, getting pregnant. Truth be told, I bet that she would have been more delighted if I had gotten knocked up in high school than the alternative.

Marco calls me a sinner and has damned me to hell. My father is in complete denial and still will not accept that I love women; everything about women. My mother constantly comes over to my apartment, begging me to at least sample some dick and then make an informed decision. Ricardo—well, that is another matter. It all comes down to the fact that I get more pussy than he does.

Women hire me to "flip" women for them; also known as turning them out. Okay, here is the gist of my profession. I love pussy. All pussy except rank pussy. When I was in school or standing out on the street and guys were whistling and checking out the females walking past them, I was clocking them just as hard. I loved the way they switched their behinds down the hallways and streets. I loved the way they flipped their hair or gently moved a loose strand from in front of their eyes. I loved the way their breasts jiggled up and down in their shirts. I loved it all; still do.

Being a genius, I decided long ago that whatever I chose as a career should be something I was passionate about. I am passionate about women and fucking women so...I started FLIP...Female Lust in Perfection. This is how it basically works. Say that Lisa has a crush on Shiron but Shiron is strictly dickly. Shiron loves dick, talks about dick all the time to Lisa...but Lisa wants Shiron to sit on her face. She makes a suggestive gesture one night. Shiron turns her down flat...asks Lisa has she lost her senses. Lisa feels dejected and tries to get over her desire for Shiron…but she cannot get her out of her fantasies. She is desperate to get inside Shiron's satin panties, to lick Shiron's Brazilian-waxed pussy. Lisa starts to reach out to some friends—fellow lesbians—and explains her problem with Shiron. One of them says, "Call the Flipper!" That is exactly where I come in.

I charge a retainer before I will even think about it. Then I charge by the hour…until I solve the problem. Once I get Shiron to give up the ass…to me, I call Lisa and tell her that Shiron is ready to be had. I ensure that Shiron cannot wait until another woman offers to go inside those panties. I turn women out; I "flip" them.

Actually, there really was a Shiron and a Lisa. Lisa called me on a Sunday afternoon—naughty girl—and asked me a slew of questions.

"Can you really make this happen?"

"Do you have a guarantee?"

"How do I know you're not a fraud?"

I responded, "Yes" to the first two questions. To the last one, I scoffed and replied, "If I can't flip her, there's not a single rat in a New York sewer."

I met Lisa the next day at the Sugar Bar. She was hot and I wanted to fuck her, but that was not the assignment. Lisa wanted to fuck Shiron and fuck Shiron she would. I had my sights on a diamond tennis bracelet at Macy's and Lisa was going to pay for that shit; point blank.

Lisa was about five-eight with legs and curves for days. She was deep chocolate—my favorite flavor—and had slanted almond eyes. I would have loved to get a peep of her parents. Both of them must have been banging and I surely would have loved to bang her mother. I love older women as well. There is nothing wrong with getting freaky after sixty. That pussy is well-seasoned and that is often the best pussy.

Lisa had a sexy smile and as she talked, I dreamed about drawing her bottom luscious lip into my mouth and suckling on it like a baby. Speaking of suckling, she had nice, perky breasts; a feast made for a saint.

We were seated at a table in the back, bottom level. She was eating her appetizer, Shrimp Al Ajillo, while I toyed with my Roasted Filet Mignon Skewers. I was too caught up in her eyes, lips, even her nose, to eat anything.

The waitress came over. "Can I get you ladies anything else to drink? Or would you like to order entrees."

Lisa gazed at me. "Order up. This is on me, after all."

She said it almost in shame. Many of my clients get hit by an embarrassing moment when they realize that they are actually arranging to pay for sex—in a roundabout sort of way.

Without looking at the waitress, or the menu, I replied, "I'll have the Catfish Meuniere with a side of Sweet Plaintains and another Apple Martini."

Lisa blushed; I have not a clue why. Then she said, "I'll take the Motherland Shrimp and a glass of Pellegrino."

"Great, it'll be right out," the waitress said before moving on.

I could not help but glance at the waitress' ass at that point. Pussy in my presence is always a distraction, even if I am already previously engaged.

Lisa cleared her throat to bring me back to home base. "So, how long have you been doing this?"

I looked at her. "What? Flipping women?"

"Yes, that." She squirmed in her seat.

I was willing to bet her pussy was wet. She was into women already so we both knew that I could get it. Shit, she had to be curious about my bedroom skills. She was paying me to capture pussy in a net that she could not begin to bait.

"I've been doing it for awhile. I don't like to discuss my personal business, though. Let's keep this professional."

She sat up straighter. "I was just wondering…Making sure that you can deliver."

"We've already been through that. I guarantee my work. If this Shiron chick doesn't give up the drawers, I refund everything except the initial retainer."

"You don't have to be so *basic*," she said, suddenly copping an attitude. "Shiron is not some *chick*. She means the world to me."

I sighed. "Okay, please, forgive me." I reached over and touched her hand, playing with her fingertips. "I will treat Shiron, and you, like queens from this moment on."

She really blushed. Yes, I could definitely get her drawers and she was truly a slut. Women kill me. One second Shiron meant the world to her and the next she was ready and willing to straddle my face. That would not have been a problem for me. Instead of the Bread Pudding with Rum Sauce for dessert, pussy and creamy thighs would suit me fine.

She pulled an envelope from her purse and handed it to me.

"Thanks," I said, shoving it into my own.

"Aren't you going to count it?"

"If it's not all there, no services will be rendered."

Lisa let out a soft, "Oh."

I had no business thinking what I was thinking…but I thought it and went into action.

"Lisa, you seem tense. You need to relax."

"I'm alright," she said, sucking down a shrimp.

She really had a thing for "skrimp." Both an appetizer and as an entrée? Made me wonder if she was a scavenger herself.

My left hand disappeared down under the table and I rubbed her knee.

"You know, I could probably see the jazz show better if I sat beside you. You mind?" I asked.

She thought about it for all of two seconds. "No, I don't mind."

By the time the waitress returned with our fresh drinks, I was beside Lisa with three fingers knuckle deep in her pussy.

The waitress gave us a knowing look. She knew what was up so I blew her a kiss. She winked, telling me that I would have to come and retrieve her drawers at a later date.

∽◯◅

"I can't believe I'm doing this!" Lisa screamed out less than two hours later as I was eating her out in the stairwell of her building. "It wasn't supposed to go down like this!"

I stopped devouring her clit for a moment and finger fucked her so I could respond. "Baby girl, I was supposed to go down… exactly like this. You know you wanted a taste, to see how I work my flip."

"But I love Shiron," she said, now in a whisper, as I went back to handling my business.

"You taste so sweet; like candy."

I lifted one of her thighs over my shoulder and teased her clit with the tip of my tongue as I gently inserted a finger into her anus. She whimpered, then settled in for the ride.

Lisa grabbed a handful of my dreadlocks and moaned with pure delight as I worked my finger deeper into her ass and snaked my tongue inside her sugary walls.

"Oooh, damn," she cried out as she came all over my tongue.

I took my finger out of her ass just long enough to stand up and press her up against the wall. I reached around her backside and stuck it back in and used my free hand to rip one of her breasts out the top of her dress. I suckled on it like she was my mother, my life force. I often wondered if that's why I love women. My mother had breastfed me as a child but she also breastfed Rosanna and she's straight-laced.

I kept digging in her ass and sucking on her breast, even when this dude walked past us and paused to take a long look.

"Shit, can I join in?" he asked in a drunken stupor.

I plopped Lisa's breast out of my mouth long enough to say, "No, man, this one is mine. Go get your own."

He winced and stared at Lisa. "Aren't you the sister in 34-B?"

Lisa was having trouble even finding her breath, rather less catching it. She tried to mouth something but finally just gave him the finger.

He chuckled. "Maybe later. I'm in 29-C, if you two want to stop by and get some dick."

I glared at him then. "I'm allergic to dick and, besides, my balls are bigger than yours."

He laughed and then continued to stumble up the stairs.

After he was out of view, I pulled Lisa away from the wall and pushed her down on the steps. I lifted my dress around my waist, exposing my bare pussy. Who the fuck needs panties!

"Now I want you to do me," I told her, climbing on top of her face and grabbing both the handrails. "Eat my pussy like this is your last night on earth."

I rode Lisa's mouth like a wave, clamping her head between my thighs and moving like a mechanical bull.

That chick loved it!

Three days later, Lisa was damn near a stalker. I had to tell her to chill, that I was on the clock and working on baiting the fresh catch of the day that she had ordered. Lisa said that she would pay me to come back over and dig her out. I declined; I never should have gone there in the first place but she was looking so damn delectable in the Sugar Bar. I wanted a taste but not to get her ass hooked.

Shiron was a personal trainer at BB & T—not the bank but a gym called Backs, Butts & Thighs. I signed up for the ten-session package and told the owner that I simply had to have Shiron because I had heard such wonderful things about her.

I showed up for my first lesson on a Thursday evening. I was too hot to trot in a pair of black spandex shorts and a white sports bra. I had rubbed ice cubes over my nipples in the locker room—I bought a juice from the concession stand before I changed—so they were hard enough to cut diamonds by the time I sashayed out into the workout area.

Shiron spotted me right away. I am hard to miss. Maybe I forgot to mention that one of the reasons that I can flip women so well is because I am fucking gorgeous on top of being brilliant. I am five-six, caramel, with long auburn dreadlocks and dark-brown eyes. So dark that many people throughout my life have insisted that they are black but they really are brown. After being teased that I was the spawn of the devil as a child, back when *The Omen* was popular, I went to an optometrist and had him confirm that my eyes were indeed brown.

"Are you Natalie?" Shiron asked in disbelief, because I was in better shape than her.

"Yes, and you must be Shiron."

We shook hands and she continued to stare me up and down. "What's wrong?" I inquired.

She sighed. "It's just that I've never had a client in such great shape. What do you need my services for?"

I held back a laugh. "Well, the biggest room in anyone's house is always the room for improvement." I walked over to the weight tree and picked up a twenty-pound set of dumbbells and started working my arms. "I'm alright," I continued, "but I really want to take it up a notch. I'm thinking about becoming a professional bodybuilder."

"No," Shiron said. "You don't need to go that route. Your breasts will disappear."

*Hmph, so she did notice my nipples!*

I put the dumbbells back and said, "Well, goodness knows, I want to keep my tatas. My lovers adore them."

I purposefully said "lovers" instead of men. That's the first hint when a person is down with the same sex, for you readers out there. When someone says "partners" or "lovers" instead of "men" or "women," they are trying to school you on something.

Shiron turned away, even though I knew she was still visualizing my nipples.

This was going to be easier than I thought. She may not have wanted to get down with the oral swirl with Lisa, but the trait was definitely there.

"Are you ready to get started?" Shiron asked.

I eyed her up and down seductively. "I was born ready to work out with you."

For the rest of the session, I flirted my ass off with Shiron. She was both nervous and fascinated. I kept rubbing up against her any chance that I got. One time, I swear that I actually took her breath away.

I asked if she wanted to go out for a smoothie after the first session but she declined. That was cool because I like a little bit of a challenge. By the time we got through the fourth session, curiosity had her cat in a frenzy and she asked me out for a hard drink.

We ended up at a local bar, in a corner booth, talking shit about this and that but really about nothing at all. I could tell that she was struggling with her feelings. That she was worried about being struck down by lightning if she touched someone else's pussy...but she wanted it.

"Shiron, you know you want it," I finally blurted out.

She almost choked on her Long Island Iced Tea. "Want what?"

"A piece of me."

She started fiddling with the ice cubes in her glass with her finger. "I don't know what you mean."

I scooted closer to her. "When we work out together...so close together...do you feel anything?"

"Natalie, you're trippin'," she replied. "I'm not into women."

"You don't have to be into women to be into me." I started caressing her thigh and then leaned in closer to whisper in her ear. "I bet your pussy is hotter than the flames of hell right about now. You know you're wondering whether or not I can make you feel...make you cum like you've never cum before."

She pushed my hand away. "No, I'm not wondering that."

I sat there for a moment, contemplating on which way to take it. I could do one of two things. I could continue to play games with her and show up for a few more sessions before going in for the kill again, or I could play hard. I decided to play hard as shit.

I scooted away from her. "Fine, it's been nice knowing you."

She was stunned. "What do you mean, it's been nice knowing me?"

"I won't ask for a refund for my remaining sessions but I won't be coming back to BB & T."

"Why not?"

"Because I'm attracted to you...I want you, Shiron. I'm not the type of woman who can constantly be around something she wants and not get it."

I downed the rest of my Hurricane and slammed the glass down on the table. Then I started gathering my things. Before I could get one leg totally out of the booth, she was grabbing onto my wrist for dear life.

"Wait. Don't go, Natalie."

*Shit, I had her!*

೮೦ಆ

We went back to her place. I never brought chicks to my crib. Most of them were potential stalkers so I was like Darkman; for all they knew, I lived underground. She had a nice apartment but I hate it when grown-ass women have dolls and stuffed animals all over their beds. I tossed all of them aside and pushed her down on the bed, ripping off her clothes. We were both still a little musty from our workout so I made a suggestion.

"Let's take a shower."

I did not wait for a response. I located the bathroom, stripped and climbed in under the heavy, warm stream. She damn near tiptoed in to join me, still worried about her decision to take a walk on the wild side.

"Get in," I commanded, holding the curtain open with one hand and rubbing a bar of soap over my breasts with the other.

Once we were both in, tit to tit, nipple to nipple, I kissed her and she almost fainted. It was so powerful; I definitely took her breath away that time.

"You never knew a woman could make you feel like this, huh?" I asked.

"One of my friends tried to get with me once." She looked down at my breasts. "I refused her."

"Probably a big mistake," I said, planting a valuable seed for Lisa. "If she was bold enough to try, that means she really wants to get with you. She'll probably turn your ass out."

She eyed me seductively. "Isn't that what you plan to do?"

"Yes, baby girl, but let me be honest before we even go there."

She stood back a few inches and said, "Yes?"

"I don't do love, and I don't do relationships. I do fucking. Now if you still want to fuck, let me know. But don't expect my ass to be sending you flowers, ringing your damn phone off the hook, and climbing into your bed on a regular basis."

"Damn, you're worse than a man."

"Then get out the shower," I told her. "I'll finish cleaning up and leave."

She started to step out but her foot lingered in midair until she placed it back inside.

"So, are you down for this or not?" I asked her.

"I want to try it." She ran her fingertips over my breasts. "You've opened up something in me."

"Taste them," I told her. "I can tell you want to."

She continued rubbing my breasts and then, without further hesitation, started sucking on my nipples.

"That's right, baby girl," I whispered. "Tonight's the beginning of a new life for you."

I let her suck on my breasts for a few more minutes but then, quite frankly, I was bored. I started fingering her pussy and then told her to place one of her feet on the side of the tub. I got down on my knees and started off slowly at first, licking the inside of her thighs and her kneecaps, making her yearn for me to get to the good part.

When my lips made contact with her pussy, she shuddered. When I bit gently on her clit, she exploded and came, just like that.

I ate her out for a good thirty minutes and Shiron had some good-ass pussy. It was going to be difficult to walk away from it, but I damn sure would.

We ended up on her bed, doing all kinds of things to each other that involved candle wax, whipped cream, and stuffing olives in each other's pussy and then sucking them out. Oftentimes, the first time that a woman gives in to her desire to be with a woman is the best. Think about it. They have thrown all caution to the wind and have basically given the world their ass to kiss.

Shiron ate more of me than I did her. At one point, I thought she was trying to draw blood as she nibbled on my clit like it was the eighth wonder of the world. We sucked, licked, ate, and proceeded back to step one; over and over again. She admitted that she had thought about women before but was too hung up on being judged to step out of her comfort zone.

"I wish that I had done this a long time ago," she whispered softly in my ear.

"Every day is a chance for a new beginning," I told her, using a tired-ass cliché.

Sometime during the wee hours of the morning, she laid her head on my chest and fell deep asleep. I pushed her off after she was sound; I don't allow cuddling. It lays the groundwork for catching feelings and never that.

೮೦೧೪

I left Shiron a note when I left the next morning, which read:

*Shiron,*
*Last night was great, but we cannot continue this. You turned me on so much that I could not bear to be around you any longer at Backs, Butts &Thighs. You can just keep the remaining money for the lessons. You earned it last night, baby girl. Maybe I'll see you around sometime.*
*You mentioned a friend who wanted to get with you. You should give her a shot. You never know. One thing is for sure; you're a pussy lover and you might as well face it. Last night may have been your first time but it definitely will not be your last. You know what they say. The best lovers often start out as friends. Just a little food for thought.*
*Take care, baby girl, and keep eating right—and I don't mean food.*
*Natalie*

I met up with Lisa to give her my final bill. She tried to get in my drawers but I refused her. I told her to give Shiron about two weeks to get hard up and desperate to have her pussy licked again. She would be good and ready by then and easy to get in the sack.

As for me, I went back to the Sugar Bar that night, for "skrimp" with a side of pussy.

If you ever need a sister flipped, look me up online. I am very easy to find.

# ZANE

୫୦୧

*Zane is the* New York Times *bestselling author of more than ten titles, the editor of numerous anthologies, and the publisher of Strebor Books, an imprint of ATRIA Books/Simon and Schuster. She is also the executive producer of several television and film projects, including* Zane's Sex Chronicles, *an original Cinemax program loosely based on her life. You can visit her online at: www.eroticanoir.com, join her mailing list by sending a blank email to eroticanoir-subscribe@topica.com or visit her MySpace page at www.myspace.com/zaneland.*

# In My Mind
## Zane

Twice a week, when I entered the classroom, I would always see her first. Well, actually, the back of her as she prepared all of her materials for class. She sat in the first row, obviously a serious student who wanted to make the best impression. I admired that.

As I walked from the rear to the front, I would brush past her and catch her distinctive whiff. She wasn't the perfume type, but she always smelled great. I recognized when she changed to the featured scent of the month at Bath and Body Works; I always did the same, but Moonlit Path would always be my favorite.

A few times I said hello to her. She whispered a soft response but never engaged in conversation with me after class, like many of the other students, especially the male students. All of them wanted to sample what they had come to know so well visually.

Never in a million years would I have imagined becoming a nude model, even though I had sketched and painted many of them when I had been an art major at the same university where I now worked. Times were hard since my mother had passed away, and I needed to pay my bills. I had obtained a little success as a painter. but no one would ever take me seriously until I was dead.

Shane was her name. One of the other students had mentioned that she was originally from Atlanta and had moved to Washington, D.C. for college. She was taller than me but, then again, so were most women. Since I measured four feet eleven inches, most girls were taller than me before they finished elementary school. Shane had long brown dreadlocks, coconut flesh and a gap between her front teeth. She wore glasses and tried to hide the fact that she was beautiful by wearing frumpy clothes and no makeup.

I did not become a lesbian until I was in my late-twenties. In retrospect, I probably always should have been one. No man had ever truly appreciated my value or respected me, not until after I was gone and they were trying to convince me to come back. Pain recognizes pain, though, and I often saw agony on Shane's face during class. I had nothing else to do but stare at everyone while they stared at my body.

The routine was always the same. I would come in, go up on the small riser, disrobe and then strike a pose, which changed weekly. The first week, the instructor had me lie on a Victorian chaise and strike a historical pose. The second week, I had to stand with my back to them and my head bent to the right so they could see my profile. I hated that. My neck had such a crick in it that I had to go home and use a heating pad. The third week, I sat on a stool with my hands folded on my lap. Now we were into the fourth week and I had to stand erect with my back slightly arched, my arms raised over my head grasping a pole, with my chin pointed a little down and to the left.

Class began and all eyes were on me. Pencils were out and the only sounds were the tips whisking across the paper and the low music playing in the background. "Bed" by J. Holiday was currently playing and all I could think about was putting Shane to bed. I had often wondered if she had ever noticed how much I stared at her over others in the class. My gaze would remain fixed on her while I made love to her over and over again in my mind. I imagined her hands running through my curly, black hair and her tongue on my nipples, that would often become hard just from the fantasy. The third week, I had actually climaxed while posing. In my mind, I had been eating Shane's pussy and she was screaming out my name: "Emile! Emile!" I hoped no one had seen the wetness of my pussy dripping down the legs of the stool. Then again, it was what it was. If I was going to sit there in the same position for three hours, twice a week, my mind had to do something. Shane had been not on my mind, but *in my mind* for so long and I decided that it was time to do something about it.

"Hello, Shane," I said while she was packing up her supplies.

"Hey, Emile," she whispered back.

"How are things going?" I asked, which took our normal conversation further than it had ever been.

She looked nervous. "I'm fine. Why do you ask?"

It was like she was trying to hide something, or feared that I had found out something. I knew next to nothing about her.

"I was just asking. We spend six hours a week together, so I was only wondering."

Shane scanned the room, full of others. "But everyone is here every week."

I shrugged, standing there in my plush robe and flip-flops. "Everyone else has at least held one conversation with me; everyone but you." I started to walk away, admitting defeat way too easily. "Sorry if I bothered you."

She grabbed my arm and, even through the thick fabric, electricity shot up my spine. My fantasy had touched me—for the first time but far from the last.

"Emile, I didn't mean to come off the wrong way. It's just that, well, it's been a rough month for me."

"I'm a great listener. Would you like to go have a drink and talk about it?"

"Oh, I wouldn't want to impose on you."

*Was that a blush?*

"Shane, it's not an imposition. Everyone needs someone to talk to, and I've had a rough year, not just a month."

"Really?"

"Yes, we all have issues, and it's important not to keep things wrapped up inside."

Shane giggled. "A drink would be nice, right about now. But only if you have the time."

I brushed one of her dreadlocks off her cheek. "Just give me ten minutes. I'll meet you out front."

"Um, okay."

୫୨୦୧

While I was getting dressed, I hoped that my touching her cheek like that hadn't scared her off. I had no idea if Shane was into men, or women, or both. I only craved for her to be into me.

When I pulled up in front of the building in my red BMW, left to me by my mother, Shane was standing on the steps.

"Get in," I said, as I pushed the passenger door open.

Twenty seconds later, we were headed to the campus exit gates.

"So what do you like to drink?" I asked.

Shane shrugged. "I'm not a big drinker, so anything fruity is cool."

"Great! I know a place in Georgetown that sells marvelous froz drinks—all flavors of Daiquiris and Margaritas."

"Cool."

"They also have a smokin' DJ. You like go-go music?"

"I really don't know that much about it, except for 'Da Butt' by E.U. Have you heard that?"

"Damn, girl, everyone's done da butt!"

We fell out laughing.

I continued, "I guess they don't have a lot of go-go in Atlanta."

There was that nervous look again. "How did you know that I'm from Atlanta?"

"Someone mentioned it." I sighed. "Can I ask you a question?"

"Um, okay," she replied hesitantly.

"Are you seeing anyone right now?"

A frown came across her face. "Why do you ask?"

"Just wondering. You seem kind of on edge and most of the time when women are on edge, it's because of relationship problems."

Shane laughed. "You're very astute. Actually, the person that I've been seeing has been tripping lately. They've been spending time with someone else, I think."

There it was. She was definitely into women. The use of "the person," "they've," and "someone else," instead of "the man," "he's," and "another woman," had said it all. It takes one to know one. I grinned like a Cheshire cat. Since she was into kitty kat, half of the battle was already won.

I decided not to fake the funk and turned the car around to head to Southeast. "I just thought of another place we can go. You'll like it a whole lot better."

80CR

We entered Too Deep, my regular spot near the Navy Yard, and Shane's eyes almost popped clear out of her head. Wall-to-wall fine women were socializing, drinking, and engaged in public displays of affection. I did not ask her if she was down with the program, but simply led her to the bar and ordered two frozen Pina Coladas.

A blob of the drink landed on Shane's chest when she picked up the overflowing cup. She was about to wipe it off with a cocktail napkin but I stopped her, leaned in closer to her and licked it off. I took my time and ran the tip of my tongue down the middle of her breasts, as much as I could with her shirt still on. I couldn't wait until I could suckle on them for hours at a time. My breasts are my most sensitive part, and thus, I like to suck on them the way I want my women to reciprocate. Knowing how much pleasure I derive from it makes me want to pleasure others.

I sat back and gazed into Shane's eyes, to gauge her reaction. Her mouth was hanging open but she didn't look upset. While her mouth was already open, I took advantage of it and slid my tongue into it. At first, she did not move hers as I explored the inside, flicking my tongue over the roof of her mouth. Then she got into it and it was on; we were making out like two teenagers and Shane was a fantastic kisser. The thought of her moving her tongue like that inside of my pussy had my panties on fire.

"U Got It Bad" by Usher started playing and I asked Shane to dance. We ended up in the middle of the dance floor, grinding on each other and my head only came up to her chest, just like a normal size woman's would to a normal-sized man. We were the perfect fit. I got lost in her, laying my head on her breast as she wrapped her arms around me and we got caught up in the words. I had it bad and I knew it. I only hoped that Shane was feeling me as much. Whoever had fucked up with her was a dumb-ass sister!

Shane had on a skirt. I reached down between her legs and worked my index finger inside her panties, which felt like cotton.

"You smell so sweet," I told her as I gazed up into her eyes. She flinched as I started fingering her pussy. It was so wet.

"You smell sweet yourself, Emile."

I pulled my finger out and licked it. "And you taste even sweeter."

I dove back into her panties, with two fingers next, and worked her damn near into a frenzy for the remainder of the song and the next: "No Love" by Kevon Edmonds.

ഇര

We left the club an hour later and headed to my apartment. Shane never asked me if I was seeing anyone and I never bothered to offer the information. For the past three years, I had been living with Madonna, but she was out of the country for four months on a contract assignment. It was my intention to end the relationship as soon as she returned. I needed a lot of attention, more importantly affection, and Madonna was too caught up in her profession to sustain me as her woman. She saw it exactly the opposite. Madonna felt that I was wasting my life away on a silly dream and that I needed to do more to contribute to the household. That was one of the reasons that I had reduced myself to nude modeling.

When we got to my place, luckily I had taken down all the pictures of Madonna and me cuddling and grinning from ear-to-ear, back when we had been happier. Sure, all of her clothes and belongings were there, but unlike a man, who has to hide hair bows and perfume bottles when a chick comes over, I was expected to have feminine items at my place.

"Wow, you're an artist!" Shane said when she noticed the easel, all the paint brushes, charcoal pencils and other supplies.

"Yes, I have an art degree from the university," I said. "That's how I knew that I could get a job there. Professor Andrews used to teach me back in the day."

"Oh, that's wild." Shane snickered. "I never would have guessed."

"Being that all you ever knew about me before tonight was my nude body, there was no way for you to have guessed."

I should not have said that. I could tell that Shane was beginning to ponder the fact that we really did not know each other. Plus, Shane had someone else. And even though her lover was probably cheating, Shane obviously still cared. I could have backed off, but Shane was *in my mind* and I had to have her—all of her.

"Why don't you make yourself comfortable on the couch?" I suggested. "I'll go get us a bottle of wine."

"Oh, I don't know if I should mix liquors," Shane said in protest.

"It'll be okay. If you don't want any, I could still use some."

I got a bottle of Chardonnay and two wine glasses from the kitchen and when I returned, I was shocked. Shane wasn't on the couch. She was standing in the middle of my living room…naked.

"I realize that my body is nowhere near as great as yours, but this is who I am," she whispered.

"You're stunning!" I set the bottle and glasses on the coffee table and started taking off my clothes. "I know you've seen this all before," I joked.

"Yes, but now I get to touch it, and lick it, and suck it."

*No, she was not turning the seduction table on me!*

"Oh, so it's like that, Shane? I never took you to be a freak!"

"Like you said, before tonight, who could have known what?" She paused. "I've wanted to suck on that pussy of yours since day one. It's always glistening, and it's shaved into a heart." She spread her legs and pointed to her own pussy. "See, we're twins."

Shane had shaved her pussy hairs into a heart, just like mine. *Damn, I was in love!*

I had first started doing it to prove to Madonna how much I cared for her, and often asked her to let me do hers, but she balked at the thought. *Fuck that bitch!*

Before I could even get over the fact that I had been in Shane's mind as much as she had been in mine, she was lifting me off the floor and carrying me to the bedroom. Yes, carrying me. She laid me on my back, spread my legs, and her warm tongue invaded my walls as I moaned in pure delight. I played with my nipples while she sucked on my hardened clit. My thighs began to shiver as she slid her finger into my asshole and started working both my holes. I grabbed a pillow and started biting on the corner to muffle a scream as I came for the first time.

Shane looked up at me. "I've wanted to taste your cum since the day you came on that stool."

I tried to catch my breath as I let go of the pillow with my teeth. "You saw that, huh?"

"Not only did I see it, I yearned to come up there and lick every drop off the stool. That was one lucky stool, to have your pussy sitting on top of it. All I could think about was that it should have been my face."

"Damn, Shane!" I said. "This is going to sound absolutely crazy, but I think I love you!"

I jumped up and pushed her on her back, demanding, "I have to taste you. Right now."

I dove in with my tongue, having never wanted to explore a woman's pussy more in my entire life. Shane tasted like the Pina Coladas we drank at Too Deep, but I could tell that she had a healthy diet, like myself. I ate her like my life depended on it. In many ways, it did. I needed her in my life and I had to do whatever I could to make sure that she would never want another.

80C3

We spent the next four hours pleasuring one another. I ate her from four different angles: spread eagle, from the back, with her on top of my face, and in the shower with her foot propped up on the side of the tub. Each time that I tasted her, it only got better and better.

When we were in the shower, I sucked on her breasts so erotically and so passionately that I came twice just from doing that. Shane gave as good as she got and turned me out in ways that I had never even imagined...*in my mind*. She ate me out on the kitchen table off a canvas and later, she shellacked my juices onto it so we could always remember our first time together.

80C3

By the time Madonna had returned from her business trip, I had moved out and in with Shane. The woman she had been tied up with had left her. As suspected, she had been cheating all along. Hell, she dropped her dime and I picked it up. Shane and I often paint and sketch each other. It had been years since I had sketched a nude and I never wanted to sketch another one outside of her.

Shane will forever be...in my mind.

80C3